SIBBY SLICKER

Sibby Series Book II

E. SLATE

Tabula Rasa Publishing

For clumsy people everywhere.

Disclaimer

No raccoons were harmed when Sibby went camping.

Chapter 1

#Sibbyinthewild #nocryinginnature

"You want to do *what?*" I asked, my mouth open in dumbfounded shock.

Aidan sat on the couch next to me. "You heard me."

"But you—and me—and—no, really?"

He nodded.

I took a deep breath, wondering if I was hallucinating. "Let me get this straight." I took another deep breath. "You want to take me on a camping trip upstate."

"Yes."

"For two weeks."

"Yes."

"With no internet."

"Yes."

"Dirt."

"Yes."

"And bugs."

Aidan sighed. "Yes."

"Many, many bugs."

"Yes Sibby, many, many bugs." He smiled, his adorable lopsided smile, which I loved.

Love had limits. And those limits took the form of not bathing for two weeks.

"But Aidan, I don't *do* nature," I whined. "I need my comforts. I'm no granola girl! I need to be clean and warm and just, no. Go with Caleb!" I suggested. "You're both from up there. You're both manly, and now that you're a full-on Brooklynite, you have more than enough flannel to get you through this. You don't need me. You don't *want* me. I promise."

Aidan reached over and grasped my hand in his. "I'm calling in the IOU."

I shook my head. "Not fair."

"Totally fair," he shot back. "Did I, or did I not spend Passover with your family?"

"You did." I looked away.

"Did I, or did I not try *gefilte* fish?"

"You did."

"Did I, or did I not drink the so-called virility tonic your mother got from her Chinese herbalist?"

I sighed. "So camping, huh?"

He nodded emphatically. "Camping."

"But why?" I demanded, making one last-ditch effort to get out of having to go.

"Because I need a break, Sibby. This city…" He shook

his head. "I've been working like a maniac. So have you. I want some time away from all the obligations and technology."

Though unplugging from the world around me did have a certain level of appeal, the idea of having it inflicted upon me irked me. But Aidan wasn't wrong—and the man *had* endured Passover. Quite graciously actually—and he'd managed to keep down the gefilte fish, too.

I sighed in defeat. "When do we leave?"

"No," Annie said, eyes wide.

"Ya."

"You? Camping?"

My best friend reached for her vodka cran and took a healthy sip. We were at one of our favorite bars. It was a shit-hole dive in the East Village. You could buy a shot, a beer, and a hot dog for five bucks. I'd never eaten the hot dog, purely for safety reasons.

"I know," I sighed. "It's really important to Aidan."

"I told you not to get married," Annie said with a roll of her eyes. "Now you're compromising and shit."

"What does marriage have to do with anything?" I demanded. "You're dating Caleb. Don't you compromise?"

"Um. I moved to Brooklyn, didn't I? And look how well that's turned out for me," she grumbled. "I'm wearing a pair of skinny jeans from Brooklyn Industries. Who the fuck am I?"

Annie had always reminded me of a modern Marilyn Monroe. Blond, curvy, total bombshell—a bombshell that cursed like a fish and drank like a sailor.

Wait, scratch that.

Reverse it.

"Can we focus, please? I have a legitimate problem. Aidan is taking me to the woods. I don't go to the woods. There are wild animals and bugs and stuff."

"And let's not forget sleeping on the ground. And what are you going to do about bathing? And getting your eyebrows waxed? You know you have to do that weekly, right? Otherwise you look kinda sasquatchy."

It was true. I had to upkeep the grooming religiously. I blamed my Russian roots. "You're not helping," I moaned. I laid my head on the bar and then felt Annie pat my hair.

"There, there," she said.

I peeked up at her.

"Did that make you feel any better?" she asked.

"No."

"Okay, I know how we can make this better."

I perked up. "Shots?"

"Shots," Annie agreed, searching for the bartender. "Doug! Shots!"

"No, wait! No shots," I called back.

The burly, tatted bartender with a Danny Zuko haircut looked at us in exasperation. "Well, what is it? Shots or no shots?"

"No shots," I said, tone firm.

Annie pouted. "Aww, shucks. You're no fun."

"And you're a bad influence. Aren't we past the stage in our life where we drink to forget our problems?"

Annie thought for a moment, her face screwed up into

a picture of introspection before grinning. "Nope, I'm overruling you. Doug, bring us two shots of vodka!"

I sighed, and threw one back with her. Setting aside the empty shot glass, I turned to her. "Now you. Go."

"My turn? Finally. My boss made her husband buy her a house in Kennebunkport."

"Because the Park Avenue penthouse, the house in Palm Beach, and the house in the Hamptons weren't enough?"

"Exactly. Which means—"

"You'll be in New York even less."

She sighed. "I used to like it, you know? Traveling, working like a dog, drinking like a frat guy. But lately, I don't know…"

"Something's missing?"

"Maybe. I don't know. I have Caleb, and that's going really well. And he's really busy with Veritas—as you know."

I did know.

Caleb and Aidan were best friends as well as business partners. They worked *all the time*. Oh. It finally clicked—why Aidan needed the camping thing.

"He never makes me feel bad that I work all the time because he's doing the same, but I'm just bored. Like, I've worked for Heather for a few years and it's getting old."

"So find a new job."

Annie looked pensive again. "Yeah."

I raised an eyebrow. "What does that mean?"

"What does what mean?"

"Your 'yeah' sounded—I don't know…"

She took a fortifying drink and then said, "I think I want something *really* different. Like, I'm done being a private chef."

"Your parents are going to kill you," I said with a rueful

laugh. Annie had gone through four years of undergrad and then moved to New York. It only took two-months of interning at Merrill Lynch to realize her actual dream of being a chef. Hello, Culinary Institute of America. Hello, hefty price tag—and hello, stress.

"No, I still want to cook," she assured me. "But I think I want to have my own restaurant. I want my own kitchen."

My eyes widened. "Doug! Another round of shots." I looked back to her. "Let's drink the crazy out of you."

"Are you really going camping?" Annie asked, drunk as a skunk, and looping her arm through mine as we walked out of the bar.

"Are you really going to open up your own restaurant?"

"Yes," she declared with drunken bravado. "I'm gonna do it. No more slaving away for a woman who yells and throws Perrier bottles at my head!"

"She throws Perrier bottles at your head?" I asked in astonishment.

"That's the French one, right?"

"Right."

"Then yeah, Perrier." She held up her hand to flag down a cab.

"Really? A cab?" I asked.

"We live in the same neighborhood."

"No, I meant, let's just call an Uber."

"What did New Yorkers do before Uber?" Annie asked, lowering her hand.

I fiddled with my phone and swiped over to the Uber app. "Um, they hailed cabs, took the subway. Or walked."

"Walked," she huffed. "What a rotten idea."

"Seriously." I tapped the screen a few times. "A car should be here in three minutes."

"Good."

I looked up at the night sky—the stars were nonexistent due to the light pollution. I wondered how I'd feel seeing them.

"Damn it, I know I have some gum in here." She was riffling through her purse, head buried in the bag, which carried her entire life. A change of clothes, her comfortable Crocs, even a toothbrush. We used to call it her One-Night Stand bag. Amazing how things changed in a few years.

I let out a laugh.

"What?" Annie asked. She found the gum, popped out a piece, and handed it to me before getting one for herself.

"Just thinking about how things change. Remember when we first moved here and everyone asked us if our lives were like *Sex and the City*?"

She laughed. "Yeah. Like we were able to sit around talking about guys at the city's best restaurants."

"I still don't own a pair of Manolos."

She smiled. "You can afford them now."

"Please don't compare me to Carrie," I warned. "Just because we're both writers."

"OMG."

"What?"

"You married an Aidan."

I groaned. "Shut up."

She bent over and let out another laugh. "I can't believe I didn't think of that before."

Our car pulled up and we scrambled inside, collapsing against the seat. I kept my eyes open as wide as I could since I had the swirlies.

"There has to be something you can do," Annie murmured. "To get out of camping. Did you offer him something sexual?"

"I was too in shock to even think clearly. He's pretty adamant, Annie. And what's two weeks? I can do two weeks. My book is with my agent. I'm free as a bird."

Annie grinned. "A camping bird."

"I love Aidan, and Aidan loves camping, ergo—"

"Ergo you love camping?"

"Fuck no. I was gonna say, ergo, I can do this. I can rough it."

She snorted. "Yeah, you can rough it. At a four-star hotel. With a spa. You're such a Jewish American Princess."

I buried my head in my hands. "Oh, God, you're right. I'm totally screwed." I looked at her. "I'm a total Sibby Slicker."

"Aidan," I whispered. "Aidan, wake up."

"Hmm," he groaned into his pillow. "What?"

Part of me felt sort of bad for waking him up. It was

four in the morning and he hadn't gotten home until two. But after I'd slept off my drinks, I'd awakened with tons of questions about camping.

The word made me shiver.

"It gets cold Upstate," I said, poking his back. He tried to bury his head deeper into the pillow, but I pressed my face in the spot between his bare shoulder blades.

"I'll keep you warm," he promised.

"Was that meant to be suggestive?"

He sighed and then wiggled his body. I removed myself from his back, and he rolled over. I snuggled into his side.

"It wasn't meant to be suggestive." His fingers found their way to my wavy hair. "Do you trust me?"

"You know I do," I replied. "But how are we going to shower?"

"I've got it covered."

My eyes narrowed. "I'm not going two weeks without washing my hair. I'm prone to dreadlocks."

"I promise to keep you safe, warm, and comfortable. September Upstate is gorgeous. It's nice during the day, cool at night. There are hardly any bugs and the bears— well, we have to make sure to keep a clean camp."

"Bears? Did you say *bears*?"

"No, I meant—" He sighed. "Yeah, bears. But they're hibernating by now." He paused. "Probably…"

"You're not reassuring me."

"We'll be fine. I promise."

"I don't have any camping clothes."

"Easily rectifiable."

"This really is important to you, isn't it?"

"Yeah, Sibby, it is."

I sighed. "Then I'll try to be a good sport."

He kissed my forehead. "Good. Can we please go back to sleep now?"

"Sure," I said. I waited until he fell back to sleep before I crept from the room. I went into my office and sat down at my desk. Before I knew it, I was on the L.L. Bean website. For safety, I opened up REI's webpage, along with Eddie Bauer.

If I was going to the woods, I wanted to be prepared. Better prepared, anyway. I considered why Aidan wanted to take me on what would've been a really fun boys-only trip and then realized this was what happened when your husband actually liked you and wanted to spend time with you.

Dammit.

I added a bunch of things to the L.L. Bean shopping cart and paid for express shipping. If I was trekking into the woods, I at least needed to look the part.

Chapter 2

#prayforwine #sos

"What do you think?" I asked, turning so Annie could get a good look at me.

"Is that a Halloween costume?" Annie's eyes widened and her hand went to her mouth as she failed to stifle a chuckle. "I think you look like a hipster Elmer Fudd."

I took off the red hunting hat and threw it at her. She caught it and fell back onto the gray comforter, snorting and guffawing like a loon.

"Oh my God!" She struggled to sit up. "Where did you

go to get those clothes? And how much money did you spend?"

I scowled and turned back to my reflection. "That army-navy store on Manhattan Avenue. And L.L. Bean." I thought I looked pretty good. "Look at my hiking boots! They have pink stripes."

"And the Mom jeans? What's up with those?"

"They're loose enough so that I can wear *gatkes*."

"Gat-what?"

"Long johns," I clarified.

"Right." She gestured to my shirt. "And the flannel? Is that a man's shirt?"

"It's Aidan's," I growled.

"I like the pigtails." She handed back the red-and-black-plaid hunting hat and I stuck it on my head. "You could totally wear that as your Halloween costume."

"Screw you," I said lightly. "I'm trying to get into this. For Aidan."

"For Aidan!" she cheered.

I rolled my eyes. "There are things we do for those we love."

"Jeez, Sibby, you sound like you're going to war."

"I *am* going to war. War against dirt, bugs, and frizzy hair."

"Your hair is always frizzy."

"Why are we best friends again?"

"Um, history? Oh, and because it would take you too long to break in a new one."

I nodded. "Right. And the best-friend divorce papers are a bitch."

"You're so weird."

Pointing to the hunting hat on my head, I nodded.

"When are you guys going upstate?" she asked with an amused grin.

"This weekend. Aidan is in full-on prep mode."

"What does that mean? Like doomsdayer stuff?"

I shrugged. "I dunno. He's buying all these meals in bags."

"Uh, what?"

"Dehydrated meals. Apparently hikers eat them." I looked at her in horror. "I didn't think about hiking. Am I gonna have to hike?"

"You mean actually move your body? Probably. You did buy the boots. Come to think of it, they are kinda cute."

"I need chocolate. Like pronto," I said, running out of the bedroom. I hauled butt to the kitchen and pulled out a chair so I could reach the top shelf of the cabinet.

"What's in the stash?" Annie asked.

I found a box and threw her a grin over my shoulder. "Entenmann's chocolate donuts."

"Double chocolate?"

"Nope. The yellow cake donut with chocolate frosting."

"Oooooh, I love it when you talk dirty. Gimme one of those."

I climbed down from my perch and opened the box. "If I give you one of these, you have to stop heckling me."

"Not a fair trade, but I'll try." She plucked a donut and stuck it in her mouth. I did the same and then made an inappropriate sound.

"Just make sure you have these in your survival bag," Annie warned. "When your blood sugar gets low, you get crabby."

"Yep. Cold, hungry or tired."

"Donuts for hunger. Pack a fifth of bourbon. That'll take care of the warmth problem."

"What happens if I get tired?"

Annie swallowed the rest of her donut. "Tell Aidan to pray."

Annie had to go grocery shopping for her diabolical boss, so she left after she helped me polish off the donuts. Aidan was still at Veritas, no doubt making sure everything was in order for his two-week absence. Though the trendy wine bar was doing well, it was still young—only a little over a year old. Restaurants and bars came and went frequently in the city, but I knew Caleb and Aidan had real staying power. Still, I worried he might be taking off too much time, but if he felt good enough leaving the business for a couple of weeks, then that was his decision to make.

After straightening up the living room and changing the sheets on the bed, I put on some water to boil and threw in the pasta just as Aidan walked through the door. "You're cooking?" he asked by way of greeting.

"I am." I poured him a glass of red wine from the open bottle on the kitchen counter into one of the wine glasses from our wedding registry.

"What did I do to deserve this?" he asked with an adorable smile as I handed him the glass.

I picked up my wine glass and clinked his. "It's an apology dinner."

He raised his eyebrows and took a sip of wine. "Nice."

He sniffed. "You opened one of the good bottles we got in Italy."

"The Chianti," I said with a dreamy sigh. For our honeymoon, Aidan and I had gone on a two-week wine tour of Italy. We'd come home with a few cases of wine—I'd wanted to bring more, but we'd recently moved into a two-bedroom apartment and didn't have a ton of storage.

"So let's get back to why this is an apology dinner," Aidan said, shrugging out of his light black jacket and hanging it on the back of a kitchen chair.

"I wasn't very—supportive. Of the camping trip." I leaned back against the counter, wine glass in hand.

He crooked a grin. "I know."

"I'm sorry."

"Do you know why we're such a good match?"

"Why?"

"Because we force each other out of our comfort zones."

I raised an eyebrow. "You're taking me camping, which is *way* out of my comfort zone. But what do I do for you?"

"You make me think differently."

"I do?" I asked.

He set his wine glass down and sauntered toward me. Plucking the wine glass from my hands, he glanced at the timer. "I've got about twenty seconds."

"For what?"

He gently put my glass on the counter, wrapped his arms around me, and kissed me. It was a good kiss. A great kiss. Our kisses had only gotten better with time. Being married totally had something to do with it; I was sure of it.

The oven timer beeped, and I sighed at our perfect moment being interrupted.

"You sit down," I told him. "I got this."

I tore into my piece of garlic bread and set it aside to let it cool. "How do I make you think differently?"

Aidan grated Parmesan over his bowtie pasta while he answered. "Because of you, I opened Veritas with Caleb."

"I can't take credit for that," I said. "That was your idea."

"True. But it came about sooner rather than later." He held up the grater and cheese wedge, and I nodded. He got up from his seat and grated cheese onto my pasta.

"Oooh, baby, you can grate my cheese anytime."

"I'm an expert grater," he said with a grin. He sat back down and put his napkin in his lap.

"As you were saying?"

His fingers pinched the stem of the wine glass, but he made no move to drink. Blue eyes rested on me, his face thoughtful. "You deserved better," he said.

I frowned. "Better? Better than what? You? There is no better than you."

A ghost of a smile flitted across his mouth. His dimples popped, like happy little beacons. "When we met I was…I don't know, content with being a restaurant manager. Content is not really the right word. It was enough—for me. But then I met you, and I knew you were the one. And I'm probably not explaining this right, but there comes a time in a man's life when he meets the woman he's supposed to be with and suddenly, he wants more—*needs* more—so he can provide for her. I needed to be able to provide for you. Owning the bar with Caleb makes me feel like I can look your father in the eye and stand proud. That I can provide for his daughter." Aidan fell silent, his eyes still on mine.

I blinked away the tears that were gathering in my eyes. He was just so damn perfect—and he *got* me in a way that no one else did.

"I made you cry," he said with smile.

"No, you didn't," I lied. "I'm allergic to emotion."

Aidan laughed.

I raised my wine glass. "Aidan Kincaid. Good at marriage."

"Sibby Goldstein-Kincaid. Good at compromise."

"Let's eat, before it gets cold."

The week passed in a blur. Whenever you dreaded something, time seemed to speed up. But when you were looking forward to something, time seemed to move backward.

Suddenly it was the weekend, and we were upstate visiting Aidan's parents for a night before we headed out to our camping destination. Every time I was around Aidan's family, I was always amazed at the differences in how we'd grown up. Aidan's family all loved the outdoors, had bonfires in the backyard, and understood boundaries. My parents had no filters, enjoyed Puerto Vallarta, and camping wasn't even in their vocabulary.

"Your parent's garage is basically an **REI** store," I marveled, standing in front of rows and stacks of outdoor gear.

He laughed. "I love all this stuff." He touched a massive blue hiking backpack, and I prayed to Moses that it was for him.

"You're not gonna make me"—I gulped—"*hike*. Are you?"

Aidan chucked me under the chin. "There's a really cool walk I want to take you on. It's easy, there's very little incline, and at the end there's a waterfall."

I crossed my arms over my chest. "Don't think you can easily substitute the word 'walk' for the word 'hike.' Call a spade a spade, okay?"

He wrapped his arms around me. "I promise it will be worth your while."

"How are we gonna stay clean? Two weeks without showers—"

"Got it covered."

"And using the bathroom—"

"Got that covered too." He kissed the end of my nose. "Trust me. I got this. I also got you a present."

"You did?"

He nodded and released me. Grabbing my hand, he tugged me to the corner of the garage where a cardboard box rested on his father's worktable.

"Go ahead," Aidan said, looking excited.

I reached for the cardboard box and managed to get it open. Inside was a knife in a pink carrying case. Aidan picked it up and clipped it to my belt.

"See? You're all decked out, ready to go. You're practically a wilderness girl."

I struggled to unsheathe the blade, but once Aidan showed me how it popped out and then locked back into place, I got the hang of it.

"You really trust me with a knife?" I asked in wry humor.

"Valid point. Please be very careful. It's wicked sharp."

"I feel like Crocodile Dundee," I said in excitement. "What other stuff do I get?"

"For now, you'll borrow everything you need. If—"

"If what?"

He cocked his head. "If I can get you into this, then we'll go full throttle and get you all the gear."

I must've blanched because Aidan laughed. "Right, baby steps."

"I know you have an agenda," I said.

"My not-so-secret agenda can wait." He smiled. "Come on. Mom's making dinner. We'll leave first thing tomorrow."

Chapter 3

#intothewoods #offroad #help #someonesaveme

We were on the road a little after ten the next morning. I'd refused to leave at the crack of dawn. Showers, people. I had to have one last good shower before I turned into a dirty, filthy, granola-eating, backpack-toting, thermal-wearing mountaineer.

There was a very good chance I was going off the deep end. But I would do this. I would do this for Aidan.

What was two weeks?

About an hour into our trip, Aidan pulled off onto a gravel road, leaving the asphalt behind. The Toyota

Tacoma that belonged to Aidan's mom rocked and bounced as we continued, the trailer hitched to the back jostling along with us.

"Um. What's happening?"

He looked at me. "We're going off road, baby."

I gripped the side of the door. "You mean this isn't your way of getting rid of me?" I teased. "Ready for a younger model already?"

"Nah, I think I'll keep you for a while longer. At least until I'm gray at the temples, and I'm a true silver fox." He reached over and quickly squeezed my thigh before putting both hands back on the wheel.

Smiling, I looked out the window. "So really, what's going on?"

"It's free to camp in any national forest in the United States. So that's what we're going to do."

My head whipped around to look at him. "You mean you're not taking me to a campsite with other people?"

"Nope."

"So it'll be just the two of us."

"Yep."

"Sleeping in a tent. With no one else to talk to. Alone with my thoughts. And bugs. Many, many bugs."

"Sibby—"

"Nope, I'm good, totally good. Not freaking out. Not freaking out at all."

He laughed. "You're freaking out a little."

"You're taking me off the grid! What if a snake bites me? Or I'm eaten by a coyote."

"You don't have to worry about either of those things," he assured me.

I breathed a sigh of relief.

"Bears on the other hand—"

"WHAT!? You said they were hibernating."

"It's unseasonably warm, but relax, I've got bear spray." He threw me a grin. "I'll teach you how to use it."

I pressed my face to the glass as we continued the drive. I didn't have a good feeling about the trip, but I held in all the feelings that wanted to come spewing out.

"My mom used to hate camping," he said.

The switch in conversation totally worked, and I peeled my face away from the glass. "Oh yeah?"

"Yeah. She said she loved nature, but she hated being dirty and inconvenienced. You know how my dad got her over that?"

"How?"

"He bought this truck and the trailer attached to it. See the flat square thing on the back of the trailer?"

I looked behind us and sure enough, there was a puffy canvas-topped square thing I had paid little attention to. "What is it?"

"It's a tent. So you unhook the trailer, the rooftop tent opens up and you climb into it using the ladder attached, and then if you have to drive off to get more supplies, you can leave everything else. And," he added, "you don't have to sleep on the ground."

"Nifty. So what's in the trailer?"

"All will be revealed in due time. But trust me, I'm about to change your idea of camping."

My idea of camping was roughing it at a Motel 6 with a questionable bedspread. This was something else all together.

"Okay, big guy. Show me what you got."

An hour later we were in a clearing.

In a forest.

I was in a forest.

Aidan cut the engine and then climbed out of the truck. "Come on," he said eagerly. "I'll show you how all this works."

I tugged on one of my pigtails, nervous and completely out of my element. There was nothing worse than feeling like a fish out of water—or in my case, a Sibby out of the city.

The tent took very little time to set up, and when I peered inside, all the bedding was in there. It was roomy, and the idea that I'd be able to see the stars before going to bed was appealing. Then he showed me the trailer. With the opening of a few doors, everything was at our fingertips. A small but efficient propane stove, a section for cooking utensils, and even a tiny refrigerator.

"How does this work?" I asked in excitement, opening the well-stocked refrigerator.

Aidan grinned. "Solar power—as well as a generator."

"Shut up."

"Told you I'd see to your comforts."

"Too early for a beer?"

"Not at all." He reached around me and pulled out two ice-cold beers. They were twist-offs, and soon I was sipping on a delicious microbrew, sitting in a camp chair, totally feeling like I could do this.

"Okay, I know I'm only like an hour into this excursion," I said as Aidan sat next to me in his own camp chair. "But this is already better than my three-week long stint at Girl Scout Camp when I was twelve."

"I need more." Aidan took a drink of his beer, his blue eyes lit with humor.

"Fourteen pre-teen girls sharing a cabin. I learned how to shave my legs that summer."

"Not very well," he murmured.

I nudged him with my foot. "It was fun—until I got my period for the first time."

"No."

"*Yes*. It was so embarrassing."

"That's not that embarrassing."

I rolled my eyes. "Have you ever been a twelve-year-old girl?"

"No," he agreed. "But I have been a twelve-year-old boy. Every time the wind blew I got an erection. Top that."

"My Hungarian camp counselor had to talk me through how to use tampons—and then the director called my parents to let them know what had happened. When my parents came to pick me up, my dad said, '*Mazel tov*.' Oh, and did I mention that I made friends with a really nice girl whose hot older brother came to get her? Well, he overheard all of it. I know he did."

"My high school English teacher was super hot, and I got a woody listening to her read *The Scarlett Letter*."

"You know, let's not do this—trade war stories about our embarrassing youths. Just tell me I win, and we can move on."

He leaned over and kissed my lips. "You win."

Aidan stood over me, looking like a sexy lumberjack fantasy come to life. His black and red flannel shirt was rolled up to his forearms, and his jeans were already dusty with dirt. His head blocked the sun, so I didn't have to squint behind my sunglasses. "What do you think, champ? You ready to go for a walk?"

"Walk?" I asked. "But I'm so comfortable."

Of course I was comfortable. I was sitting in a camp chair, nursing a beer, relaxing in the sun. The late September weather was holding on to an Indian summer, and fall was nowhere to be seen except for the slight changing of the leaves. I prayed it stayed that way for the next two weeks.

"If you go on a walk with me, I'll cook you dinner."

"Hmm…"

"And clean up."

I grinned. "You're pulling out all the stops, huh?"

"I want to ensure we stay married." He held out his hand, and I grasped it. He hauled me up and wrapped his arms around me. "Thanks for doing this," he said into my hair.

Squeezing him around the middle, I buried my face in his flannel shirt. He smelled like the woods, earthy and masculine. He smelled like Aidan.

I nuzzled deeper.

"What are you doing?" he asked with a chuckle.

"Seducing you in the woods. Duh."

"You're not trying to get out of the hike, are you?"

I laughed. "Service me now, and I'll hike with you tomorrow."

Aidan started backing me toward the tent ladder.

"You have really good ideas," Aidan said. His breathing was returning to normal as we lay on the surprisingly comfortable foam mattress in the tent. The vents were open, and air filtered through. Late afternoon sunshine peered through the flaps. As far as an afternoon romp went, it was definitely top five.

"I think I like camping."

He laughed and pulled me into his arms. I rested my head against his chest. "I needed this. So much."

"Sex?" I quipped.

He pinched my side and made me squirm. "This."

I dragged my finger up and down his arm. "You're not like, having a midlife crisis are you? Like you're not gonna suddenly insist we leave the city, move upstate, and grow vegetables. I mean, don't get me wrong, I love farm-to-table, sustainable, traceable, all that stuff, but I'm not ready to—"

"I don't want to move." Aidan looked unperturbed by my outburst. He continued to lie there, all sexy with those bedroom eyes.

"But you *do* want something." I sat up and reached for my black tank top. "Tell me what's going on. Because I feel like there's something going on with you—and it's not just about the need to go camping."

"You're reading into things," he said.

My eyes widened. "Now I *know* there's something to read into."

He shifted his position, making the muscles of his chest dance.

"Don't try to nippulate me into distraction," I stated, pointing to his sculpted body.

"I love the city," he began, ignoring my jest. "You know that."

I nodded. We both loved the city. Sure, it was congested and expensive, and sometimes we saw inappropriate things on the subway, but what city didn't have its issues? At least ours had amazing food and culture. And our best friends.

"You're ready for a dog. That's what this conversation is about," I said. "Your puppy parent genes are kicking in. We can get a dog. A cute little rescue pup. I'm game. Let's—"

"I want a kid," he blurted out.

I blinked. "I need you to repeat that."

He took a deep breath and sat up, placed his hands on my crossed legs, and looked into my eyes. "I want a kid."

"With me?"

He rolled his eyes. "No, Sibby. With Mrs. Nowacki. Of course with you."

"I think if her parts were still working, she'd be totally game."

Our seventy-five-year-old Polish neighbor was hot for Aidan. I looked around for the rest of my clothes. It was suddenly too warm in the tent, and I felt like I needed to escape.

"Sibby—"

"Just one question. Have you been talking to my mom?"

He shook his head. "No."

"Really? Because you both seem keen on this kid thing."

"This isn't about your mother. This is about us, and what we want."

"I'm not ready," I stated. "I'm not ready to quit drinking or to eat my meat well done. Or give up oysters and certain types of cheese. I'm not ready to be all healthy and generally put together and go to prenatal yoga and drink kale smoothies."

"You don't have to go to prenatal yoga and drink kale smoothies," Aidan said, blue eyes wide and searching.

"Yes," I nodded with emphasis. "I do. Because I won't do it unless I do it right."

Aidan ran a hand across his mouth, trying to hide his smile and failing. "See, you'd make a great mom."

"I'm not ready, okay? My career… I just got my dream, Aidan. I get to tell dirty stories for a living. Please don't ask me to put it on the back burner. Not yet."

"I'd never ask that of you. You know that, right?"

"I do." I looked away, hating that I was the one who had to tell him no—not forever, but just for right now. "But here's the thing, my career *will* go on the back burner if we have a kid. It's inevitable. I already work from home. You work sixty hours a week out of the house. So please, Aidan. Can we wait?"

"For how long?"

"I don't know. I don't want to put a time stamp on it."

Everyone always talked about a woman's biological clock, but it had nothing on a guy who was ready.

Aidan managed to slide into his jeans and then buckled his belt. He threw on his flannel, covering his delectable body from my sight.

I sighed. "You're not mad at me, are you?"

"Come here," he said, his voice soft. I collapsed against his chest and pressed my closed eyelids to soft, worn flannel. "I'm not mad. Not at all."

We fell silent as Aidan stroked my hair. Though he was understanding now, I wondered how much time I had before he got antsy and brought up the kid talk again.

Chapter 4

#check4critters #glamptastic #noshowersnoservice

True to his word, Aidan cooked me dinner while I sat by the campfire he had also made.

I could get used to this.

But I couldn't get our earlier conversation out of my head, and I desperately needed my friends. Part of me wondered if Aidan had dropped the kid bomb on me while we were in the middle of nowhere so I'd have no one to freak out to, forcing me to talk to him about it. But sometimes, you needed your gang of girls to talk to.

Natalie had moved with her husband and toddler to

Houston to be closer to her parents, and as someone who'd had motherhood accidentally thrust upon her, I thought she'd be a good person to talk to. I dug out my cell phone, silently rejoicing when I saw that I had one bar. I fired off a text, but the screen immediately read, *Message Failed to Send.*

"Damn!" I lifted the phone higher, trying to find service.

"Who are you trying to text?" Aidan called to me from the trailer. "Annie?"

"Natalie," I called back, not taking my eyes off the screen.

There! One bar!

I held my phone over my head until I heard the swoosh sound of the message sending.

"Success!" I walked to the trailer and watched Aidan stir a pot with a wooden spoon. "What are we eating?"

"Chili."

"From a can?"

"From my mother."

"Oooh. This'll be good."

Aidan held up the spoon to give me a taste. I blew on it and then sampled. "Yep. Knew it. Best chili ever."

He took a small bite. "Needs some salt." After grinding some salt into the pot, he began to stir again. "So, you're still freaking out, huh?"

"Oh yeah," I admitted blithely.

"And since Natalie has a baby, you thought to text her instead of Annie."

"Annie would tell Caleb."

Aidan kept his eyes on his task. "Caleb already knows."

"Oh he does, does he? How many people knew what you wanted before I did?"

"Just Caleb," he assured me. Pause. "And my older sisters."

"Both of them?"

"Yeah." He sighed. "And my mom. But that's it, I swear."

I inhaled and then exhaled deeply. "As long as you didn't tell my mom. I'd never hear the end of it."

"I have to say, you're taking my admission rather well."

"I've had two beers since you told me. I'm sedated."

"Ah."

I looked around the campsite. "Aidan?"

"Yeah?"

"I have to…you know…"

He grinned. "There's a shovel. You can dig a hole."

"You're kidding."

He laughed, a booming sound that was loud in the otherwise quiet forest. "Of course I'm kidding. Remember the small blue tent I set up? That's our bathroom. Don't forget to check for critters!"

"Just say no to bugs!" I called back, smiling. Halfway to the loo tent, I stopped and looked at him. "You kinda lied to me."

"Did I?"

"This isn't camping—this is *glamping*."

He grinned. "I know my audience."

"Now if only I had my computer."

"You can't write by hand?" Aidan asked.

I blinked. "You're kidding, right?"

"Yeah. Totally kidding," he backtracked.

"Liar."

"Well, it's a good thing I packed your computer."

"You didn't."

He looked immensely pleased with himself. "I did. I

know you. And I know that when you need to write, you *need* to write."

"But how will I be able to charge it?"

"The trailer has a generator, Sib. Remember?"

"I'm stupid in love with you. You know that right?"

He laughed.

"You don't have a couch hiding out in that Mary Poppins trailer, do you?" I asked with a wide grin and a lot of hope.

"Sorry. You'll have to settle for the camp chairs. Now, go do your thing and then come back. Dinner is almost ready."

I got to the loo tent and my phone chimed. Apparently, we weren't as off the grid as Aidan would've had me believe. I opened my screen.

Natalie: Hi! The monster has been projectile vomiting all day. It's in my hair, in the carpet, on the dog. He's fine, but I'm a bit tied up. Talk soon?

Projectile vomit. *Eeshk.* If that wasn't a billboard for birth control, I didn't know what was.

The sun started to set, and the temperature began to drop, so I snuggled into Aidan's side while we looked up at the stars, the fire blazing. I'd forgotten how clear and bright they were—there was too much light pollution from the city to ever be able to see the stars, even on a cloudless night.

"This is nice," I murmured, resting my head against his shoulder.

"It is," he agreed, cuddling me closer.

"Know what's missing?"

"Hmm?"

"A dog."

He chuckled. "You think a furry baby will distract me from wanting a human baby?"

"Is that such a terrible idea? Think about it. The dog could hang out with you at the bar. It could be the Veritas mascot."

"I like that idea. But I also like the idea of a tiny human."

"Nat had to clean up projectile vomit today—because her own tiny human puked everywhere. And when I say everywhere, I mean *everywhere*."

He laughed. "Yep, sounds about right."

Aidan didn't sound at all appalled, which meant I was failing at misdirection. I dangled the dog carrot and had only gotten a nibble.

"Dogs are easier," I said. "They potty train really fast."

"I get it, Sibby. You're not ready. I'm okay with that." He looked down at me and kissed my lips.

It was going to be one of those things that kept popping up in conversations and fights. And if the idea of projectile vomit didn't scare him off, then I knew he was totally serious.

Aidan was ready for a kid.

I was ready for bourbon.

I woke up to roving hands trying to work their way under my T-shirt. "Psst," Aidan whispered. "You awake?"

Cracking an eyelid, I licked my dry lips. "Someone's frisky this morning," I commented.

His hands headed south, and though I was half-asleep, needed coffee, and a good tooth-brushing, I couldn't say I was disappointed by Aidan's attention.

"I feel like a man out here."

His pants were already down, and I felt his hard length against me. "Guess you don't need any caffeine."

"What do you say?" He grinned, blue eyes twinkling with good humor. "Up for an early morning romp?"

I looped my arms around his neck. "Persuade me."

An hour later, we were finishing breakfast, happy smiles on both our faces. "You ready to go on that walk?"

"No way to get out of it, huh?" I teased.

"Come on, it'll be fun."

I liked fun—in the form of sitting. The morning had been crisp, but it was warming up, and the idea of walking hand-in-hand so Aidan could show me one of his favorite spots was definitely appealing.

"Okay, let's do it."

It was amazing what you could hear when there weren't any distractions. No garbage trucks, no construction workers, no dogs barking. All I heard was the wind in the trees, an occasional call of a bird as leaves crunched under our booted feet.

"So," I began as we walked shoulder-to-shoulder, "have you tried contacting Caleb?"

Aidan threw me a sheepish grin. "I might have checked in with him."

I laughed. "I'm glad I'm not the only one."

"I'm impressed, Sibby. You've only reached for your phone a few times since we've been here."

"I made a 'Sibby in the Wild' video last night and posted it to Instagram."

"Last night? When did you do that?" he wondered.

"You were already asleep." I winked. "And now I know which tree to stand by to get cell service."

"You know what this reminds me of?" Aidan took my hand and brought my knuckles to his lips.

"What?" I knew my cheeks were flushed. Not from the exercise, but from how Aidan was looking at me. Like he wanted to make very good use of the large boulders next to the trail. Apparently, nature made Aidan insatiable. Hmmm. Something to remember for future reference.

"This reminds me of our honeymoon."

"This does not look like Italy."

"I know that, smart-ass," he quipped. "But remember how we walked hand-in-hand down cobblestone streets, laughing, talking, just being with each other?"

I sighed as beautiful memories filled my head. "Yeah. I do."

"Sometimes I feel like we're fighting so many things for each other's attention. You know?"

"I guess," I said, a bit uncomfortable. "You don't think —are we in a rut?"

"Not a rut, per se, but—it's nice, Sib. Having you all to

myself. No book deadlines. No bar. None of that. Just you and me."

I didn't want to bring up the kid conversation again, but it seemed inevitable. "A baby complicates everything, Aidan. If what you're saying is true, that we don't spend enough time together, we'll have even less time together if we have a baby."

We stopped walking and Aidan dropped my hand. He stared off into the trees, like he was searching for words that would make sense to me.

"I feel like something is missing," he admitted quietly.

My breath hitched.

"No," he stated with emphasis, nearly yanking me into his arms, crushing me against him so I didn't tromp away. "I don't mean with you. I just feel—I don't know. What I'm doing—the bar, the rat race… I feel like it's meaning-less. It's all bullshit. I want a family. I'm ready for a family."

I didn't say anything for a long time. We stood on the forest path at a literal fork in the road I hadn't seen. There were only two directions to go—both forward, but I wasn't sure I wanted to take either of them.

"When we met," I said slowly, "my whole life had just gone up in flames. I'd never lived with that kind of instability."

"You fought me, you know. Fought being with me."

I nodded. "Yeah. I fought you. I fought myself. I'd just gotten out of a relationship, and I wanted to figure out who I was before being part of a couple again. What I felt for you back then"—I looked at him—"how fast I fell for you." I shook my head. "I didn't know if it was real, or if I was just making another shitty life choice."

He smiled. "How long did you wait for the shoe to drop?"

I grinned playfully. "Still waiting. You can't be this amazing."

"Sure I can," he teased.

My smile slipped. "I want to give you everything you want. But Aidan…" I took another deep breath. "I'm not ready to give up that last piece of me. We have a baby and everything changes. We change."

His blue eyes were earnest. "For the better, though. Don't you think? Sometimes you just have to leap; otherwise you're stuck in the same place. I don't want to be stuck."

"Why do people have kids? Answer me that."

"Because they want them," he said simply. "Do you want a family, Sibby?"

"I have a family." My words were slow, careful. "What we're doing now, our lives, it's enough for me. I'd like a dog. I wasn't joking about that."

Aidan's eyes remained locked on mine. "Are you saying you might actually *not* want to have kids?"

"I'm saying I don't want the pressure. I get enough of that from my mother."

"When have I pressured you?"

"You haven't," I stated. "Not in the real sense. But knowing you're ready and I'm not, that now lurks in the back of my head."

Did I want kids? Maybe. In the vague sense of the word.

"So what do we do?" Aidan asked, his face a shield—a shield I saw through.

"Right now? We walk."

I picked the left fork and hoped it got us where we wanted to be.

Chapter 5

#arewedoneyet #justkeepdrinking

We fell into an uncomfortable silence as we walked deeper and deeper into the woods. Though both of us tried to pretend we hadn't had a deep heart-to-heart a few minutes prior, we couldn't sweep it under the forest floor.

Aidan was ready for kids.

I wasn't.

I wasn't even sure I wanted them. Not really. I enjoyed doing what I wanted when I wanted to do it. Both of us worked like maniacs—and we'd only been married a year.

I'd hoped to have a few more years alone together before we changed the family dynamic.

If we had a kid now, would I resent Aidan? Would I resent the baby? See? I was not in any rational frame of mind to even consider procreating.

"Are we almost there?" I asked Aidan who was walking a few steps ahead of me.

"Yeah. We're almost there." He didn't turn around to look at me.

I swallowed a lump of tears in my throat and continued to trek after him. Ten minutes later, Aidan reached down to help me up onto a boulder. The hike had been mild, and it had felt like we'd only managed to do a steady incline, but it turned out that we were on the side of a mountain. Aidan had promised me a view of a waterfall, and he'd more than delivered. Afternoon sunlight glinted in golden speckles as the water slathered the rocks and then pooled below.

"Oh, wow," I breathed.

Aidan finally looked at me. His shoulders slouched as he released the tension. "Come here," he said, voice as rough as the rocks.

I moved into his embrace and snuggled against him. "I don't want to lose you." The words were garbled from emotion, but I knew he heard me by the way he held me tighter.

"You won't."

"Promise?"

"Promise. I'll make you another promise." He leaned back so he could stare down into my eyes, and his hands came up to cup my cheeks. "I promise I won't say any more about it on this trip. This trip will just be for us."

I inhaled a breath as tears continued to spill down my cheeks. "Sometimes I don't think I deserve you."

He hauled me close to him again and buried his face in my hair. "I feel that way about you. All the time."

"I think I have low blood sugar."

He released me just enough so he could rummage in his jacket pocket. "Here." Aidan handed me a granola bar. "Do you need some water?"

I shook my head. "I'm good."

"Let's head back," he suggested, hopping down off the rock. He helped me down as I tore into the granola bar. "We'll make some lunch."

"And then?"

"What do you mean, 'and then'?" He smiled at me and reached for my hand.

I chewed and swallowed before replying. "Well, we hiked, we had the sex. What's next after food?"

"You relax. I'll set up a hammock."

I shook my head. "Nope. I don't do hammocks."

"Why not?"

"Clumsy people and hammocks do not mix."

He grinned. "Ah, gotcha."

"Shut up." I playfully swatted him. My chest lightened of pressure, and suddenly the somber mood from our earlier talk seemed to drift away. I wasn't great at living in the moment, but I desperately wanted to. It wasn't the worst thing in the world to slow down.

We got back to camp, and I helped Aidan prep lunch. I let him do the fixing since the trailer area wasn't big enough for two. While he made lunch, I grabbed napkins and beers. We'd eat in our camp chairs.

"It's ready!" he called.

I got up and took a step toward the trailer back. "Ow." I winced.

Aidan looked up from setting our sandwiches onto two paper plates. "What's wrong?"

"I think I have blisters."

"From your hiking boots?"

I nodded.

"Didn't you tell me you'd worn them before?

"I have worn them before."

"Sibby," he said in that voice he used when he knew I had stretched the truth.

"Um…I have worn them before." I sighed and then admitted, "While I was watching TV."

"So you didn't break them in."

"Nope."

"And now you have blisters."

"Yep."

His smile was rueful. "Let's eat and then we'll tend to your feet."

After we ate, Aidan heated up a bucket of warm water using the propane stove. I grimaced and gingerly removed my boots and socks.

"You have blisters everywhere!" Aidan stated in surprise.

"I think my blisters have blisters." I winced as I dunked my feet.

"I've got a cure-all."

"You're not about to make some frat boy penis joke, are you?"

"Had to go there, huh?"

"What's this cure-all?" I demanded.

He hopped up from his chair and went to the trailer. A moment later he was back, handing me a bottle of Jack Daniel's Tennessee Honey Whiskey.

"And then the kingdom rejoiced. The end." I unscrewed the lid and took a swig. It went down smooth and warm. I had another nip.

"Easy there, champ. It's not even dark yet," he teased.

I glanced at my phone resting on my lap. "It's happy hour."

"Cheers." He clinked his beer bottle against the whiskey. "You good here for a bit?"

I nodded. "What are you doing?"

"I want to scout for some more firewood. Tonight, I'm cooking you steak over an open flame."

"Why do you keep me around?" I wondered aloud.

"I like lookin' atcha." He kissed me quickly. "I wont be far."

"Wait! How am I supposed to entertain myself?"

He reached into the back pocket of his jeans. "Here." Aidan tossed a book at me.

I caught it. Glancing at the title, I shook my head. "Ass."

"Have fun!" he called and started walking away.

The jerk had given me a dog-eared copy of *Walden Pond*.

I stood by the tree where I could get cell service. It was spotty, and every now and then I had to put the phone on speaker and hold it over my head just so I could have a conversation.

Like now.

"This is my worst nightmare realized," I said.

Annie laughed. "I do not envy you. Like, at all."

"Shut up," I growled. "He took me fishing yesterday morning."

"He didn't."

"Yup. We got up when it was still dark, and we walked to a lake in the middle of nowhere."

"Catch anything?"

I sighed. "No. My allergies went haywire, and I started sneezing. Aidan said I scared off all the fish."

Annie laughed again. "Where's Aidan?"

"Collecting firewood." There was noise in the background over the phone, voices, and the sound of silverware clinking. "Where are you? Are you at work?"

"Nope. Got the night off. I'm having dinner at the bar at TAO."

"You're eating Asian Fusion *without* me?"

"Yes," my best friend answered, not sounding a bit contrite.

"What are you drinking?" I demanded.

"Vodka gimlet."

"Bitch!" I paused. "Do you think I can order Seamless up here?"

"Try it," she suggested. "Aside from your lack of ethnic cuisine, how is it? Planning to go all *Walden Pond*?"

"Don't make me Thoreau up." I hiccoughed.

"Are you drunk?"

"Yes. I've put away a fifth of Tennessee Honey since I got here. Funny thing, you mentioned *Walden Pond*. That was one of the books Aidan brought. The other was *The Hitchhiker's Guide to the Galaxy*. I've taken a shower with water heated by the sun. I'm dying. My soul is dying."

"I'd rather go to the gynecologist than go to the woods."

"I haven't seen anyone except Aidan in days. I'm going stir crazy. I'm also secretly afraid that Aidan is going to realize I'm just a hot piece of ass with frizzy hair and a decent sense of humor and then decide to leave me for some granola-girl who loves homemade deodorant and doesn't own a TV."

"You're squirrelier than normal," Annie commented. "What's really going on? Is this about the woods?"

"Nothing's going on."

"Sibby, you're a shit liar, and I've known you for a decade. Tell me what's going on."

"He wants a baby."

"No."

"*Yes.*"

"Do you? Want a baby?"

I paused before answering. "I don't know."

She sighed. "Oy."

"Yeah, oy," I agreed.

"Sibby!" I heard Aidan call.

"Coming!" I yelled back. "Gotta go. Don't tell Caleb."

"Iron vault," she assured me.

"Stop at one gimlet and then I might believe you."

"I've already had two—hey, if you do get knocked up, who the hell am I going to drink with?"

"Sibby!" Aidan called again.

"Way to make my drama all about you," I hissed at my best friend.

"You breeders are all the same."

"I'm not a breeder!" I protested.

"Not yet. But your husband has dimples that charmed the pants off you. I bet his sperm has dimples that will charm your egg into fertilization."

"You've had more than two drinks," I accused.

"Guilty!"

"I so hate you!" I hung up on her and then trekked back to camp. Aidan had lit a fire and was sticking a marshmallow onto a stick. It had become our nightly routine. It was sweet and cute, and I was sick to death of it. I wanted to take the bag of marshmallows and throw them into the fire. Instead, I forced a smile and sat down.

"How's Annie?" Aidan asked with a wry grin.

I gaped. "How did you know?"

"Please." He snorted. "You found a spot that has service, and you make up excuses to go over there every time you want to check social media, send a text, or call someone."

"Are you mad?"

"Mad? No." He peered at me. "I'm the one who brought your computer for you."

I nodded. He was correct. He had brought my computer for me. I'd even opened it a few times and tried to write. Unfortunately, "AHHHHHHHHHHH" didn't translate into a decent story.

I was never asking Aidan for anything ever again. Not if it meant being dragged to the middle of nowhere where I had to sit and contemplate my life choices. Okay, so I was shallow. I admitted it. I liked internet, couches, and showers every day. I didn't want to have to climb a ladder to get into my bed, and I liked being able to groom properly. I hadn't looked in a mirror for days, but I was pretty sure I looked like a Neanderthal.

And yet…

I felt closer to Aidan than I ever had before. It was just the two of us, no distractions, no work.

"What are you thinking about?" Aidan asked as he ate a burnt marshmallow. He put another one on the end of the stick and then handed it to me.

"A book idea," I lied.

"Yeah? Inspired up here?"

"Uh, yeah. Sure."

"What's the book about?"

A husband that drove his wife to insanity.

"Not sure yet," I hedged. I twirled the stick, letting the marshmallow turn a golden brown.

"Sibby?"

"Hmm?"

"Can you look at me for a second?"

I was afraid if I looked at him, I'd tell him how much I hated all of this and that I wanted to go back to the city immediately. But somehow, I schooled my expression into drunken bemusement and looked at him.

"What's wrong with your face?" he asked.

"Um. How am I supposed to answer that?"

He shook his head. "No, I just mean—did you walk through a bush. Did your face brush against any leaves…or white flowers?"

"I don't remember. Why?"

"It's…well…red."

"I've been drinking," I admitted. "A lot."

"Yeah, it's not flushed from drinking. Come closer." As I scooted toward him, he turned on his headlamp. I winced and closed my eyes at the brightness. "Sorry. Turn your head. No, the other way."

"Well?" I demanded. "What is it? Why aren't you saying anything?"

"I think you walked into something poisonous."

"Poison Ivy? Oak? What?"

"If I had to guess, it was Cow Parsnip. And"—he sighed—"you've got a really bad rash."

Chapter 6

#creatureofthenight #notavampire #quarantined

"It's exacerbated by sunlight," Aidan said as he pressed a cool compress to my skin. "So you have to stay out of the sun tomorrow."

My face felt like it was on fire—it itched like hell.

"You're telling me, that on top of looking like a swamp thing, I have to stay out of direct sunlight?"

"Yeah, Sibby, you have to stay out of direct sunlight— and please spare me the vampire jokes."

"It would've been too easy," I muttered.

"Lean back," Aidan said, urging me to lie down. He

was doctoring me in the tent, and due to all the booze, I was getting sleepy.

"Will this have any long-lasting effects?"

"Not if you stay out of the sun." I felt his fingers running through my hair. "Ready to call it quits?"

"Hmmm? No, don't stop that. Keep going." I reached up to urge his fingers to continue their effective detangling of my hair.

"Sibby?"

"What?" I asked, drowsy and oddly content—had to have been the bourbon.

"Do you want to go home?"

"No, I don't want to go home," I said.

Well, that was a surprise.

"You sure?" Aidan pressed. "Because I can absolutely—"

"No, I want to stay. You're having fun. And I'll be okay. This isn't serious, is it?"

"Not unless it blisters."

"Wow, don't become a doctor," I quipped. "Your bedside manner sucks."

He chuckled. "You're sure you're okay to stay?"

"I'm fine. I'll be fine." I struggled to sit up.

"What are you doing?"

"I need help de-robing. I want my pajamas, maybe a Benadryl to knock me unconscious, and to wake up to a new day tomorrow."

"Well, I can help with the pajamas—and I packed some Benadryl, so if you give me a few minutes I'll find it for you."

Aidan helped me into pajamas, all the while leaving the cold compress on my face. He tucked me into the sleeping bag and said, "I'll be right back, okay?"

"I'll be here," I muttered.

I fell asleep before he made it back with the Benadryl.

"On a scale of one to ten, how bad do I look?" I asked the next morning.

"You're beautiful," Aidan said.

"Liar."

He shook his head and looked away, trying to hide his grin. And failed. Failed hard. In fact, his shoulders shook and a moment later, he was bent over at the waist. When he straightened back up, he wiped the tears from his eyes.

"You done?"

"Yeah," he choked out. "I'm done." He looked at me and then burst into laughter again. "You look like a mummy!"

"You told me to wrap my entire face!" I shouted.

"I can't—stop—laughing!"

"I'm gonna punch you. I'm gonna punch you so hard."

"It would be worth it," he wheezed. Somehow he stopped laughing and got himself under control. He scooted toward the exit of the tent, unzipping the protective screen. "I'll make you coffee."

"Uh huh."

"And breakfast."

"Great."

"And I'll even give you a foot rub tonight by the fire."

"Just go." I flung my hand in the direction of the privacy screen. "And leave me to my suffering."

"So dramatic," he called over his shoulder, stupidly cute dimples on display.

When he was gone, I flopped down on my back. I reached for my phone by my side. We lived in an age where everything needed to be documented for social media or it didn't happen. And though the rational part of me was horrified that I was willing to share this moment with Instagram, another part of me said, "Screw it. Bring on the laughter" because I was desperately in need of some laughter—and I knew other people could use it too.

I never had a problem poking fun at myself. Two years prior, someone had recorded a video of me opening a bottle of champagne. The stubborn cork had refused to budge, and then suddenly it had shot off like a rocket— nailing my ex-boyfriend in the eye.

Yeah, it went viral. Thus launching my writing career before it had really begun. But that was neither here nor there. I wasn't documenting my camping excursions because I wanted to be discovered or to perpetuate the idea that I was some great social influencer. And what the hell did that mean anyway? No, I did these videos because I knew—*knew*—there were women out there subjected to nature, to their men's desire to be in nature, just like I was.

At least I had a man who cared enough about me and my wishes to make me as comfortable as humanly possible.

So I pressed record and smiled for the camera.

I finished the video and got it ready to upload. Unfor- tunately, there was no cell service in the tent, so I'd have to wait until the cover of darkness, head to the tree where I knew I could get a few bars, and then upload it.

Time was dragging to the point where I felt like Superman was flying around the earth, turning it backwards. Aidan had brought me food and coffee, and after he cleaned up, he joined me in the tent. He tossed a deck of cards down.

"Strip poker?" I asked.

"I was thinking Go Fish."

"Yep. I knew it."

"Knew what?" he demanded, shrugging out of his black jacket and tossing it in the corner.

"You don't find mummies attractive. Just don't look at my face. Look at my body. Come on! Objectify me!"

"It's kind of hard to objectify you when—"

"Are you going to shuffle those cards, or what?"

"Got you something," he said with a grin. "Dig around in my jacket pocket."

I leaned over to grab his jacket, sticking my hands in his pockets. I pulled out a packet of Peanut M&M's. "You've been holding out on me."

"Extreme measures."

I ripped open the top of the bag and poured a few of my favorite candy into my hand. "Deal those cards, sucker. I plan to take all your fish."

Though the side vent of the tent was open, I could only see darkness. I'd fallen asleep after our card tournament, and it was nighttime when I awoke. Aidan was somewhere out there, talking to someone. He must've found his own cell service hub. I thought about calling out to him, to tell him I was finally awake, when threads of his conversation became audible.

"Dude, I think she might divorce me," I heard Aidan say.

I stilled my movements, and despite the fact that I had to pee I didn't dare move so I didn't make any noise.

"No, I'm not being dramatic," Aidan nearly snapped. "First, I guilt her into coming to the woods with no one but me for conversation. And it's been one thing or another since we got here. Nothing has gone right. She got blisters from a hike and just as she started to recover she walked into Cow Parsnip. She's been asleep all day in the tent with bandages on her face—stop laughing! Come on, man."

I sat up, hoping that would relieve the pressure on my bladder.

"And I clobbered her emotionally by telling her I want a kid—and now she thinks I'm baby hungry and in cahoots with her mother."

Pause.

"I am *not* baby hungry. You're missing the point. Just get up here, and bring Annie."

Ah, so he was talking to Caleb.

But there was *no way* Annie was coming up here. If I hated nature, Annie hated it even more. No way would she come up here. Not happening.

The conversation ended, and I heard Aidan sigh. I wanted to wait a few minutes, let him move away from the tent before pretending I had just woken up. But my stomach chose that moment to let out a noise resembling the Sarlacc, the creature that looked like a pit of teeth from *Return of the Jedi*.

"Sibby?" he called.

"Yeah?"

Aidan sighed. "How much of that did you hear?"

"I heard nothing."

"I don't believe you."

"I heard all of it," I admitted. "Can I come out now? I really have to pee."

"Yeah."

I poked my head out of the tent. Aidan stood below the ladder, looking up at me. I could see his face because the lantern had been lit and so had a campfire.

"What time is it?" I asked, turning around and wiggling my body down the ladder.

"You didn't check your phone?"

"It died before I fell asleep."

"You should have said something. I would've charged it for you."

"Aidan, stop."

He cocked his head to one side. "Stop? Stop what?"

"Stop walking on eggshells around me."

"I'm not—"

"You are," I insisted. "I heard that conversation with Caleb. Stop feeling bad for telling me what you needed."

"But we don't want the same things, and I'm worried that—"

I jumped into his arms and hugged him close, my gauze-covered face hitting his chest. "I don't think I'm cut out for camping. That's a given. As far as the kid thing, I just need time. Okay?"

His arms crushed me to him. "I'm not driving you away? You still love me?"

I leaned back, so I could look at him. I sniffed the air like a rodent searching for predators. "Are you drunk?"

"No! Well, maybe a little."

"Oh, Aidan," I said with a smile and hugged him again. "I missed you today."

"I missed you."

"Sorry I passed out."

"Sorry I dragged you to the woods and you got a rash. How do you feel?"

"You know that guy from *Braveheart*—Robert the Bruce's father?"

"Yeah."

"Do I look like that guy?"

He chuckled. "No."

"You swear?"

"I swear."

"Good. Can I make you dinner?"

"You're going to make *me* dinner?" he asked in amusement as we walked toward the campfire.

"I was gonna open a can of soup and call it a day. How do you feel about that?"

He reached up to touch my face and then chuckled when he realized I was still covered in gauze. "I think that would be very, very nice."

The next day the gauze came off, and I had my face again. It was a little redder than normal, and it was definitely itchy, but anything was better than looking like an extra from a *Grey's Anatomy* episode.

After breakfast, I heard the sound of a motor approaching. I looked at Aidan who was grinning. He was back to his affable self and hadn't even suffered a hangover.

"Let me guess… Caleb?"

"Yep. Texted me this morning."

"You have to show me your hotspot," I said.

"What will you give me for it?" he teased.

"Half my PayDay bar."

"Gimme."

Caleb rolled into the clearing, and before he'd even parked his blue Subaru, Annie was jumping out of the front seat.

"Savior!" I yelled, hopping up from my chair and running toward her.

"You have seen nothing yet," Annie said. She released me and then went to the front seat of the car and pulled out a bottle of vodka. She raised an eyebrow. "Got any orange juice?"

I waved her toward the trailer. "This way." Shaking my head, I looked at her. "How the hell did Caleb get you to leave the city?"

Though Annie wasn't a born and raised New Yorker she acted like one. She rarely felt inclined to leave Manhattan, and she got oddly nutso when she couldn't order Chinese food at any hour.

"You were in a dire situation," she remarked. "You needed me. What kind of friend could I call myself if I didn't relieve you of your suffering—nice face, by the way."

"You're a jerk." I stuck my head into the refrigerator and pulled out a plastic jug of OJ. "What's the real reason you came?"

"You were the real reason," she assured me.

I looked at her over my shoulder and waited.

She sighed and gave in. "Fine, I got a promise from Caleb."

"What kind of promise?"

"He will not ask me to marry him again for at least another six months."

"Ah." I set the OJ on the counter and reached for the vodka.

"How's the uterus embargo?"

I rolled my eyes. "Let's just drink."

Chapter 7

#burnbabyburn #discoinferno #allhailthepyrogods

"Come on," I said. "Setting up your tent shouldn't be that hard. We can do it. We're strong women. We're wilderness women. We got this."

"You're drunk," Annie said, looking at me with glassy eyes. "Or you've had a lobotomy. We can't set up this tent ourselves!"

"Look, the boys went on a hike, no doubt to talk about us—and what we're *not* giving them. Wouldn't it be nice if when they came back, the tent was already set up and we had cooked dinner?"

"No, actually, it wouldn't." Annie crossed her arms over her chest.

I placed my hands on my hips. "You're a selfish bitch."

She scoffed. "You're one to talk."

"Caleb wants to marry you—why won't you say yes? You've been in a relationship for two years. You know how many women would kill to have a guy like him want them that way? Pull the trigger already."

She bent over at the waist and laughed. "*Me* pull the trigger? Get knocked up already! What, are you afraid you can't juggle a career and motherhood at the same time? Newsflash, you're right, something has to give. No one can do it all, and you know who suffers? The woman. It's always the woman."

I didn't like how Annie was spewing my deepest, darkest fears, letting them out in the open to breathe. "Are my fears really your fears?" I asked. "Because this whole time, I thought you were commitment shy. If that's the case, then break up with Caleb now and don't string him along anymore."

"I tried!" she yelled.

"Um, what?" I blinked. "Hold on. What do you mean *you tried?* And when?"

Annie looked down at the ground. "Few weeks ago. It didn't stick."

"You didn't tell me," I said softly. "Why didn't you tell me?"

"You were on a book deadline."

"Still—Annie, this is something you share. You shouldn't have kept it to yourself."

She shrugged, looking like a morose teen. "Like I said, it didn't stick. Caleb wouldn't let it."

"What happened, Annie? What brought this on?"

"I don't want to talk about it."

"Well, we're going to talk about it!"

"Let's talk about you," she shot back. "Why don't you want a baby?"

"People can not want babies."

She shrugged. "People can not want to get married."

I put my hands to my head. "I think we drank too much."

"Sibby—"

"I'm sorry, okay? I'm sorry I wasn't there for you, I'm sorry I don't understand why you're having issues committing to Caleb, I'm sorry I'm so drunk, and I doubt I'll remember every detail of this conversation—"

"SIBBY!"

"WHAT?"

"The camp chair is on fire!"

I turned and sure enough, the camp chair had fallen into the fire. Annie and I looked at each other, both stunned stupid.

"What do we do?" she yelled.

"We put it out, you dink!" I shouted back, running toward the fire.

"Okay! But with what?"

As Annie had her flight moment, I was having a fight moment. The fire gods would only get half my chair if I had anything to say about it. I lugged over a water container and called to Annie. "Drag the chair off the fire!"

"But—"

"Do it!"

She snapped into action, yanked the chair out of the fire, and then I doused the flaming sucker. Because it was me, I somehow got soaked in the process.

"Sibby's fucking Law," I muttered. "Every damn time." I tossed the empty water container aside.

Annie giggled.

Then I giggled.

And then the guys walked back into camp. They exchanged a look.

"What happened?" Caleb asked, taking in the burnt chair, my wet clothes, the sizzling firewood.

Annie and I both pointed at one another and said at the exact same time, "She did it."

"Did you guys have fun on your hike?" I asked Aidan that night while we were in our tent. Caleb and Annie were in their own ground tent. We'd had dinner together, and that had gone a long way into sobering me up.

"Yeah," Aidan said and then stopped talking.

"You know something," I accused.

"I know nothing."

"What do you know?" I demanded.

"What do *you* know?" he asked back.

"Ummmm."

"Ah ha! I knew you knew something."

"But you know something, too," I said. "I wonder if you know what I know or if you just think you know what I know."

"What?" he asked.

I leaned up on my elbows and looked down on him. "Spill. And then I'll spill."

"Bro-code."

"Wife-code."

"Damn it. That trumps all the codes." He grinned and then sobered. "Okay. So apparently Annie tried to break up with Caleb a few weeks ago." Aidan paused, gauging my reaction.

"That's all? That's all you got?"

"What have you got?" he demanded.

"Same as you."

"Caleb wasn't very forthcoming. I don't think he knew what set her off."

"Annie's always been…commitment shy? I don't know. It was weird. In college, she did this thing where she dated guys—serial monogamy, right? Almost like she thought she was supposed to. When she didn't graduate engaged, it was kind of hard on her."

"I can't imagine being engaged at twenty-two."

"Yeah. But she comes from one of those families, ya know? Southern. They expect things of her. Moving to New York and going to culinary school was against everything her parents wanted for her."

"And yet they paid for her school."

I shrugged. "She went crazy for a bit."

"I've never seen Caleb so happy—and so confused."

"Annie's confused," I said quietly. "Getting what you think you want and then realizing it's all good, that there's nothing to worry about… Some people can't handle that."

"Hmmm. Come here."

I lay down and snuggled into his side. "Thanks for calling them."

"Is the trip better now?"

His fingers wove their way through my hair, making me drowsy and comfortable. "Yeah. I didn't realize how much I would miss people."

"It's been five days, Sibby."

I laughed. "Yeah and my life is tied to the internet and a computer screen. It's a lot to adjust to."

"Yeah…but it hasn't been all terrible, right?"

Lifting up so that I could look him in the eyes, I smiled. "No. Not all terrible."

"Camping isn't that hard," Annie said the next morning as she bit into a homemade breakfast burrito.

"How many camp showers have you taken?" I demanded. I pointed to a tree and a tent. "See that? That's our privacy tent. We have to heat water, put it in a plastic bag with a hose and a glorified sprayer on it and then spray ourselves down, soap up, and then rinse—all in like two minutes before the water is gone. I can't even get a brush through my hair when I'm done."

Annie leaned closer so she could touch my locks, which were currently in braids. "Hmmm. When was the last time you conditioned?"

I smacked her hand away. "Eat your burrito."

She grinned and took another huge bite of the sausage and egg burrito.

"Were you guys warm last night?" Aidan asked, sipping on his cup of coffee. He was sitting on a milk crate—considering we were down one chair. Caleb had only brought two; one for him, one for Annie.

"I was warm," Annie announced.

"Because you stole all the covers," Caleb stated.

She shrugged and then offered him her burrito. He grabbed it and sent her a steamy look.

I didn't understand their dynamic. They got along, they had fun, they were adventurous. Both of them loved food and wine. What was Annie's deal? There was something important she wasn't telling me. But that girl kept stuff on lockdown. She didn't like dealing with emotions, and subsequently she wasn't really good at it.

Then again, who was?

"How are you guys doing on supplies?" Caleb asked.

Aidan scratched his jaw. He was sporting a beard, and it looked good on him. "We should probably go into town and get more stuff."

"Yeah, you're almost out of beer." Caleb grinned. "And you will be by the time we leave."

I perked up. "There's a town nearby?"

Aidan nodded.

"With cell service?"

"Maybe." Aidan reached for a fallen piece of sausage on his plate.

I hopped up. "What are we waiting for? Let's go!"

"Sibby's been without legit email," Aidan explained.

"You sound like I'm insane for needing technology."

"No, not insane," he assured me. "A little kooky at times, but not insane."

I grasped his hand and tried to haul him off the milk crate, but he was tall and steadfastly planted. "Come on, come on, *come on*. If you take me to town where there's cell service and I can check my email, I'll be your best friend."

"I already have a best friend," Aidan quipped, pointing to Caleb.

"I slither on top of you naked. Does he do that?"

"Slither?" Caleb repeated. "What do you mean you *slither*?"

I made a face. "Oops, I forgot we weren't alone."

"Seriously, what's this slithering thing?" Caleb demanded. He looked at Annie. "Can we try it?"

Ignoring the direction of their conversation, I dropped Aidan's hand and removed the plate from his lap so I could plop down. "Please, please, please. Can we go?"

"Yeah, Sibby, we can go."

"Yippee!" I jumped off him and ran to the truck. I scrambled into the front seat and waited.

Civilization, here I come!

This wasn't civilization.

It looked like a ghost town. It was just a tiny section of old buildings with peeling paint and a dirt road down the strip called Main Street. And about four stores. Total.

"Was this what you were expecting?" Annie asked.

"You think Upstate, and you think quaint little towns with funky art and jewelry. Organic farm-to-table restaurants. Not"—I glanced around—"this."

"Oh, good. You're totally confused too." Annie nodded, frowning. "I haven't seen one human being since we drove in."

"Clearly there are humans here," I muttered. "The

guys went into the general store to fill up the propane tank, so—"

"I don't even see a Starbucks. And they exist everywhere!" Annie announced. "Literally everywhere."

"What do you think would happen if Amazon, Starbucks, and Google had a ménage romance going on?"

"Then all my dreams would come true."

She walked up the street, and I followed her. "What do you see?" I asked.

Annie peered around like she was scoping out the place. She lifted her nose to the sky and sniffed. "That way." She pointed ahead. "About twenty feet. A bar."

"You smelled out a bar?"

"I'm a Monahan," she explained. "It's what we do. And also—I read the sign." She grinned.

"I'll text Aidan and tell him where we are."

Though it was late afternoon, you couldn't tell when you walked in. It was dark and divey. Just the kind of place Annie and I liked in our college years. There was something comforting about the scarred pool table and the half-lit-up jukebox. A few locals wearing baseball hats sat at the bar, nursing their beers. They all looked at us like we were specimens in a museum.

A middle-aged guy wearing an army green button-down kept his gaze on us as we bellied up to the bar.

"Do you have any cider on draft?" I asked.

The bartender's expression didn't change as he looked me up and down. "Beer."

"How about a Pinot Gris?"

"I got one white," he all but growled.

"I'll take it." I looked at Annie. "You're up."

"IPA on draft," she said. "And can you turn up the sound on the TV. I want to catch that replay."

The bartender grinned and lifted the remote to the TV,

increasing the sound. He poured her an IPA. "Five bucks." He looked at me. "Eight for yours."

"Do you take cards?" I asked.

"Are you trying to get us thrown out?" Annie asked me. She fished around in her back pocket and set a twenty on the bar. "For the drinks—and maybe a few rounds of pool?"

The bartender filched the money and smiled. "You got it, sweetheart."

We took our drinks and headed to the single pool table. "So, how did you get time off? I thought Heather was in the throes of dinner party season."

Annie kept her eyes on the rack as she rolled them to the dot on the green felt. "I quit."

I gasped. "What? When?"

"Um. About a week ago?"

"And the secrets keep coming out," I marveled. "Do you even confide in me any more?"

"I'm not like you, Sibby. I don't just dump emotion on anyone who will listen."

I frowned. "I don't do that."

"You have a hard time hiding your feelings."

"Yeah, but you hide yours *too* well," I threw back. "What did Caleb say when you told him you quit?"

"He doesn't know."

I stared at her, gripping the pool cue so tight my knuckles turned white. "Why not?"

She shrugged.

"Wow. Okay." I picked up my glass of wine and took a sip. It was worse than Franzia, if that was possible. "I've never had a front row seat to watch someone self-destruct. What else you got coming? Hmm?"

She glared at me. "I'm not self-destructing."

"Breaking up with Caleb for no reason. Quitting your

job for—well, it's about time, actually. But you didn't tell me. Or Caleb. I want to know why."

"Time for a change. That's all."

"Bullshit."

We were in the middle of a stare down when someone asked, "Can we join you guys?"

Chapter 8

#blackandblue #nottalkingaboutsteak

Two locals, both burly and muscled, clutching two beers, waited for us to answer. I was about to open my mouth and say no when Annie replied, "Sure."

I frowned at her. Not only were we in the middle of a best friend fight—which we seemed to be doing a lot lately—but we were also not single. I didn't want to be joined by two random dudes. I wanted to choke down the rest of my wine, play a game of pool, and wait for Aidan to show up and tell me we could go back to the woods.

Did I say that?

The woods weren't *that* bad. My rash had cleared up, and the weather was still gorgeous. I totally had the showering thing down. It wasn't ideal, but it was manageable. And Aidan's libido was off the charts. Fresh air did the boy good.

And going to sleep with the tent vents open so I could hear the sounds of nature…well, I never thought I'd like it. But I did. Snuggling close to Aidan and smelling the scent of a campfire on his clothes and skin…it made me all—

"Buy me a shot?" Annie asked the brown-haired Hulk. I swore the guy had no neck, like, just shoulder muscles with a little head on top.

"Sure," he said, smiling down at her. They walked away from the pool table, leaving me with Trucker Hat.

"So—"

"I'm married," I interrupted. "And I'm waiting for my husband." I held up my ring finger to show him I wasn't lying.

"Have a nice night," he said and slunk away. He took his drink back to the bar, leaving me alone at the pool table.

I heard a feminine giggle.

Annie was getting into trouble, and she wasn't listening to me. My oldest friend in the world was going through something, and she was actively keeping me out of it. But there was only so much I could do. I couldn't stop her behavior—she was an adult, but I sure as hell would not aid her.

I pulled out my phone and sent a text to Aidan. Caleb was Annie's boyfriend, and it was up to him to decide if he wanted to get involved. Then again, the guy wanted to marry her, so I couldn't imagine he'd be at all okay seeing Annie flirting and giggling with some other guy.

I grabbed my drink and went to the bar. I found a seat

in the corner to nurse the swill they called wine. Also, from the seat I had chosen, I could see Annie. She was leaning forward, brushing her breasts against the burly guy's chest. Throwing her head back, she laughed.

I drank more wine.

The door to the bar opened, and Aidan's tall form stepped through. He turned his head and found me. Caleb was one step behind him.

"What the fuck?" I heard Caleb say. "Is she drunk?" He looked at me when he asked the question.

"As far as I know, no," I said.

Caleb sauntered toward Annie and the dude she was standing next to. Aidan came to me. "Did you try and stop her?"

"No, I actually pushed her in that guy's direction." I rolled my eyes. "Of course I tried to stop her. She doesn't want to be stopped."

I watched Caleb put his hand on Annie's arm, and then Hulk stepped forward, his face darkening with a scowl.

"I'm her boyfriend," Caleb said. He was a few inches shorter than Hulk and definitely leaner. "And we're ready to get out of here."

"She doesn't look like she wants to leave," Hulk said. He pushed out his chest, trying to appear bigger, which wasn't necessary.

"Annie, come on. Let's go."

"I'm not ready to leave. I'm having fun." She swayed on her feet. Guess she'd done a few more shots I hadn't seen.

"You're drunk," Caleb said, reaching for her hand. "Let's go sleep it off."

"No!" she yelled and shrugged out of his grip. "You're always trying to tell me what to do!"

Caleb took a step forward, in between Annie and Hulk. "We can talk about this at home."

Everything happened pretty fast after that. Insanity ensued. Shouts, curses, and then Aidan jumped into the fray and took a punch to the nose. The cluster-fuck ended when the bartender dumped a bucket of ice onto Hulk, Caleb, and Aidan.

"Not in my bar!" the bartender yelled. "Get out! The four of ya!"

I ran to Annie who was standing by in stupid shock. Grabbing her arm, I made sure she had her purse, and then I tugged her toward the exit. Aidan and Caleb stumbled out after us. Caleb's shirt was ripped, and even in the dying afternoon light, I could tell his right eye was red. It would be black by the following morning.

"Fuck, my nose is bleeding," Aidan said, leaning over on the sidewalk. I dropped Annie's hand and ran to him.

I removed my black, long-sleeved shirt and handed it to him. He pressed it to his nose and remained hunched over to tend to himself. Caleb was also bent over, breathing hard.

"You okay?" I called to him, shivering in my tank-top and running my hands up and down my arms.

He managed a nod. "Got the wind knocked out of me. I'll be fine."

I glanced at Annie who was standing off to the side, staring down at Caleb with a glazed look. A wave of anger overcame me, but I clenched my jaw shut. She was drunk, and there was no use fighting with her about her behavior even though she'd gotten her own boyfriend punched in the eye, not to mention Aidan had been injured trying to break up the fight.

"How attached are you to this?" Aidan asked, rising.

His nose had stopped bleeding, and my shirt was crumbled in his hand.

"I'm not."

"I'm gonna get rid of it. Don't want to bring it back to camp."

I nodded. He found a public trashcan a few feet from the bar and threw away my ruined shirt. He came back, and I wrapped him in my arms. "How's the nose?"

"I'll need some Advil pretty soon. It's throbbing already."

"Broken?"

"Nah. I got lucky, it's just bruised." Aidan leaned over and kissed the top of my head. "I don't want him driving. I don't think he's in the head space for it."

"His eye's swelling shut too," I commented.

"Why don't you drive Caleb's car. Annie can ride with you. Caleb will ride with me."

Seething, I climbed into the driver's side of Caleb's blue Subaru. I adjusted the seat and mirrors, waiting for Annie to get her ass into the car. It was painful watching Caleb and Annie interact through the windshield. I couldn't hear what they were saying to each other, but Caleb's shoulders were tight with tension, his mouth rigid. Annie looked completely confused, like she didn't know how she'd gotten there.

Vodka, I wanted to shout at her. But it wasn't the vodka. The vodka had only been what had allowed her twisted behavior to come out.

The passenger side of the car opened, and she slid inside. She slowly buckled herself in, keeping her eyes forward. She took a deep breath; I knew she was about to speak, but I cut her off.

"Don't," I warned. "Just don't."

"Okay," she said, voice sounding small.

She was my oldest friend in the world, and I loved her. But at that moment, I really didn't like her.

We drove back to our camp in complete silence. When I parked, she unbuckled her seatbelt and was out before I'd even unlatched myself. When I opened the door, I heard it: the sound of her puking.

Aidan and Caleb were just climbing out of the truck when they glanced at me.

"I'll go," I volunteered. "Let me just get her some water." I headed for the water cooler and Aidan followed me. Out of the corner of my eye, I saw Caleb go into the tent he was sharing with Annie.

"He doesn't want to stay with her tonight," Aidan told me, his voice low.

I sighed. "Can't blame him."

"Do you mind if you swap places with Caleb? Will you crash with Annie? He wants some time away from her before driving back to the city."

"All right. I'll bunk with her. But I have to say, she's not my favorite person at the moment."

"What's going on with her?" he asked.

I shrugged. "She won't confide in me, Aidan."

Caleb came out of his shared tent with Annie, holding some personal belongings. He shot Aidan a questioning glance and looked relieved when Aidan nodded. As I passed Caleb, I placed my hand on his arm in a show of compassion before heading toward my drunken friend.

She was about ten feet away, bent over, resting her head on a tree. Even in the dying sunlight, I could tell she wasn't just physically feeling bad, but emotionally, too.

"I'm never drinking vodka again," she vowed.

"Until the next time," I said in dry humor. "Here." I held out the bottle of water. She stood up slowly and grasped it.

Leaning against the tree, she unscrewed the lid. She drank half the bottle before coming up for air. "Is he—"

"Still here," I said. "But spending the night with Aidan in the rooftop tent."

Annie clutched the bottle of water. "I've really screwed this all up, haven't I?"

"Yep, you have."

"You're pissed at me."

"More worried than pissed. But yeah, I'm pissed."

A light behind us flared to life, and I heard the sound of white gas hissing in the distance. Aidan had lit the lantern, and it cast a warm glow over the campsite. When it went dark, there would be no problem walking around. Caleb was nowhere to be seen—I imagined he'd curled up in the tent with a bottle of bourbon and would pass out soon.

"You hungry?" I asked.

She shook her head. "I think I just want to go to bed."

The sun had fully set, and Aidan and I were sitting by the campfire. Both Annie and Caleb were passed out in different tents, sleeping off their emotional hangovers.

"I think this is my fault," Aidan said.

I placed my hand on his thigh. "Why would you even say that?"

He shrugged. "I invited them up here, didn't I? All because of"—he looked at me—"what's going on with us."

Pulling my hand away, I hunched toward the warmth of the fire. "Their issues aren't our issues. And they would've come out anyway. She quit her job and didn't tell him. She didn't even tell me. I only found out today."

"Maybe she's having a mid-life crisis." He paused. "Fifteen years too early."

"I don't know. Maybe she's freaked out because she's turning thirty."

"Thirty is a weird birthday," he admitted. "It's like, 'Oh, God, I'm thirty. I have to have my shit together!'"

"How did that work out for you?" I asked with a smirk.

"Caleb and I spent most of it drunk and morose," he quipped.

Aidan had been thirty-one when we'd met. Apparently, I'd missed the show.

"I think for women, it's like, I don't know…a crossroads? Like if you're unhappy at your job, you wonder if you should stick it out because you don't want to be seen as flighty or a quitter. You marry the guy you've been with for a few years even though you think about what else is out there. And also…" I swallowed. "That's when the clock starts ticking."

"Do you feel any of that?" he asked. "Are you unhappy in any—"

I placed my hand on his leg again. "God, no. I'm the opposite of unhappy." I smiled. "I'm so glad I got fired from that mediocre job and Matt and I broke up. All of that led to you. And to writing."

He smiled slightly. "I remember the night we met like it was yesterday."

Annie had been trying to cheer me up after the demise of my job and my relationship, so we'd partied on the Upper East Side where we'd met Aidan and Caleb. I'd gone home with Aidan, and she'd gone home with Caleb.

I snorted.

"What?"

"Just, weird. I was thinking about the night we all met. I ended up marrying you." I grinned and then my smile slipped. "And Annie…"

"Has her own shit to figure out."

I buried my head in my hands. "Ugh. This is going to be so awful. We're going to have to choose sides. I hate choosing sides."

"I choose him," Aidan said quietly.

Swallowing, I hated to think that sometimes history with a friend wasn't enough. "I'd choose him, too."

#seriously #Sibbyout #stormisgonnacome

"Sibby?"

If I pretended to be asleep, would she give up?

"Sibby," she said a bit louder.

"What," I snapped into the pillow, my face squashed.

"I hear something outside the tent."

"You only think you do," I explained. "You'll get used to it. Go back to sleep."

"I know I hear something!" Annie hissed.

Because it was pitch black in the tent, she couldn't see

me roll over and stick out my tongue. "Crap, now I'm awake, and I have to pee."

It had taken me an hour to fall asleep. First of all, the rooftop tent was stupid comfortable. It had a one-inch memory foam mattress and it was always a perfectly flat surface no matter what the ground beneath the trailer was like. To go from that to sleeping on the uneven ground on a foam mattress in their tent wasn't cool.

And now I had to get up, assuage Annie's fear that there wasn't an animal lurking around outside the tent and then use the bathroom.

"I have a flashlight in here somewhere," I muttered, rooting around near my head. I found it underneath my pillow. "Light is coming on."

I'd gone to sleep in sweats and a hoodie, and my UGGs were in the corner. I slipped them on and then looked over my shoulder at Annie who hadn't moved from her sleeping bag.

"I'm going to open the tent and prove to you there's nothing out there, okay?"

She nodded warily.

"Okay." I unzipped the tent, shined the light outside and immediately encountered a pair of beady black eyes with centers that glowed green. I screamed and dropped the flashlight. The beam illuminated the hind end of a scurrying beast with a ringed tail.

"Sibby?" Aidan called as he climbed down the ladder of the rooftop tent, his headlamp on its highest setting. He hit the ground and ran toward me. "What happened? I heard you scream!"

I pointed in the direction of the retreating animal. "I think a raccoon was trying to get into the tent."

"Told you," Annie muttered.

"Did either of you bring food into the tent?" he asked.

We shook our heads.

Aidan raised an eyebrow like he didn't believe me. "You sure?"

"Yes, Aidan, I'm sure. You don't have to sound so condescending." I crossed my arms over my chest.

My jacket was in the corner of the tent. He crouched down, stuck a hand in one pocket, and came up empty.

"See? Told you, there's nothing—"

His hand went into the other pocket and pulled out a half-eaten PayDay bar. "You were saying?" he asked in amusement.

"Everything okay?" Caleb called, sticking his head out of the rooftop tent.

"Sibby moment," Aidan called back.

"Hey." I lightly smacked his chest. "That's not a thing. Don't make that a thing."

"What time is it?" Annie asked. I heard her stifle a yawn.

Aidan looked at his watch. "About five thirty." He leaned in close to whisper, "How did you sleep?"

"My neck is kinda tight." I rubbed the back of it. "How do people sleep on the ground, anyway?"

He smiled. "Got you hooked on my way of camping, huh?"

"Don't put words into my mouth." My stomach growled. "Put food in my mouth."

He laughed. "You don't want to try to go back to sleep?"

I sidled up to him. "Maybe a midday nap?"

"It's five thirty in the morning and you're frisky. Nature agrees with you."

Leaning down, I gave him a nice view and a suggestive wiggle.

"You know I can hear you, right?" Annie said.

I stepped outside to zip up the tent. "Go back to bed. You're grumpy."

Caleb and Annie left three hours later. They'd loaded the car in silence, and I imagined the drive back to the city would be just as quiet and super awkward. My goodbye with Annie had been strained. There was nothing to say at this point. She was determined to spiral out of control and I wasn't her mother. She knew everyone was pissed and that she'd screwed up.

"Do you think she'll be okay?" I asked Aidan.

He finished the bite of hamburger before answering. "I don't know."

"Didn't think for a second to lie to me, huh?"

"Two things could happen. She'll hit rock bottom and alienate everyone around her, and then she'll eventually climb out of the hole. Or—"

"Or?"

He sighed. "Or she'll be the girl who never gets her shit together. And you'll have to decide if you're okay having her in your life."

The idea that Annie and I would someday not be friends jarred me to the core. She'd been in my life so long. I'd gone to her grandfather's funeral with her. She'd spent the winter holidays with my family when her parents couldn't be bothered to tell her they were going on a last-minute vacation without her. She'd been there for me through every stupid college breakup, post-college breakup, doubts about life and my direction moving forward. She'd encouraged me to write a book. Her career had inspired me to write dirty chick lit. She was tied to every aspect of my life. She listened when I had writer's block, read parts of my work that didn't fit in anything I was working on, and encouraged me to keep going.

She never judged me.

"I'm a terrible, terrible friend," I said quietly.

"What? You're not."

"No," I insisted. "I am. So Annie is going through a really hard time, and what do I do? Make her feel worse by judging her. Okay, so I don't understand her way of coping. But as her best friend, I should just be there for her. Not try and change her. She doesn't need my advice, she just needs to know I'm here for her. Always."

I reached for my phone so I could shoot off a text to her, but Aidan's hand stopped me. "Have that conversation in person. If you feel that way, say it face-to-face, and maybe there's a chance she'll really hear you."

"I just wanted to tell her I love her, and that we'll talk soon."

He smiled. "Yeah, do that."

After I went to the tree to send the text, I came back and finished lunch. "What should we do today?"

"Whatever we want," he said with a charming grin. "I gotta question for you."

"Uh oh. Will I like this question?"

He threw me a look. "How would you feel about buying a place Upstate? So we could have a weekend place."

"We're not really in a position to buy," I pointed out.

We had very little in savings. All of our money was tied

up in Veritas, and it was still a new bar. It was turning a small profit, but every penny aside from living expenses went right back into the business. I made a decent living, but book advances were not what they used to be. And I was still an unknown. A traditional publisher had only taken a chance on me because I'd had a decent social media following—and that was because I'd made an ass out of myself on YouTube. I'd hit *The New York Times* once, but that didn't mean I was swimming in a pile of gold coins Scrooge McDuck style.

I was a millennial cliché.

"I—ah—my grandmother," Aidan said. "Offered."

"The one in Florida or the one in New Jersey?"

"The one in Florida," he said. "She just sold her house and is moving to a retiree community on the beach."

"Living the dream," I mused.

He smiled. "Something like that. Anyway, she knows how expensive it all is up here. She wants to help."

"That's sweet of her."

"Anyway. Think about it. It might be nice for us when…"

I knew what he was going to say: when we had kids.

There was no stopping this train, I realized. Aidan had boarded the baby express. His biological cock was ticking. I needed to hop on.

And soon.

"A storm's coming," I announced.

Aidan looked up at the clear blue sky. "I've been checking the GPS weather app. Nothing is showing up."

I blew my already red nose—I'd woken up with a stuffy head. "I'm telling you, a storm is coming. I never pay attention to weather apps. This"—I pointed to my nose—"is the only app I need. I'm a regular barometer."

"Are you sure you're not just sickly?"

"Shut up."

Sure enough, three hours later, the temperature dropped, gray clouds rolled in, and snow flurries began to fall.

"How did you know?" Aidan asked in amazement.

"I told you. It's a magical gift."

It was too cold for me to enjoy a campfire, so we got into the tent. We drank mini bottles of scotch and played cards as the flurries turned into full-on snow.

"Your magical gift can't tell us how many inches we're expecting, can it?" Aidan asked.

We were lying down, snuggled up together, warm and cozy enjoying our privacy. I couldn't believe it had already been a week and a half since Aidan had brought me here.

"Sorry, it doesn't work like that."

"How are you? Are you cold?"

"I'm wearing a thermal, a hoodie, and a jacket."

"So you're cold," he teased. "What are my chances of getting you naked?"

"Pretty good. But I'm not taking off the wool socks."

"Deal," he said.

Aidan and I hadn't been married a long time, but I already had a rule: never say no to sex unless you really didn't feel well, and even then, the best cure for a headache was sex. I'd done my own study on the matter.

My mother's first rule of marriage: never let your

husband see you in a pair of sweatpants. She claimed this was why she and my father still had an active sex life— she'd also chosen to share this wisdom with me on my wedding day. Thankfully, I'd had enough champagne to douse the image of my parents being anything other than parents. I chose to believe I came from a cabbage patch. It was just easier.

"That was nice," I said when Aidan rolled off me.

"Yeah, it was."

We took a few moments to clean up—which was difficult in the tent, but we made it work. "There's something really enjoyable about being out of the city," I admitted when I climbed into the sleeping bag.

"So what you're saying is you want to do this regularly," Aidan said, fluffing up a pillow behind his head.

"Not even a little bit." I grinned. "But once in a while, yeah. And maybe in the summertime. The weather's been pretty good, but"—I gestured to the outside—"I could do without the random snow storms."

"I hear ya. But if we camp in summer, you're going to deal with mosquitoes. And gnats."

I sighed. "Bugs love me."

"It's because you're sweet meat. I'm gonna start calling you that."

"Veto." I smiled and leaned over to kiss him. "Good night, love."

"Good night."

The next morning, I woke up before Aidan. I peeked outside and didn't see any white. The snow hadn't stuck, which was nice. I quietly climbed out of the tent so as not to disturb him. I gingerly made my way toward the loo, but my foot hit a patch of frost on a hidden tree root. Because I was me, I tripped and tumbled with all the grace of a drunken hippo. I hit the ground with an audible *thump*.

Hoping to stop my fall, my hands reached out in front of me. My right wrist took the brunt of it, and I heard the snap of bone.

I cursed and screamed, and tears leaked down my cheeks. Aidan came running, his boots only halfway laced up. He crouched down next to me.

"What happened?" he demanded.

"Tripped," I said between a gasp and a moan. I cradled my wrist, wondering if it was too early for Jack Daniels Tennessee Honey.

"You get whatever you want for however long you want," Aidan said.

I looked up at him and gave him what was surely a dopey grin. "You're pretty."

Aidan looked at the nurse who was monitoring my pulse. "Whatever you gave her…thanks. She loves me again. At least for now."

"Love you always," I gushed.

"Let me guess," the middle-aged nurse remarked. "Newlyweds?"

"He wants a baby," I blurted out.

The nurse leaned close to me and stage whispered, "Honey, if my husband looked like your husband, we'd have six children."

I stared at Aidan and sighed. "He would make pretty puppies. That's for sure."

"Sibby," Aidan said, trying to keep a straight face. "How are you feeling?"

Gesturing to my blue-casted wrist, I grinned. "I don't hurt."

"That's good."

"I want sweet potato fries," I murmured. "With chipotle aioli."

"You guys are from the city, aren't you?" the nurse asked.

Aidan scratched his beard. "That obvious?"

I reached up and stroked his chin. "This is nice."

"I'm just gonna leave you two alone," the nurse said with a wink.

"I'm sorry I'm klutzy," I said. "Now our camping trip is cut short."

"Don't apologize for that, Sib. I'm just sorry you broke your wrist."

After I'd tripped and fallen, Aidan had rushed me to the nearest hospital. My right wrist would be in a cast for six weeks. I had no idea how I was going to write, but at the moment, I didn't care because drugs.

"Will you sign my cast?" I asked. "I've never had a cast, and I want this one signed."

"You've never had a cast? As clumsy as you are?"

"Born under a lucky star."

He touched my shoulder. "Let me go find a Sharpie at the nurses' station. I'm sure they have one."

"Did you know the French word for hospital is *hôpital?*"

"I did not know that."

"I like French. Maybe you can write me a French poem on my cast."

"Maybe," he said with a soft grin. "Let me go find that Sharpie, okay?"

Aidan left.

My cell phone rang on the hospital bedside table. I stared at it for a moment. "Oh!" I picked it up. "Um, hello?"

"Sibby?"

"Mom?"

"Yes, it's me. Why are you answering your phone?"

"Because it's my phone?"

"I thought you were out of service for a few more days."

"Change of plans."

"You sound funny. Are you smoking the reefer?"

"What? No—"

"It's okay if you are. I'm not judging. In fact, studies have shown that marijuana opens the consciousness."

"So does Oxy," I murmured.

My mother paused. "Oxy? Are you on Oxy?"

"Um, maybe?"

"What have you done to yourself, Sibyl Ruth?"

My mother just middle-named me. This was my fault for answering the phone while under the influence of a narcotic.

"I might've broken my wrist."

"Doing what?"

"Uh, walking."

"Where's Aidan?"

"Getting a Sharpie so he can sign my cast."

At that moment, Aidan reappeared, Sharpie in hand. "Who are you talking to?"

Chapter 10

#backtocivilization #yayinternet

I held out the phone to him. "It's Mrs. Goldstein."

"Your mother? Why are you calling her Mrs. Goldstein?"

"She's in a mood."

"I heard that!" came my mother's voice from the speaker.

"I gave her the setting of this dark comedy."

Aidan rolled his eyes and took my phone. "Hi, Mom… Yeah, she tripped…on a tree root. She's fine." He paused.

"About six weeks. No, I promise. Okay. Love you too." He hung up and set my phone aside.

"What did you promise her?"

"That I wouldn't let you get hooked on Benzos."

"I'm not even on Benzos," I muttered. "Can we please get out of here?"

"Yep. You're all checked out. I've got your prescription for pain pills in my pocket. And"—he held up the Sharpie—"one of these bad boys. Let me sign it. You still want a French poem? I could Google one real fast."

"Nope. English is fine."

"I'm really sorry, Sibby," Aidan said as we walked to the elevator.

"For what? Dragging me to the woods," I teased.

His face sobered. "Yeah. None of this would've happened if—"

"Aidan, I'm fine. I'm okay."

"You walked into Cow Parsnip and wound up with a terrible rash."

"Yeah."

"And the raccoon—"

"Didn't get the PayDay bar."

"I took you from cell service and email, and now your wrist is broken," Aidan stated, sounding desperate.

"My best friend got you punched in the nose," I reminded him. The swelling on the bridge of his nose had gone down, and he hadn't taken any Advil the last two days, so he was on the mend. "You know, despite all the crap, I had fun."

"Yeah?"

"Yeah. But Aidan," I said quietly.

"Yeah, Sib?"

"If you don't take me back to the city so I can order from Seamless, I might have to kill you."

He laughed and wrapped an arm around me. The elevator doors dinged open. "I love how you didn't demand a real shower first."

I sighed and pushed the button for the lobby. "Would you believe me if I told you I was sick of beef products? I need some Indian food in my diet."

"God, I'd kill for a pizza."

"Make you a deal," I said. "We get back to the city and for the next few days that we were supposed to still be Upstate, we'll have a staycation and order food from all our favorite restaurants."

"Deal."

"Bed!" I yelled and flopped down onto my back. "Oh, God, Aidan. Come feel this mattress."

Aidan climbed onto the bed next to me. "Glorious. Jesus. I've missed this."

"I'm never leaving this bed ever again. This bed is *perfect.*"

We'd debated spending the night at his parents' house, but we'd decided to take the train home, not caring how late we'd get back to Brooklyn. While I'd been in the hospital, Aidan's dad and sister had gone to the campsite to pack it up. There had been nothing for us to do, and I, for one, was incredibly grateful for that.

"How's your wrist? It's almost time for another pain pill."

"I'm okay," I said truthfully. "And I'd like to find a way not to take the meds if I can help it."

"Take one tonight so you can sleep. Trust me. You don't want to wake up in the middle of the night in pain."

I smiled. "You mean you don't want me to wake *you* up in the middle of the night because I'm in pain."

"That too," he agreed with a grin. "Well, there's good news and there's bad news."

"Bad news first please."

"Our favorite Indian place closed an hour ago."

"Good news?"

"The Thai place is open."

I pouted. "But it's pick-up only."

He leaned over and kissed my nose. "I'll wrap your wrist, you'll get into the shower, and I'll go get the food when you get out."

"Your guilt is really working for me, isn't it?"

Aidan laughed. "You could probably ask for the moon, and I'd find a way to get it for you."

"Just get me Thai food and a shower and I'm good."

"You're too easy."

"Hey!" I laughed, smothering his face in kisses.

"You walked right into that one," Aidan said, pulling me to him, mindful of my wrist. "You really had fun?"

"For the most part. Yeah, I did."

"That shit with Annie is weighing on you." His hand stroked up and down my arm, and it was so soothing I was in danger of falling asleep.

I sat up and rubbed my left hand down my face. "Have you talked to Caleb?"

He paused.

"How bad?" I asked.

"Bad. He's moving out."

"Shit," I muttered.

"Did she even text you back?"

I shook my head.

"What are you going to do? Call her?"

"Right now?" I lifted my shoulders in a defeated shrug. "I'm going to shower."

The next morning I awoke with a throbbing wrist. Aidan was out of bed and on his way to the kitchen before I could utter a moan. He brought me some toast with melted butter, strawberry preserves, and two pain killers.

"Can't have you downing those on an empty stomach," he warned.

I hardly chewed. And then I was popping pills like Judy Garland in her heyday. "Easy there, tiger," Aidan said.

"This is worse than when I smashed my nose into the swinging door at Antonio's."

A slow smile crept across his face.

"You dirty perv. You're remembering our secret affair…"

"Ah, the early days of our courtship." He grinned, his eyes a little glazed.

"Hey. You love me for my mind, too, right?"

"I do, yeah."

"And my humor…"

"Definitely."

"But you really love me for my butt. Don't lie."

"It was a major selling point in the early stages. Frankly, sometimes I thought you were a little more trouble than you were worth."

"Liar!" I laughed.

"Okay, your turn."

"My turn what?"

"Objectify me," he clarified.

"Not without a cup of coffee." I climbed out of bed. "You're not going to believe this, but I'm totally used to that tent."

"Yes!" He held out his fist for a bump. "My mission is complete."

"Put that fist away, bro," I teased.

He made the explosion noise accompanied by his fist opening.

"You're keeping the lumberjack beard, right?"

He scratched his jaw. "If you like it."

"I *love* it."

"Great. I'm another hipster with a beard in Brooklyn."

I rolled my eyes. "Who owns a bar. It's totally gonna work for you and you know it." I went into the kitchen and got the coffee going. Only then did I realize that we were low on groceries.

"We're out of half and half."

"I'll run to the corner bodega and grab some," Aidan said.

"You're the best."

"And you're the invalid." He threw on his clothes, pressed a kiss to my lips, and was out the door. I waited about five seconds before going for my phone. I checked Instagram, pleased with the number of likes and views on my camping videos. But the video of me doped up in the hospital was by far the biggest success.

Was it wrong that I enjoyed it?

I debated a moment before calling Annie. She still hadn't replied to my text. I wasn't sure what to say to her, and now that Caleb was moving out, I knew she'd need me more than ever. Before I could talk myself out of calling, I dialed her number from my favorites list. It rang and rang and then went to voicemail. I left a stilted message, telling her I'd heard about the break-up and that I was there for her if she wanted to talk.

Honestly, I didn't expect to hear from her. Not for a while at least.

Sighing, I set aside my phone and then went to pour a cup of coffee. I was ready to suffer through it black   that's how badly I needed the caffeine. My cell rang and I jumped to answer it, thinking it might've been Annie. But it wasn't.

It was my agent.

"Hi, Alex."

"I didn't expect you to answer," she said. "I thought you were still on vacation."

"Er—we cut the trip short. What's up?"

She paused a moment, and I felt an instant sense of dread.

"What is it?" I demanded. "Just tell me."

"No one bid on your book."

"No one?" I repeated.

"Correct."

"Did anyone tell you why?"

Alex paused before replying. "They didn't like your heroine."

"You're not supposed to like the heroine," I explained. "She's a bitch. Until the end, when she has her redeemable moment, and then you understand why she is the way she is."

"Well, apparently her come-to-Jesus moment happens too late. And by the end, no one cared."

"They *all* told you this?"

"Pretty much. Or some version of it."

"Fuck. What about Mandy? What did Mandy say?"

Mandy had edited all three of my dirty chick lit chef romances.

"She was the first to pass."

"Motherfuckfuckshitonastick."

"That about sums up how I feel too." Alex's tone was sympathetic, and yet…

"What did *you* think of the book?" I asked.

"I didn't like your heroine."

It was like a punch in the throat. With a chair. "You didn't think to tell me this when you read through it?"

"I tried to say it—maybe I was too gentle."

"Tact is overrated. In this business, writers need to have a thick skin. So come on. Lay it on me."

"Your heroine is a raging cunt who is mean to everyone in her life, and she somehow manages to win the heart of the nicest, sweetest, most deserving guy in the world. It's totally unrealistic and people hate her."

"Thanks for not mincing words." I felt like I was back in one of my creative writing classes where my teacher ripped everyone's story to shreds in front of each other. Failed writers were mean to other writers on purpose.

"And Sibby…"

"Hmmm?" I was suddenly winded.

"Your voice changed in this book. It didn't sound like you were the one who wrote it."

I took a long moment, and then I asked, "So, what do we do?"

"I could shop it around at some of the other houses, but frankly I think you'll have the same outcome. I'd suggest writing another book. Maybe outline a three-book series. One similar to your dirty chef stuff. Shelve this one and don't look back. And don't shop it around anymore…"

"I don't want to write another series like that one," I protested.

"Well, it would sell."

"So I've gotten to that point already, huh? Art as a business? They call that selling out, you know? Do I really have to decide if I want to be true to my muse or put food on the table?"

#WriterProblems

Alex sighed. "Think about what you want to do and give me a call a little later, okay?"

"Okay." The word came out in one long breath.

I hung up with Alex and stuck my tongue out at the phone. I was lost in thought when Aidan finally returned.

"Sorry, sorry, I know that took way longer than expected, but I ended up at the grocery store instead. They had Marshmallow Fluff on sale and—Sibby? What's wrong?"

Chapter 11

#realitysucks #saynotoadulting

"This is a fucking nightmare," I said, spooning out a bite of Marshmallow Fluff and slathering it on a Graham Cracker. I mashed in a layer of Nutella and then shoved the concoction into my mouth.

Apparently, loss and disappointment were delicious.

"How is this a nightmare? Aidan asked.

I stared at him.

"No, I'm being serious."

"I write book. Agent takes book to publishing house. Editors not bid on book, author doesn't sell book. Author and husband become destitute, and have to move in with crazy, overbearing Jewish parents."

"First of all, thanks for breaking down the industry into digestible statements for my benefit." He smiled. "Okay, so no editor wanted your book. So publish it yourself."

"I can't just publish it myself," I retorted.

"Why not? You have the social media following. Your Instagram account alone is—"

"Is for people who like it when I spill things. Or get in clumsy accidents. I'm like Tim 'The Tool Man' Taylor, except Jewish…and a writer…"

"And not a contractor. Or fictional," he pointed out. "Are they right?"

"Is who right?"

"The editors, your agent. Is your heroine a bitch?"

"Yeah, she's a bitch. No question about it. But she's supposed to be redeemed by the end of the book, and they all said she wasn't even *likable* by the end."

"What do you think?"

I sighed. "I think they're all people who've been in the industry for years, and they know what they're talking about."

"Not always," he remarked. "Sometimes you have to do your own thing, knowing you're ahead of the curve. They'll catch up."

"Or they won't. They're very…hesitant to take a risk. Alex also said my voice had changed for this book. That it didn't sound like me or my dirty chef trilogy."

"So fuck them."

I blinked. "Fuck them?"

"Yeah, fuck them! Go out on a limb, Sib. Publish it yourself. See what the masses say. *Fifty Shades of Grey* was a wild success, and so the industry came to E.L. James."

"Oh my God!" I exclaimed in amazement.

"What?"

"You *listen* when I talk!"

He laughed, but then levity fled. "You take constructive criticism, Sibby. You take it really well. You listened when Alex and Mandy made suggestions for your chef trilogy. You didn't fight—it was like you knew they were making your books stronger, better. So you have to ask yourself why you're balking at taking their criticism now."

"Ego?"

"Don't think so. You get uncomfortable telling people you're a successful author. You've got very little ego. So what is it about this book that has you not wanting to change it?"

I shrugged. "I dunno. I guess…I read all these books about reformed assholes. Right? I mean these heroes are such dicks! And yet they meet the one, and they end up changing and being worthy. I wanted to do that with a prickly heroine. It's just a double standard, ya know? Assholes are redeemable, but bitches aren't? Why?"

"Sing it, sister." He held out a doctored-up Graham Cracker. "So your new book has an agenda?"

"I wouldn't call it an *agenda*. That makes it sound like I did it on purpose. I really didn't. But I started writing this character, and she came out different than I was expecting."

"Be true to you, Sibby. The rest will fall into place."

"Even if I never sell another book to another publisher?"

Aidan chuckled. "Even then." He leaned over and placed his hand on mine. "You can do it, you know? Be a success on your own. You don't need the backing of a publisher."

I squeezed his fingers. "You have faith in me. Why?"

"Aside from that whole thing of loving your spouse and supporting their dreams?"

"You're like, really good at life."

"I try."

Four days later, our staycation was over and Indian summer had officially disappeared. The restaurant my friend Zeb managed was switching over to an autumn menu that resembled a squash-pumpkin-gourd orgy.

"This soup is the best thing I've ever had," I told him. "New chef?"

Zeb nodded and sipped on his espresso. "She started about a month ago. Fresh out of culinary school."

"Let me guess, you found her," I said with a grin.

Zeb had the magic touch. We'd both been servers together at Antonio's. When I'd left—ahem—gotten fired, Zeb had left soon after for a management position at a small, failing restaurant. It had taken him four months to turn the place around from the brink of closure to one of the city's newest gems. And then he left. As soon as a place started doing well, he found another spot. He loved the challenge.

"How much longer do you have at this place?" I asked.

"I'd say another three months."

"And that would make how many restaurants you've turned around?"

"Four. No, five," he said with a smile. "Who would've thought my greatest talent would be turning around failing restaurants?"

"You're like a better looking, gay Gordon Ramsey. You so need your own TV show!"

He put his hand to his heart. "Thank you for saying that! And by the way, I'm not convinced Gordon is straight."

I leaned forward. "What have you heard through the restaurateur grapevine?"

"Nothing. I'm just convinced I could turn him if we ever met." Waving his hand away, he lifted it higher to signal the server waiting on us.

"You know you're not supposed to do that, right?" I teased. "Wave down a server?"

"You'll tip well to make up for my bad behavior."

I shook my head in exasperation.

"We're ready for the next course, please," Zeb said to the gangly youth.

"Thank you," I added. "The food is excellent."

"I'll tell the chef," the server said, taking away our empty bowls and Zeb's espresso cup.

"Okay, lady," Zeb said as he rested his arms on the white tablecloth. "Tell me what you're really doing here."

"What do you mean?" I asked. "I came to catch up."

"Mm-hmm." Zeb's expression said he clearly didn't believe me. "You're newly wed and busy with your hunk, all your writing dreams came true and you have a career you should be focusing on, and now you pop up out of nowhere just to catch up…"

"I haven't really fallen off the radar, have I?"

"Nat moved to Houston to raise that little hellion—"

"Who is your godchild."

He grinned and went on. "Then you go and disappear on me."

"You've been working eighty-hour weeks," I pointed out. "Do you have time to go out?"

"Honey, there's always time to go out and do coke off a stripper."

"When was the last time you did that?"

Zeb thought for a moment. "It's been too long." He sighed. "The idea doesn't even really appeal to me anymore. Sad, I've gotten old."

"Plus, Terry would have a field day," I commented, mentioning his boyfriend. "You look great."

And he did. For someone who worked all the time, his skin had a healthy, youthful glow.

"I just got back from five days in the Dominican Republic. Terry surprised me."

"Explains your fresh complexion."

"Out with it, Sibby."

"I'm not sure where to start."

"What's the most pressing?" he asked.

"Um… Aidan wants a baby."

"Ew. Why?"

"I really have no idea," I said with a sigh.

"And do *you* want a baby?"

"I don't know. Yes. Someday. I don't know. Maybe?"

"Oh, man, we should've started lunch with a couple of cocktails."

"I'm not drinking," I stated.

"Uh, why?"

"That leads me to my second problem—my book." I filled him in on my conversation with Alex, including the not-so-delicate input she gave about the heroine. "I don't drink when I'm in writing-mode. I'm supposed to start writing a new book. Something more in line with the dirty chef trilogy."

"So you have to peck at the keyboard with one hand, and you're not allowed to drink while doing it? That's the stupidest thing ever," he scoffed. "You've heard of Ernest Hemingway?"

"Yes."

"And F. Scott Fitzgerald."

"Yes."

"And Snookie?"

I let out a laugh. "I've got a process." I thought for a moment. "So do you think Aidan is right? Do you think I should publish the book myself, or write another one and have Alex try to sell it?"

The server interrupted us and set our food down. Two plates of handmade, ultra fresh pumpkin ravioli sprinkled with pumpkin seeds and Parmesan sat steaming in front of us. After thanking the server, who quietly disappeared, I turned back to our conversation.

"Is the book good?" he asked.

"I think it is."

"Did you write it for you, or for your fans?"

"Me."

"Then publish it yourself. I'm with Aidan. You've got the fan base. Fuck what other people have to say. It's your life, your happiness."

I sat back in my chair. "What the hell happened to you in the Dominican Republic?"

He smirked. "I'll never tell."

"Not fair."

"You can read about it in my posthumous autobiography: *A Gay Grows in Queens*."

"I look forward to it," I drawled.

"Try the ravioli. You're gonna *plotz*."

I was in the middle of unlocking the apartment with a grocery bag in my good hand when my phone rang. For a brief moment, I hoped it was Annie, but she'd gone so far underground she was probably finding oil.

Answering my phone, I stumbled into the foyer. "Hello? Hold on."

"Okay!" came the chirp on the other end of the phone.

I knew that voice—and it wasn't Annie.

"Before we start, you're not covered in any of your kid's fluids, are you?"

Natalie let out a laugh. "Nope. But that's because I stuck the little monster with Tad. I'm in New York!"

"You're not!"

"Surprise!"

"Ohmygod!" I squealed. "Did I know you were coming? Did I forget you were coming?"

"Last-minute trip. Meeting with a very high-maintenance children's author later this week who insisted on seeing the illustrations in person."

"Oh, those quirky writer types," I mocked. "We're terrible, aren't we?"

"The worst," she agreed. "Anyway, I have some free time tomorrow night."

"Pencil me in."

"I can't wait to see you."

Nat and her husband had moved the year before from

New Jersey to Houston, Texas, and I felt her loss every day. Even though she had a kid and I didn't, we were still close. She was a talented illustrator who'd been doodling as long as I'd been scribbling. Now, we were both successful artists. Though we didn't talk as frequently, we still made time for a weekly phone call. I'd missed it the last few weeks since I'd been out of consistent cell service.

There was so much to catch up on.

"You haven't changed at all," I remarked when Nat strolled into the coffee shop the next day. She was dressed in skinny black jeans, black ankle boots, and a sexy leather jacket. She'd chopped her long hair into a sleek bob months ago, and because she sent me a selfie from the salon chair, it wasn't a shock. A delicate gold chain was around her neck, and I admired the subtle grace she possessed. If Nat had been taller, she could have easily been a model. She didn't even look like she'd popped out a kid.

"That's not true," she said, releasing me from a hug. "I got a new tattoo."

"That makes number four or number five?"

"Six." Pulling back the right side of her hair, she grinned. Below her ear was a tiny black bird. "I'm in love."

"So am I—and I don't even have any tattoos!"

"The only untatted person in Brooklyn."

"Aidan doesn't have any tattoos, either."

"A match made in heaven." She leaned back in the red booth of our favorite coffee shop. It was near Antonio's, and we'd spent many afternoons before work drinking coffee and talking about our dreams of being paid for our art.

I rested my casted arm on the table. "It needs adornment."

#ifitwalkslikeaduck #baglady

"Tell it again." Nat laughed and raised the steaming cappuccino to her lips. Her brown eyes danced with humor as she surveyed me over the peak of foam.

"Why is it so funny?" I demanded.

"Because it was a *raccoon!*" Laughter pealed from her lips. "God, this is better than the last movie night out Tad and I had."

For the past hour, I'd recounted what had occurred on the camping trip. From me showering using a privacy tent to the rash on my face and of course, Mr. Raccoon.

"I'm glad my pain amuses you." I held up my casted-wrist and raised an eyebrow.

"Well, that does suck," she agreed. "But I made it really pretty."

"You did," I agreed, enjoying the sight of the cast covered in Sharpie. She'd managed to draw and shade the cast to look like a piece of tree bark.

"Be glad I travel with my felt tips."

"All hail. I bow down to thee."

She laughed again and then peered at me with a knowing look. "You look troubled."

"Do I?" I let out a sigh. "I've got a lot on my mind."

"Tell me."

"I've talked to Aidan and Zeb and yet—there's no clarity."

"What about Annie? Have you talked to her?" Nat asked. The two of them had gotten to know each other well because both of them had been in my bridal party. So had Zeb. What could I say? I was nontraditional.

"She's part of what's got me all mixed up, but I'm not ready to talk about it yet," I admitted. I hadn't heard from her—and neither had Caleb. I really didn't want to tell Nat about Annie. It felt…disloyal.

"Okay, so you don't want to talk about Annie," Nat said. "What else has got you in knots?"

"Did you want kids? Before you got pregnant?" I blurted out.

"Blunt is your middle name." She looked at me in amusement. "I was sort of ambivalent. Do you want kids?"

"Aidan does."

"Ah."

"He's not pressuring me," I rushed to say. "But I feel that pressure anyway."

"Yeah. Tad wants another one."

"Already? The monster is not even two!"

"Everyone always talks about women being baby hungry. Don't buy into it. It's the guys."

"So, what are you going to do?" I asked.

"Have another one. Eventually. But I'm good with how things are right now."

I nodded in agreement. "*I'm* good with how things are, too. I'm not ready for a baby."

"Let me give you a piece of advice, and you can do with it what you will. It's never a good time to have a kid. Period. Yeah, you can be more financially stable, or have more space in one home or apartment versus another. But think about it. What if you have a kid when your career is in the toilet? You're going to have to jump back into work to get where you want to be. Or what if your career is skyrocketing? You're gonna leave that, lose momentum, just because you want a kid? See what I mean? It's all shit timing, Sibby. So you make a choice—if it's important to you, you'll do it."

"I think I'd like a baby," I said slowly. "But I kind of wish it wouldn't turn into a teenager."

"Look at it this way," she said. "When it's a teenager, you're no longer breast feeding, which means you can drink. A lot. That's how I plan on getting through the monster's teenage years."

I leaned back and shook my head. "You've got this mothering thing on lockdown."

She winked. "If only I'd remembered to spike this cappuccino with Baileys…and on that note, let's get out of here. I'm ready for a real drink."

When we walked into Veritas, Aidan jumped over the bar and onto the floor in front of us. He rushed at Nat and gave her a big bear hug.

"When do you leave?" he asked. He released her and then greeted me with a kiss before taking the leisurely path back around the bar.

"I have four more child-free days, and I plan to make the most of them," she said with a laugh. "I'm thinking karaoke one night."

Aidan slid a drink menu in front of her and waited.

"I'll try a Heartbreaker, please," she said.

"What's a Heartbreaker?" I asked.

Aidan's mouth flattened as he shook the martini shaker. "Caleb's new cocktail." A few moments later, he set the drink down in front of her.

She took a sip. "Wow. That's really good."

"Pain inspires art, eh?" I remarked dryly.

"How's he doing?" Nat asked.

Aidan sighed. "Good. All things considered. He's been working here nonstop. I sent him home and took his shift. He's burnt."

"He moved out of their apartment, right?" Nat pressed.

Aidan looked at me.

"I had to catch her up to speed. I wasn't gossiping," I defended. "I *wasn't*."

"Right." He scooped some ice into a glass, and with the bar's fountain gun, filled it with water. Setting down the glass on a coaster, he said, "He's staying with a friend on the Upper East Side."

"A friend," Nat said slowly.

"A friend," Aidan reiterated.

"A female friend? Is that what you're not saying?" I demanded.

"Maybe."

"You mean Caleb breaks up with his girlfriend of two years, and the first thing he does is fall into another woman's vagina?"

"*She* cut him lose, Sibby," Aidan reminded me. "Actually, she backed his ass into a corner, made him feel like shit—*for months*—and never had the courage to end it."

"She tried," I argued back.

"Not hard enough." His voice had risen. "She treated him like shit! So what if he's hooking up with a hot girl? It's not your concern."

I pressed my hands to the bar and stood. "Hot? Did you just say she was *hot?*"

"Oh, boy," Nat muttered. To Aidan she said, "Now you've done it."

"You've met her, haven't you?" I demanded, glaring at him.

"I know her," he admitted slowly.

"How?"

He remained frozen, body filled with tension, face pale.

"How, Aidan?"

Aidan sighed. "I used to date her."

Gemma Peters.

Her name was Gemma Peters.

How could best friends sleep with the same girl and not care? I'd asked Aidan this moments before stomping out of Veritas, in a complete blind rage. Although I couldn't say exactly why I was so upset, except that halfway out the door, I didn't want to turn around and admit I was being irrational.

Annie and Caleb were not together. However he got his ego back was his deal. But the fact that Aidan, *my husband*, had once upon a time, slept with this Gemma Peters…well, it just didn't sit well with me. Kind of like three-day-old Kung Pao Chicken.

In fact, I was feeling really nauseated.

"Men," I muttered.

"Preach!" the homeless bag lady with a shopping cart full of treasures shouted back at me.

I stopped walking and looked at her. Her tin foil hat was crooked, and she was wearing one red sock and one purple sock, but suddenly, I felt like she was capable of being an objective observer about my life.

"Can I ask you something?"

"Gimme a quarter," she demanded.

I rooted around at the bottom of my bag and found some change. I gave it all to her. She pressed her hands together and bowed. "Ask your question, frizzy-haired girl."

My hand immediately went to my ponytail. "Why do some guys sleep with the same girl but none of them care?"

"I need more details," she said, sounding strangely lucid and non-crazy.

"My husband and his best friend have both hooked up with the same woman. Neither seem to care that she's been with both of them."

Shopping cart lady placed a hand to her chin and struck a thoughtful pose. "I do believe it's because neither of them are serious about her. Your husband didn't want to marry her, did he?"

"No," I said that with confidence. I knew all about Aidan's serious past relationships. He'd never once mentioned Gemma.

"And his friend doesn't want to marry her either?" she went on.

"He just got dumped."

"Ah. Ego. He needs to feel like a man again."

"Thank you. I needed to hear that."

"*Quack. Quack, quack, quack…*"

Lucid moment over.

With a wave, I continued walking. I wandered through the neighborhood, stopping off for an ice cream cone. Nothing better than ice cream when it was chilly out. A few blocks later, ice cream gone, I was standing on Annie's front stoop. I had no idea if she was home or if she'd let me in. But I had to try.

I pressed the buzzer for her apartment. A moment later, the intercom crackled to life. "Hello?"

"It's me," I said, relief that she was home pouring through me. "Can we talk?" For a moment, Annie didn't say anything, and I worried she'd say no, but then the buzzer buzzed.

I opened the front door and nearly ran to the stairs. I took them two at a time until I got to the third floor. Annie was leaning against the doorframe when I stumbled out of breath.

Bent over at the waist, I inhaled sharply.

"What happened to your wrist?" she exclaimed.

"I went camping," I reminded her. "Slipped on a frosty tree root."

"Seriously?"

"Seriously."

"You do clumsy with such flair."

I lifted my eyes. "You're just now figuring this out?"

"I've been aware for quite awhile. You coming in, or do you want to wheeze out in the hallway?"

"I can wheeze from inside your apartment," I quipped, following her inside. The apartment looked sparse, and I faltered when I realized it was because all the masculine touches were gone. Caleb had taken his belongings and left. Most of them anyway. There were some boxes stacked along the living room wall.

"He hasn't picked up the rest of his stuff?" I asked.

"Those boxes are mine," she said quietly.

"Yours?"

"I'm—moving."

"Where?" I asked.

"Montauk."

"What's up there? A job?"

"My uncle owns a seafood restaurant. I'm gonna cook there for a while. Until I can figure out things."

"When are you leaving?"

She sighed. "Few weeks. Trying to sublet the rest of my lease."

"Were you going to tell me?" I asked.

Annie nodded and then shrugged. "Probably—if I could've ever gotten over my embarrassment."

I took a moment to study my best friend. She was sad, that much was obvious. But there was something else, too. She looked…hopeless.

"I love you, you know," I said.

"I know."

"Do you? You're the sister I never had."

"Yeah."

"No, I mean it," I stated. "If I've ever done anything to make you doubt that, then I'm a shit friend."

"You're not a shit friend," she said, finally showing a little life. Her blue eyes were lit with truth. "You've stood by me even though I've behaved badly—you're like my conscience, Sibby."

"I don't want to be your conscience. I want to be your friend. Why won't you let me?"

"My parents are getting divorced," she blurted out. "They've been separated for months. And I just—marriage doesn't work."

"My marriage—"

"Is new and yet it still has its issues. You guys don't even want the same things."

"That's not true."

"Isn't it? Come on, Sibby, be honest with me. Or at least be honest with yourself. If you really wanted a kid you wouldn't be fighting it this hard."

"Oh, I get it." I crossed my arms over my chest and glared defiantly at her. "You aren't happy, so you want to take everyone else down with you."

"Is that what you think of me? Really?"

I clamped my jaw shut in mulish anger.

"You don't know me at all. I was your maid-of-honor."

"Did you mean your maid-of-honor speech?" I tossed back. "Did you really mean what you said? About looking at us and knowing we were going to last."

"Yes, I meant it," she snapped.

"Then how can you stand there and tell me you can't have the same thing?"

She blinked. "Because your parents are still together. Because your entire childhood of happy moments isn't a lie. Because your parents *wanted* you."

"Your parents wanted you," I insisted.

Annie sighed, her chest heaving with emotion. "No, Sibby, they didn't. I was an accident and they got married because of it."

Chapter 13

#inicecreamveritas #sibbyslaw

"That can't be true," I said once I'd recovered from shock.

"It's true." Her expression was bitter. "Believe me, it's true."

"Did you always know about this?"

She shook her head. "It came out in one of my screaming matches with my mother."

"Lovely," I muttered, my own tone bitter.

"Right? My mother, ladies and gentlemen, who always wanted more from life than to be a wife and mother."

"So she blamed you for holding her back? Nice."

She cocked her head to one side. "But isn't that how you feel? About impending motherhood."

Did I feel that way? Would I resent a baby? Resent the time it took away from my writing, away from Aidan? My life wouldn't be my own anymore.

"There's a difference between resentment because you had a kid and not being ready to have a kid."

"When are you going to be ready?"

I shrugged. "Maybe when I'm on speaking terms with the make-believe kid's father."

"What does that mean?"

I smacked my forehead. "I left Nat at Veritas."

"Rewind," Annie said.

"Nat's in town. We were hanging out at Veritas. Aidan might've given me some news that had me flying off the handle."

"What kind of news?"

"No news," I backtracked.

"Sibby. Have you had sugar?"

"No."

"*Sibby?*"

"Yes!" My arms flew up in exasperation. "I had sugar, okay? But this is not a sugar spell, I promise. I had the smallest ice cream cone in the world! A kiddie scoop, even."

"Sprinkles?"

"No!"

"Sibby, come clean already."

"Fine! I had a strawberry ice cream with waffle cone mixed in. And it wasn't a kiddie size; it was the biggest size they had! It was amazing!"

My best friend blinked at me but didn't seem at all fazed by my sugar-induced outrage. I was hypoglycemic, and technically, I should've been more cognizant of my sugar intake. But I'd really wanted an ice cream and—

"You hate strawberry ice cream," Annie said, calm and matter-of-fact.

I froze.

"You hate strawberry ice cream," Annie repeated. "You call it the devil's torment."

"Frozen strawberries are too cold, and they're always freezer-burned," I murmured.

She made a face. "And how did your ice cream taste today?"

"Like the best thing in the worl—"

Annie inhaled a slow breath. "Do you think—can you possibly—"

"Don't say it."

"Are you pregnant?"

"Gah! Why did you say that? Now it's a *real* possibility!"

"And it wasn't before?"

I put my hands over my ears. "La la la la la! I can't hear you! La la la!"

Annie gently pulled my hands down and held them. "When was your last period?"

"What's the date today?"

She told me.

"Oh no," I whispered.

"Maybe you're stressed. You've been stressed. I stress you out."

"True." I shook my head. "I've been regular. I've *always* been regular. Even when I was eighteen and got mono and dropped a bunch of weight, I was regular."

"Okay, let's not panic. There's a first time for everything, right?" She marched me toward the bathroom.

"What are you doing?" I demanded. "Stop pushing me!"

She paused. "I've got a pregnancy test you can borrow."

"Borrow?" I snorted. "I'm not gonna give it back. And why do *you* have a pregnancy test?"

"Because most women go through scares." She began shoving me into the bathroom.

"I don't have to go. I can't pee on a stick when I'm empty!"

"Wait here!" She ran to the kitchen. A moment later, I heard a cabinet open and then the sound of running water. Annie rushed back, spilling water on the wooden floor. Thrusting it at me, she said, "Drink all of it."

I took the glass and looked at it.

"What are you waiting for?" she screeched. "Pound it! Like you did in college!"

With a deep breath, I went in. I chugged. I chugged until there was nothing left.

"I can't anymore," I moaned as she tried to shove round three at me.

"How do you feel?"

"Like I'm at sea," I muttered.

"How's the bladder?"

"Too personal. Even for us."

"This? You called me in the middle of the night after you lost your virginity."

I glowered. "I thought I'd done it wrong!"

"How can you even—fine. Whatever."

"You do realize we're in a slapstick comedy routine, don't you?" I asked, feeling hysteria rise in my throat.

She put both hands on my shoulders and looked deep into my eyes. "Do. You. Have. To. Pee?"

"Yes!" I squeaked, sounding like a chipmunk who'd sucked helium.

Annie grabbed my hand and stalked toward the bathroom.

"I can't do it! I can't pee on a stick!"

"Sure you can. It's really easy, you just get your leg—"

I threw her off. "No, you don't get it. I can't do this. I can't find out if I'm pregnant. Not yet."

"I don't get it."

"What if…"

"Yeah?"

Shaking my head, I felt my insides quake. "What if he did this on purpose? What if he poked holes in the condoms while I was sleeping, and I—"

"Aidan? Aidan Kincaid? Your *husband*." Annie looked at me like I'd lost my marbles.

"Yes, my husband," I snapped. "The one hungry for a legacy. The one who wants to fill my womb with his dimpled Irish swimmers."

"And I'm asking again. You really think Aidan would do that to you?"

My shoulders slumped. "No. I don't. But if that's not the case, then…"

"Then what?" she demanded.

"Then Sibby's Law."

"Sibby's Law," she repeated in understanding.

"How's it going in there?" Annie called through the closed door of the bathroom.

"Can you not say anything for like, five minutes? I have stage fright." I sighed. "Waterfall, waterfall, waterfall…"

And I thought the SATs would be the hardest test I'd ever have to take.

I set the stick on the wrapper on the bathroom counter. Washing my hands, I stared at it out of the corner of my eye. Plus sign, minus sign. The test was idiot proof. I just had to wait.

"Come on," I muttered at the stick. Somewhere in the distance, I heard my cell phone ring.

"Should I get that for you?" Annie asked.

"It's probably Aidan," I called back. "And no. Don't get it. I'm not ready to—no. Let it go to voicemail."

Annie's phone trumpeted for a moment, and then it stopped. "Timer's done."

Moment of truth.

I leaned over the counter and peered at the stick.

One big, fat, bright pink plus sign.

Light-headed, I sank to the floor. I brought my legs up and curled into the fetal position. The bathroom door burst open, and Annie loomed above me.

"Sibby?"

"I'm with child," I said, breathless.

"God, you're so fucking dramatic," she stated. She dropped onto the floor to my level. I wormed my head into her lap, and she started stroking my hair. "This is not the end of the world."

"It's not?" I sniffed.

"No. You have a husband who loves you. You love him. Your kid is gonna be gorgeous and more importantly it's going to have me for an aunt."

"I can't believe this is happening."

"Believe it."

"This is so surreal," I murmured.

"Yeah, I bet it is. It's going to be okay, though."

"My kid is gonna be short, have frizzy hair, allergies, and be fated to have it's own version of Sibby's Law."

"Only half Sibby's Law," she said. "Aidan's genes should counterbalance the klutzy."

"It's gonna need braces."

"Probably."

"It's gonna cry a lot."

"Definitely.

"And it's gonna tell me I'm the worst mother in the world!" I burst into tears.

"Uh, that title already belongs to my mother," Annie said, tone dry. "It's gonna love you so much, Sibby."

"It might be a boy!" I wailed.

"It might."

"Or a girl!" I went on.

"Well, it's got a fifty-fifty chance."

"I don't know what to do with either. Kids pick their noses—and then wipe it in places."

"Dude, most adults do that," she pointed out.

I moaned.

"You're not looking at this the right way," Annie said. "Sit up."

As I wiped the tears from my cheeks, I grabbed the end of the toilet paper roll and pulled. "How am I supposed to look at it?"

"Aidan wanted a kid; he gets a kid. You know what you get?"

I shook my head.

"A grateful husband who will do anything you want. You want pickles and Oreos in the middle of the night, he'll go get them for you."

"Ew, that sounds—hmmm, good actually?"

She raised a blond brow. "Really?"

"No, it sounds awful. What else do I have to look forward to?"

"Er—"

"You were winging that speech, weren't you?" I said with a laugh.

"Maybe. How'd I do?"

"It's over already? Please, I need a bit more."

She blew out a breath, startling her bangs. "Okay. Give me a second. Oh, I got it!"

"Yeah?"

"You can finally use the phrase, 'Because I said so.' And they can't really argue."

"Pretty sure the kid will argue."

"It'll be cute. Really fucking cute."

"Yeah."

"It'll make you happy. And sad, and angry, and every emotion in between. You're a writer. You can use all that."

I grabbed her hand and gave it a squeeze. "That might've been better than your maid-of-honor speech."

"Are you gonna be okay?" Annie asked, hugging me goodbye at her door.

"Think so," I said. I refused to let go of her and just held on. "What about you?"

"Think so," she mirrored. "Just need some time, you know? I need to get my head on straight."

"Yeah." I pulled back. "I get that. But no more radio silence, okay?"

"Promise."

"I'm gonna need you," I whispered. "I have no idea what the fuck I'm doing."

"No one has any idea what they're doing. I think they call that life."

"When did you get so philosophical?" I demanded.

"After my second vodka cran."

"You drank? When?"

"When you were peeing on the stick. I had two. One for me, one for you. Since, you know, you can't drink anymore."

"And you just had to go there, didn't you? I won't even miss the booze."

We stared at each other for a long minute before both saying at the same time, "Lie."

"Are you going to tell him tonight?" she asked.

"Yeah. I'm no good at keeping secrets."

"How do you feel about it?"

"Don't know yet. Still kinda in shock."

She nodded. "Makes sense to me. Text when you get home?"

"Yeah, I will. Drink another vodka cran for me?"

"Count on it." Annie grinned and then pulled me into another hug.

My phone rang again. "I better get that. It's the third time he's called." I pressed a button and put the phone to my ear. "Hello?"

"Sibby? Sibby, where are you?" Aidan demanded, sounding frantic.

"With Annie," I said, voice totally calm and normal.

Too normal. Too Stepford Wife. "You do know you have the 'find your wife' app on your phone, right?"

"Forgot about it," he admitted. "I'm home. I got John to come in and cover. Sibby, listen, Gemma meant—"

"I don't care about Gemma." It was the truth. I didn't care that Aidan had been with her at some point before we got together. I just didn't like that Aidan had called her hot, and that made me start to wonder how early pregnancy hormones kicked in. And I also didn't like that Caleb was already out sowing his oats, but then again, it wasn't any of my business.

"You don't?" He sounded surprised.

"I don't," I reiterated. "I'm on my way home. See you in a few."

"Yeah. Love you, Sib," he said, tone husky.

Tears welled in my eyes. "Love you, too." I hung up with him and looked at Annie.

"You guys are disgusting."

I smiled. "Thank you."

"Sugary sweet, and far too happy."

"I know."

She hugged me again. "I'm really glad."

Chapter 14

#untothebreach #momisgonnakillme

I got to the front door of the apartment and stared at it. I knew that as long as I stood in the hallway, I was still Sibby: klutzy, sarcastic, bumbling Sibby. But the moment I went through that door I would become someone else. Someone accountable. Someone who had to be responsible for another human in a few months. Someone *not* Sibby.

It scared the living shit out of me.

With a deep breath, I unlocked the door. Aidan was sitting on the couch watching TV, but the moment he saw me he clicked the remote and the TV went dark. He jumped up and came to me, wrapping me in his arms.

"I feel like things have been off with us," he said into my hair. "And I don't know if it's because Annie and Caleb split, and we inevitably chose sides, but—"

"Aidan, stop." He quieted and I squeezed my arms tighter around him.

"Nat said to tell you she'd see you later," he drawled.

"Ah, crap. I left her high and dry, didn't I? I'll call her tomorrow."

"It's okay. I gave her a few drinks, made her sit and talk to me."

"Hmmm."

"What are you thinking about?" he asked, stroking my hair.

"Kids."

"What about kids?"

"I think…giving one a shot isn't a bad idea."

He pulled back, so he could look down at me. His eyes searched mine. "I don't understand. Just yesterday you weren't ready."

I inhaled. "Yesterday, I didn't know I was pregnant."

Aidan blinked blue eyes—eyes I really hoped our baby had. And his dimples. And his heart. He had such a good heart, and he loved me with all of it.

"Sibby," he whispered. "Are you—"

"Yeah, Aidan. I'm pregnant."

"How did this happen? We weren't trying."

"Not sure, honestly. But birth control fails all the time. I'm still kinda in shock, actually."

His expression was concerned, his touch comforting. "But are you…happy about it?"

"Yeah." I nodded slowly. "I am."

His smile was slow, and then it became a full grin. He

swept me into his arms and spun me around the room, dusting my face with noisy kisses before setting me down. "You sure you're happy?"

Laughing, I snuggled against his chest. "I'm sure."

"You found out with Annie, didn't you?"

"She's the one who told me I needed to take a pregnancy test. I had strawberry ice cream without thinking about it and she knew," I explained. "Are you mad? That you weren't the first to know?"

"You needed your girl. I'm glad she was there for you."

"I'm glad she was, too."

We were curled up in bed, and I was near comatose due to Aidan's exuberant show of virility. Not that I was complaining.

"So how do you think it happened?" Aidan asked. His fingers ran up and down my arm, lulling me into an even deeper trance.

I snorted. "When a sperm and egg go out for drinks—"

"Hey!" He gently poked me in the side, making me squirm. "I know how it works."

"Oh, good. Because that was about to be a really awkward talk."

Aidan chuckled. "Can you be serious for one moment?"

"Nope. Not in my wife contract."

He moved so he was looking down at me, his expression tender. "You've made me so happy, Sibby. You made me the happiest man in the world when you married me. And you did it again when you told me you were pregnant. I'm just"—he leaned over to give me a kiss—"I don't even know what to say."

"Say nothing. Just go back to rubbing me."

Aidan laughed again. "I guess I just got some insight into the next many months."

I looked down at my still-flat belly, picturing it huge and mountainous. Then I thought it might be better not to think of it, or hyperventilation might occur.

My phone pinged. I didn't even move from my comfortable spot. I felt Aidan lean over me to the bedside table. "It's Annie."

I cracked an eyelid. "You read it. I'm too tired."

"It's a link to a website."

My eyes drifted closed. "Hmmm."

"*Why condoms fail.*" He was quiet for a moment and then said, "Sibby, wake up—you gotta read this."

I didn't move. "Why don't you read it to me."

He sighed. "Remember we had a random cold front move in when we were camping?"

"Uh, yeah. I remember."

"And remember how we had sex that day?"

"Yes."

"Remember how it dropped dramatically in temperature?"

"Spit it out, Aidan," I groused. "I want to go to sleep."

"The condoms froze overnight, and then thawed out the next day. So our protection became *defective*."

"This is so me," I muttered. "Only I would get knocked up while trying to use protection and being prepared."

"You're a rotten Girl Scout."

"Don't I know it."

The next day, my doctor was able to squeeze me in for a quick appointment. After confirming my pregnancy and projecting my due date for the end of June, she congratulated me and then gave me a prescription for prenatal vitamins.

I'd just gotten my prescription filled, the bottle of vitamins resting in my hand basket when I heard someone ask, "Are you Sibby Goldstein?"

A young woman with a blond bob and hot pink tips stood in front of me, a hopeful smile on her face.

"Hi," I greeted. "I'm Sibby. Have we met "

She shook her head, sending pink tips swinging back and forth. "No, we've never met. I recognized you from your Instagram account." She glanced at the wrist. "How's it healing?"

"It's okay," I answered, wondering how she seemed to know what had happened to me with out asking about it. And then I remembered that I shared my klutzy with the world.

"I'm a huge fan. I'm Stacy." She held out her hand. I gave her an awkward shake with my casted wrist. "I've been following you since you shot off that cork and hit your ex with it."

I let out an uncomfortable laugh. "Total fluke. I swear I

didn't plan it."

"Would you mind if I got a picture of us together?" Her brown eyes were hopeful.

"Ah, sure." I really wasn't in the mood for a photo-op, but it wasn't Stacy's fault I had a ton on my mind. She smushed close to me and got her camera into position.

"Smile," she said, snapping a bajillion photos. When Stacy was satisfied she'd gotten enough, she tucked her phone away. "Thanks, Sibby."

"My pleasure."

With a wave, Stacy went on her way but kept glancing back at me every few seconds. I held my smile until I was sure she was out of sight. I looked down at the prenatal vitamins in the basket and hoped she hadn't seen them.

On my way home from running errands, I texted Nat and apologized for storming out and leaving her to her own devices. She replied right away telling me all was good. I debated on whether or not to break the news to her I was pregnant, but I decided to keep it to myself. After all, I hadn't even called my own parents yet to tell them. I knew the moment I told my mother, she'd blab it to the entire family, not to mention all her friends. I wasn't ready for the barrage of phone calls and emails, all the well-wishers.

Soon, the baby thing would completely take over my life—but right now I was still thinking about my book. Alex had called a few times, but I'd let her roll to voicemail. I didn't know what to tell her because I still hadn't even come to any conclusions about what to do about my book with my hated heroine.

I could always beef up the ending, I supposed. Give her a John Cusack-type of moment where she really made an ass of herself to win back the hero. Everyone seemed to have a problem with the hero forgiving her too soon. Like, they really wanted her to have to work for it. But at what point did that just draw out the story for no reason? They loved each other, so wouldn't the hero forgive her quickly? Not every story had to be ridiculously dramatic.

I needed to speak to someone who could be completely objective, and I could think of no one better to talk to than my college creative writing professor.

When I got home, I set my grocery bags on the kitchen table and took out my phone, intending to call Milton Brandford. My eyes widened when I saw my screen light up with notification after notification. My Instagram account was going berserk.

"What the hell?" I asked aloud, unlocking my phone.

That. Bitch.

Stacy had tagged a photo of us together and written, "Obsessed with the Dirty Chef Series! Congrats @Sibby-Goldstein". In the bottom of the picture, the label on the bottle of prenatal vitamins was clearly visible.

She'd outed my pregnancy to the entire internet— before I'd even told my mother.

I was *so* busted.

Once the news of my pregnancy had broken, due to the fact that there was no such thing as privacy anymore, I'd done the adult thing and taken a nice deep breath and then gone on an epic cursing rampage.

I knew there was no point in calling Aidan—he wasn't a professional firefighter, after all—so I waited until he came home from the bar to tell him that our very private news was no longer private.

"She's got fifty-five thousand Instagram followers!" Aidan remarked in bemusement.

"Good for her," I muttered from underneath a gray couch pillow.

"Holy shit, she's got even more Facebook followers… and a makeup tutorial YouTube channel."

"Stop, Aidan, I don't care. That bitch—"

"Is a book blogger," he interrupted.

I threw off the pillow, letting it hit the floor. "What?"

Aidan clicked a few times and a beautiful, professional website popped up. "Whoa. This looks legit."

"This is karma, you know," I told him, getting up off the couch and heading to the kitchen.

"How do you figure?"

I poured a glass of orange juice. "I was the reason everyone at Antonio's found out about Nat's pregnancy. This is just the universe getting me back in spectacular fashion."

"Little bit," he mused.

Clutching the glass of juice, I nodded. "I know. Let's just hope my mom—"

My cell phone rang.

Aidan looked at it. With a grimace, he held it up to me.

Chapter 15

#hurricane5hitsNY #thebubbehaslanded

I stared at my phone like it was a hostile entity. I took it from Aidan's hand and then set it down, turning off the ringer. It vibrated across the coffee table, dancing, mocking, demanding to be answered.

"You will not break me," I muttered.

"Just answer it."

"No."

"Why not? Ten bucks says she saw the Instagram photo."

"That's my stupid fault." I ran a hand across my face.

"I'm the one who set up her account so she could follow me. I have no one to blame but myself."

"She follows me, too," Aidan commented. "And she sends me cat videos."

I looked at him. "Yeah? When did that start?"

"Few weeks ago."

The phone fell silent and then immediately started vibrating again.

"You're going to make her year," he said with a soft smile. "She's finally going to become a grandmother."

"Make her year? This is going to make her entire life. From the moment I was born, she's waited for this, trust me." I sighed. "Why are you not more upset about Stacy? Or about my mother finding out?"

"Oh, I'm royally pissed off at Stacy. But I'm also happy in a way. So even though I hate that she took away our chance to share the news and stole our privacy, I'm glad people know."

"I wish we'd had more time to keep this to ourselves."

"How much time were you hoping for?"

"Ten years?"

"Sibby—"

"You answer the phone, Aidan. Give me this. I'm housing your child. If you're nice to me, I'll make sure it's a boy so you can do boy stuff together, like throw a ball around, or commiserate about the stock market."

"I'm sorry, are you giving birth to a forty-five-year-old accountant? And don't you know it's the sperm's job to decide the gender? Did you even pass sex ed? Your dad's a doctor!"

I pointed at him. "Not the way to win."

He grasped my finger and brought it to his lips. "We went to the doctor. We were going to tell them anyway—"

"No, we weren't," I countered.

"We weren't?" Aidan raised an eyebrow and then took the glass of orange juice from me and drank the rest.

"Not until the three month mark. In Judaism, it's bad luck to announce a pregnancy before the end of the first trimester. Some women even wear a piece of ruby jewelry because they believe it protects against miscarriage."

"That's cool about the ruby. But the cat's out of the bag, isn't it?"

We both glanced at the cell phone. It had gone silent again, and then it gave a little vibration letting us know there was a voicemail waiting.

"It's only gonna get harder," he warned. "The last thing you want to do is let your mother spin herself into a tizzy."

My shoulders sank. "You're right. That'll just make it worse. My mother is a category five hurricane on the path to grandmother-hood. Nothing and no one will get in her way. Not even her daughter. I already miss drinking," I said with a sigh. "I never realized how much I relied on liquid courage."

"You don't need it; you have me." He wrapped his arm around my shoulders and pulled me close.

"I'll listen to the voicemail," I said with great reluctance. I picked up my cell phone and pressed a button. My mother's voice blasted through the device, making it sound like she was in the same room.

"I'M GOING TO BE A GRANDMOTHER!" she shouted and then the line went silent.

I looked at the phone and then at Aidan. "Was that it?"

"I think so," he said, equally as confused.

"That wasn't that bad," I remarked.

"Yeah, that was subdued for her. I don't get it."

"I don't either."

My phone chimed with an incoming text. "From my father," I told Aidan. "Oh. No."

"What?"

"Mom is at the Atlanta airport—she's flying to New York." Looking at Aidan, I felt my pulse speed up. "Category five just became category six."

"There is no category—oh right. I need a drink," Aidan muttered.

"Sibyl Ruth Goldstein Hyphen Kincaid, I could absolutely kill you!" My mother yelled as she wrapped her arms around my middle and pressed her cheek to my stomach.

"It wasn't my fault," I got out. When it was clear she had no intention of letting go of my belly, I sighed. "Ma, I'm up here. I'm not an incubator."

"I wanted to be the first one to hug my grandchild. Three more seconds. Okay five."

I rolled my eyes heavenward. Did you know you could be completely claustrophobic in your own body?

Mom pushed back and then finally gave me a real hug, her scowl diffusing into a beautiful, happy smile. "Your father told me I should've waited to get confirmation from you, but knowing you, you were dodging my phone calls."

"Er—"

Mom pushed me aside and went for Aidan. "And you —you glorious, handsome son-in-law of mine, get over here so I can thank you for *finally* getting the job done. That virility tonic from my herbalist was like a tiny Red Bull for your boys."

Color suffused Aidan's cheeks as he dutifully bent over to give my five-foot-two Tasmanian Devil of a mom a hug. He shot me a look over her shoulder, and I mouthed, *Told ya.*

My mother let go of Aidan and sauntered into the apartment. "The old me would've killed you both for allowing me to find out I was going to be a grandmother via social media. But the new me, the *zen* me, is okay with this knowledge. I am at peace with it."

Aidan threw me a look and I shrugged. "So, when's Dad showing up?" I asked.

"He's not coming; he's speaking at a heart conference."

I swallowed. "It's just you?"

"Just me," she chirped.

"And you leave when?"

"I have to be back on Tuesday for my pottery class."

Five days.

Mrs. Goldstein would be here for five days.

"Are you"—Aidan cleared his throat—"staying in a hotel?"

She laughed. "Oh you silly boy, of course not! I will stay right here on your new pull-out couch. I don't want to waste any time commuting, you know. We have so much to get done! This place is in no shape for a baby..." She kept gabbing as she went for her phone to make a list, but I tuned her out. While she was in full on grandmother mode, I looked at Aidan.

"Am I having a stroke?" I whispered.

"I was going to ask you the same thing," he murmured, completely dazed. He touched his face. "I can't feel anything."

Mom clapped her hands, turning her focus back to us. "Come on you two. We have a lot to do!"

"Who's ready for dinner?" I asked.

"I could eat," Aidan said.

Mom didn't acknowledge the question. She was too busy leafing through a *Ralph Lauren* magazine for baby clothes. "I'm sorry I didn't have time to pick up any books for you before I got on the plane."

I blinked. Glancing at Aidan, I said, "Can you order the pizza?"

My mother set the magazine down on her lap. "Sibby, now that you're pregnant, you need to pay attention to your diet. You can't live off of pizza and Peanut M&M's. You need a balanced diet. Lots of grilled chicken and spinach. You can have red meat once in a while, but it has to be well-done."

"Blasphemy."

She ignored me. "No more soft cheeses. And do you have any oysters in the house? You should throw those out immediately."

"Ma, when have I ever had oysters in my refrigerator?" I demanded.

"How about pizza tonight and grilled chicken tomorrow?" Aidan asked, ever the peacekeeper.

"I suppose that would be fine," my mother allowed,

turning her attention back to the magazine. She dog-eared a page, and I wondered what ridiculous outfit she was hoping to buy for my unborn child.

"Pizza is on the way," Aidan said a few minutes later, setting down his cell phone.

I curled my feet under myself and reached for the blanket resting on the back of the couch. Aidan helped cover me and then scooted close. My mother watched us from the matching chair with a smile on her face.

This hadn't been the first time she'd shown up unannounced. A few years ago, she and my father had made an unexpected trip to New York. I'd filled them in that not only had I split from my boyfriend of two years, but I'd also lost my office job. I'd presented Aidan to them and admitted I was a waitress in an Italian restaurant. Once they'd gotten over their shock, they'd been incredibly supportive.

"So, I didn't know you were in a pottery class," Aidan said, trying to diffuse the strange tension in the room.

"Oh yeah. I started…three weeks ago? It's super fun. I get to be creative and drink wine while doing it!"

"Cool," I said.

"Yes. And the teacher is a young sculptor with a firm *tuchus.*"

My eyes widened. "I'm glad for you?"

Mom laughed, taking in my expression. "I'm married, Sibby, not dead. I still have a very healthy sex—"

"Who wants a beer?" Aidan interjected, standing up. "I'm getting a beer. OJ for you, Sibby?"

"Sure. I like to live on the edge," I said. "Mom?"

"I'll have a beer, too. That sounds nice."

My mom was a wine type of woman, and vodka martinis when she went to weddings. Told me they made her feel wicked and dangerous. I could count on my hands how many times I'd seen my mother drink a beer.

Shaking my head, I wondered if I'd fallen into a parallel universe.

"Great, I'll be right back," Aidan said. He went to the kitchen, which had an open floor plan, but at least he'd escaped. Marginally.

"I'd like to talk about what this grandchild will call me." Mom set aside the magazine and gave me her undivided attention.

"I thought you wanted to be called *Bubbe*?"

"*Bubbe* sounds so…old. And German."

"Your family *is* German," I pointed out.

"My family is also French. I was thinking *Grandmère*."

"Ohhhhhh-kay."

"Or Grand-Ma-Ma. Emphasis on the second syllable."

Yep. Parallel universe, indeed.

"Would you like the kid to speak with an English accent when it calls you 'Grand-Ma-Ma'?" I asked, tone dry.

I heard Aidan choke on a laugh.

"Let's not call my grandbaby a 'kid,' okay? Let's come up with a unisex nickname."

Aidan returned with our drinks. He handed my mother a pint of beer and then set the glass of OJ on a black slate coaster. "I like that idea."

"What idea?" I demanded.

"We need a name to call the baby while it's in utero," my mother went on. "No more calling it 'kid' or 'it.'"

"Oh, I see. You want to give it a cutesy nickname," I drawled.

"Exactly." Mrs. Goldstein beamed.

"How about peanut?" Aidan suggested.

"No."

"Sprout," my mother suggested.

"Veto."

"I got it," Aidan said in excitement. "Nugget!"

"Hell n—"

"Oh! I love that!" My mother clapped her hands. "Nugget! Yes! I have a grand-nugget! That's the cutest thing *ever*!"

"I know!" Aidan agreed.

"Pierogi!" I shouted.

They both looked at me. Aidan frowned. "You want a pierogi? I can run out and get you—"

"No, I don't *want* a pierogi. I refuse to call my unborn child a nugget. We live in a Polish neighborhood; I want the nickname to be ethnic, okay? Pierogi."

My mother blinked. "You can't call a baby a pierogi."

I crossed my arms over my chest. "My uterus, my rules."

Chapter 16

#fuckkale #fuckallthekale #notarabbit

The next morning, I woke up alone. Aidan didn't have to be at the bar until three, and he'd promised to spend most of the day running interference between my mother and me.

I loved my mother. I did. In small doses. From a distance. She usually traveled with my father, who somehow counteracted her energy. He was like a human version of Benadryl. He calmed my mother in a way no one else could.

Four days and counting.

"Aidan?" I called, rolling out of bed. I padded my way into the living room. The pull-out sofa was put back together, the bedding folded up and stacked on the chair.

My mother and Aidan were nowhere to be found.

They must've run out to grab breakfast, letting me sleep. I went into the kitchen intending to make coffee. Unfortunately, I couldn't find any. I frowned. I knew we hadn't gone through it all, but when I opened the cabinets, I found only empty shelves.

Except for the lone box of naturally decaffeinated mint tea.

"What the hell is this?" I demanded.

There was no caffeine in my apartment. None. Did my mother throw it all out?

Didn't she know how dangerous that was?

I looked in the refrigerator. Empty too, except for a carton of orange juice and a plastic to-go cup filled with green sludge.

Time to find out what the hell was going on. I located my phone and shot off an all-caps text to Aidan. He called immediately.

"Hey, Sib," he greeted. "Sleep well?"

"Yeah, great," I groused. "Aidan, where is all the caffeine?"

"We threw it out," he said, confirming my suspicions.

I took a deep breath, striving for calm. "Why?"

"Because caffeine isn't good for Pierogi."

And so it has begun, I thought darkly.

"And all the food? Where's all the food?"

"It was all processed junk," he said. "Mom and I are at Whole Foods. We're just finishing placing our order."

"Order? What order?"

There was the sound of shuffling, and then my mother's voice came through the phone. "Whole Foods delivers.

We're getting you and Pierogi a lot of healthy foods. Wheatgrass, kale, Brussels sprouts, peas—"

"I get enough peas when I order Aloo Mater Gobi every week," I interjected.

"Balance, Sibby," she reminded me. "Organic chicken breast, organic turkey breast—"

"Bacon? Please tell me you at least got me some bacon."

"Too fatty."

I was slowly losing my will to live.

No caffeine? No bacon?

"And I got you every type of herbal tea they have. So you'll have plenty to drink in the mornings. We have to keep you hydrated!"

"Fantastic," I muttered.

Mom didn't even register the sarcasm. She'd gone down the Grand-Ma-Ma rabbit hole.

"We've got one more stop to make," Mom went on, "and then we'll be home. In the meantime, drink the kale smoothie in the refrigerator."

"Is that what that is?" I demanded.

"It's good for you. It's got coconut oil, protein powder, kale, and mango. The mango makes it sweeter."

And yet it still didn't look appetizing.

"See you in a bit!" She clicked off.

I stared down at the cell phone in dumb shock. When I came to, I went to my favorites list and pressed Annie's name. While it rang, I grabbed the kale concoction.

"Hello?" came Annie's sleepy voice.

"She took my caffeine," I stated.

She yawned. "Who?"

"My mother."

"Mama Goldstein is in town? Why?"

I told her about the Instagram photo exploding my

social media. Annie had deleted all social media apps from her phone, saying it was so she could refocus her life. But I knew it was so she wouldn't stalk Caleb.

"Not only that, she hijacked Aidan! They're at Whole Foods, buying every organic herbal tea in existence. And I'm about to drink a kale smoothie!"

"Ew!"

"I know." I sniffed. "It's the only thing left in my house."

"Are you gonna try it?"

"I'm starving," I admitted. "So I don't think I have a choice."

"I need a video of this, please."

"Stand by."

I hung up with Annie and then situated my phone so I was in the frame. Tying my hair into a messy bun, I tried to make myself presentable. I grabbed the smoothie and pressed record.

The video of me choking down a smoothie the color of the Wicked Witch of the West had a thousand views by the time Aidan and my mother returned. Not even the viral validation was enough to make me benevolent. I didn't forgive them for throwing out the coffee—or the Mint Milanos, though I had a sneaking suspicion the two of them shared the rest of the bag for breakfast, leaving me de-glutenized.

Aidan set down two big shopping bags with the Barnes & Noble logo onto the coffee table. "Look what we got!" he said in excitement as he made a tower of baby books in front of me.

There were some I recognized and some I didn't.

"This one is supposed to be really good," Aidan said, handing me the thickest. "Each week will tell us the size of Pierogi."

"Using fruits," Mom interjected.

I gave them a thumbs up, suddenly feeling exhausted. It could've been the lack of caffeine, or it could've been that I felt completely steamrolled.

Wasn't I a person outside of this baby? It was like the moment I'd found out I was pregnant, my wants and needs had been pushed aside, all to make room for…Pierogi.

Okay, I had to admit the nickname was kind of adorable.

My mother held up *The Complete Book of Baby Names* with a smile. "I'm gonna put a few of these on your bedside table." Mom nearly skipped to the bedroom, her arms loaded with baby books. As soon as she disappeared, I was on Aidan immediately.

"I thought you were on my team," I whispered.

He frowned in confusion. "What are you talking about?"

"You ditched the coffee without telling me. You didn't even ask for my input."

"Your mother said—"

"Is my mother having your baby?" I snapped.

He backed up, instinct to preserve his man-bits kicking in. "No."

"Who's having your baby?"

"You."

"Any more big changes, you run by me first. Got it?"

"Got it."

"Sibby? What color was your pee this morning?" called my mother.

Aidan froze.

"Is she trying to make our marriage sexless?" I demanded.

My chastised husband opened his mouth to speak, but my mother's voice sounded again. "And your poop? Did you poop this morning?"

Four. More. Days.

The next morning, I snuck out of the apartment to hit up the closest Starbucks. Both Aidan and my mother slept like the dead, so it was easy to get past them.

Now, I was waiting for the tired barista to finish my Pumpkin Spice Latte with a dollop of whipped cream.

"Here you go," she said, setting it on the wooden ledge next to the espresso machine.

"Thank you!" I took off the lid and breathed in the delicious aroma of syrup and sugar.

Mama was about to get her fix!

"Drop it!" boomed a voice—way too loud for the early morning crowd at Starbucks. I turned slowly, my mouth hanging open. There stood my mother, wearing a stretchy black exercise suit.

A few bleary-eyed patrons sitting in chairs and sofas turned with their morning coffees. Some even appeared more awake due to the spectacle unfolding.

"How did you know I was here?" I demanded.

My mother marched over and snatched the latte from my grip. "I heard you tiptoe past me. You're not as quiet as you think you are."

"I've done some reading, Mom. I'm allowed to have one cup of coffee."

She held up the latte. "This is not black coffee. This is sugar and chemicals and—"

"And it's delicious," I bellowed, finally losing my temper.

"Don't take that tone with me, Sibyl Ruth!"

"Don't treat me like a child! You threw out everything in my cupboards! You got Aidan on your side! You've even got me calling this baby Pierogi! I have no self-respect left!"

"Ladies," the cashier said in a placating tone, "maybe it's best if you—"

"Shut up!" my mother and I both yelled at her. She blinked and then her mouth trembled. *Great.* On top of going through caffeine withdrawal, I was also making a twenty-year-old barista cry.

My tone softened. "Listen, I'm really sorry. I'm hormonal and she"—I pointed to my mother—"stole all the coffee in my house."

The trembling of the barista's chin stabilized. "That sounds awful."

"It's for your own good," my mother said. The anger in her tone had disappeared, and she suddenly sounded tired.

"You haven't involved me," I told her. "You and Aidan have talked and bulldozed over my feelings, my wants."

Her shoulders sagged. "I got carried away, didn't I?"

"Maybe a little."

"I'm sorry, Sibby. I'm just excited and I—It's no excuse. You're right. You're a grown woman. You and Aidan can handle this yourself."

I let out a laugh. "Like hell we can! I'm terrified."

"You are?"

"Yes. I need you, Mom."

"You do?"

I nodded. "But maybe, I could need you from Atlanta?"

She laughed and moved to hug me with one arm, the Pumpkin Spice Latte in the other hand. There was the sound of clapping, and when my mother pulled away, there were tears at the corners of her eyes.

"Look at us, making a scene." She wiped her cheeks and looked down at the latte. She took a sip, her eyes lighting up. "Oh my goodness, that's delicious!"

I wrapped my arm around my mother's shoulders. "You're my mom and I love you. But if you don't give that back and get your own, I might have to hurt you."

My mother stood by the apartment door, her wheeled suitcase packed and ready to go. She'd changed her flight and had even sweet-talked the customer service rep to upgrade her to first class. My mother had mad phone skills. "Call me if you need anything."

"I will," I said, giving her a hug.

"You too," she told Aidan.

He bent down to hug my mother. "Thanks for everything."

"Yeah, Mom. Thanks."

She raised an eyebrow. "That almost sounded sincere."

I rolled my eyes. "It *was* sincere."

"There's my girl." She touched my cheek and leaned in to whisper. "You're gonna be fine."

Tears gathered in the corners of my eyes. I hadn't realized how much I needed to hear that until that very moment. "Thank you."

"One more hug," she said. "Then I've got to go before the Uber guy drives off."

"Let me grab your suitcase," Aidan said, wheeling the baggage out into the hall and carrying it downstairs.

"Don't be mad at him," Mom said to me softly.

"I'm not mad at Aidan."

She cocked her head to one side. "Yes, you are. It wasn't his fault. It wasn't your fault. But accidents happen, and you of all people should know that sometimes the best detours lead you to some pretty spectacular places."

My throat closed with emotion. "He talked to you, didn't he?"

She nodded.

I wasn't sure I liked my mother knowing such personal details about my marriage.

"You'll be fine. You both will be fine."

"Yeah, now that I have coffee back in the house."

She laughed. "Moderation. That's all I'm saying."

I hugged her again and said into her hair, "Thanks again, Mom. We'll see you and Dad soon."

"For Thanksgiving?" she asked hopefully.

"We'll see."

She left, and a moment later Aidan came back, shutting the door behind him. "She's off," he said.

"We're alone again?" I asked.

"We are."

"Good." I jumped into his arms and wrapped my legs around his waist. "I missed you these last few days."

His blue eyes lit with desire. "I've missed you too."

"You still think I'm sexy?"

"Incredibly."

"Then let's get in bed and do the horizontal hora. It's the one dance I'm actually good at."

Chapter 17

#saltmeetwound #outlikeatrout

"YAY!" Nat squealed, hugging me to her. "You're having a baby!"

"Don't remind her," Annie said. She sat in the red diner booth, sipping on weak coffee. "Her mom reminds her every five seconds."

Nat shrugged off her boho bag and slid into the unoccupied booth across from Annie. "She left, right?"

"Yesterday. I have my apartment back," I said. "And my husband back."

"Tell her what happened with your mother at Starbucks," Annie needled.

I glared at her as I took a seat next to Nat. I couldn't show my face in that Starbucks ever again. Even after leaving a massive tip, I'd always be remembered as the pregnant girl with a dramatic mother.

"Something happened at Starbucks?" Nat asked. "Tell me everything!"

I'd told Nat countless stories of my mother. She'd always listened with equal parts fascination and disbelief. After I recounted what had occurred at Starbucks and Nat stopped laughing, I said, "Can we not talk about it? Please? It was a rough few days."

"Parents get weird when they're about to be grandparents," Nat said in commiseration. "Tad's mother turned into a full-on nightmare."

"I thought she was already a nightmare," Annie interjected.

"A nightmare on steroids. At least your mother loves you, Sibby. I'm just the girl Tad knocked up and then married."

"I'm sure she doesn't think that," I said.

"Oh, yes, she does. Last Christmas, she got drunk and told me this."

I stared at her in mute horror.

"That's pretty bad," Annie said. "Last Christmas, my mom got drunk and threw a fork at my father."

"Why did she throw a fork at your father?" Nat wondered.

"Because he's my father." She took a sip of her coffee as if her explanation was an actual explanation. Then again, it made total sense why they were divorcing.

"I'm glad I celebrate Hanukkah," I said. "I popped so

many bubbles in fifth grade when I told the entire class that Santa wasn't real."

Nat and Annie laughed.

"I had no filter."

"What's changed?" Annie teased.

"I miss this," Nat wailed in feigned misery. "I miss you guys. I hate that I have to leave tonight. I love New York. I'd move back in a heartbeat."

"Tell Annie not to leave," I demanded. "She's ditching me, just like you ditched me."

"You're leaving the city?" Nat asked, mouth agape. "Why the hell would you do that?"

"Need a change," Annie said.

Nat looked at me and then at Annie. We all understood what Annie really meant: she wanted a change of scene that didn't remind her of Caleb.

"Where are you going?" Nat asked, skating past what could've been an awkward emotional moment.

"Montauk. My uncle owns a seafood restaurant, and I'm going to go up there and cook for him. Get my head on straight, hopefully."

"Live on the beach? Get a tan?" Nat asked.

Annie laughed. "Yeah."

"Okay, never mind. Fuck Manhattan, I want to go to Montauk."

"Next summer, you both should come up there. It's gorgeous in the summer."

"Next summer, I'll be ready to drop Pierogi. My due date is the end of June," I explained, looking around for the absent waitress. Seriously, my blood sugar was dropping to dangerous levels.

Annie frowned in confusion. "Pierogi?"

My cheeks flushed with heat. "Yeah." I cleared my

throat. "Pierogi is the nickname we gave—" I gestured to my stomach. "So we don't have to keep calling it—*it*."

"Wow." Annie leaned back in the booth. "You did it. You became *that* person."

"Yeah, I know." I drummed my fingers on the table. "Was I this bad when I waited tables at Antonio's?"

Nat snorted. "No. You were very attentive."

The sound of silverware and plates dropping from somewhere behind the closed kitchen door clanged through the diner.

I looked at Nat. "That could've been me."

Nat laughed. "Oh yeah. That definitely could've been you."

"What'll you have?" a waitress asked, appearing as if our hangriness had summoned her like a genie in a bottle.

"The Tootie Fruitie waffle, extra whipped cream, please," Annie said, closing her menu.

Nat stared at the menu and pointed. "I'll have the steak and eggs. Medium and over easy, please."

"And for you?" the waitress asked.

"The granola, fruit, and yogurt. A side of steamed spinach. Oh, and a large orange juice." I handed the waitress my menu and then she left.

"What the hell kind of order was that?" Annie demanded.

I sighed. "I became *that* person, remember?"

After breakfast, the three of us said goodbye and went our separate ways. Nat had to get back to her hotel and check out, and Annie still had packing to do. It was amazing how we were all at these different points in our lives: Nat was a mother, Annie was as lost as she'd ever been, and I...well, I was somewhere in between.

Sometimes I felt like I'd just figured out my place in the

world—and then *bam*. I was fired, or dumped, or knocked up.

It was time to take some control back.

I walked into Veritas and sat down at the bar. It was the middle of the day, and the bar wasn't technically open, which was why I'd come now instead of later when it got busy.

His back was to me, and he was holding a clipboard, cataloguing the liquors. "You've been avoiding me," he said without turning.

"Yeah, I have been," I admitted quietly.

Caleb clipped the pencil to the top of the clipboard and then set it aside. "I suppose congratulations are in order?" He turned to look at me, a small smile on his lips.

"If you're feeling charitable."

"Congratulations, Sibby. Aidan's over the moon. I'm happy for you both." There were shadows underneath his eyes, and he looked leaner than the last time I'd seen him.

"How are you doing?" I asked him.

"Hanging in there. Working a lot." He retrieved a pint glass and filled it with water. Setting it down in front of me, he waited.

I picked up the glass of water and took a sip. "What she did to you was complete and utter shit."

He blinked and then smiled. "It was complete and utter shit, wasn't it?"

"Absolutely," I agreed. "She's wrong in how she handled her emotions, and she's wrong in how she treated you."

"Do you…" He swallowed. "Do you know *why*? Because for the life of me, I never could get her to talk to me."

"She's clammed shut. Annie's…not like me. I'm sure you know how I handle things." I smiled.

"Aidan might've clued me in," Caleb evaded with a rueful grin.

"I came here to make it right with you—you and me."

"I get it, Sib. I'm Aidan's best friend and business partner. I was Annie's boyfriend. But you and I—we don't have to be friends."

I reached over the bar and bopped him on the head. "Are you being serious right now?"

He rubbed his head and frowned. "Uh, that hurt."

"No, it didn't." I rolled my eyes. "Seriously, Caleb. I thought we were friends in our own right. Are you telling me that's not the case?"

"I—what are you going to do when I start dating other women? You want me to tell you about it?"

I crossed my arms over my chest. "How's what's-her-face?"

"How did you—*Aidan*." He shook his head. "And I'm not dating Gemma."

"You're just getting your groove back, right?"

"Are you judging me?"

"Nope. I'm not. Seriously, I know you probably don't believe me."

He paused and glanced away. "Is she seeing anyone?"

"Would either answer make you feel any better?"

"Why do you have to answer a question with a question?"

"Why do you?" I threw back.

Caleb sighed. "See? How can we be friends if you won't be honest with me? You're honest with Annie. So be honest with me."

"You want honesty? Fine. No. She's not seeing anyone. She's moving to Montauk to get some perspective. She quit her job, blew up her life, her parents are divorcing, and she has no idea who she is or what she wants. I'm not going to tell you that I understand how the first thing you could do after breaking up was fall into bed with someone else—then again, I'm not a guy. But hey, you have your own way of figuring out your own shit and who am I—"

"I wanted to marry her, Sib," he interrupted, voice hard. "I thought I'd found the person I was going to spend the rest of my life with and she—"

"Is fucked in the head because her parents weren't a good example for her."

"Well, that's a bullshit excuse."

I raised an eyebrow. "Is it?"

"You don't just give up because—"

"You don't understand her," I said, coming to the realization. "Do you? Because if you did, you would've stopped asking her to marry you and tried to figure out a way to help her get over her fear of commitment."

"I was *there*! I was committed. We lived together. How much more could I have done for her?"

"Did you give her room to breathe? Did you allow her to be herself, or did you try and change her?"

He fell silent.

"Maybe you liked the idea of a project."

"She's *not* a project. I love her—and she threw that in my face when she got drunk and flirted with that guy and kept pushing me away." He picked up his clipboard. "You say you want to be friends, but you chose her long ago. And you're choosing her now. You're even excusing away her shitty behavior, and I get it. I do. She left me, Sibby. She left me before we even broke up, but she never left you. She'll never leave you. And that's why you'll always choose her, no matter how bad her decisions, no matter how destructive she gets." His face hardened. "Good. I'm glad she's going to Montauk. I don't want to see her ever again."

Chapter 18

#Pierogi1Sibby0 #heifer

"What did you say to Caleb?" Aidan asked the moment he walked through the door.

I slowly closed the lid of my laptop and looked at him. "Hi, honey, how was your night at work? My night was pretty uneventful. I fell down the mommy pregnancy blog rabbit hole, and now I'm terrified and over loaded with information, most of which probably isn't even true. I would drink wine to cope, but I can't now. So I've been drinking herbal tea like it's going out of style, and now I have to pee like an old man in the middle of the night."

Aidan closed the front door, his face softening when he looked at me. "Google is a dangerous thing."

I gestured to the stack of books my mother had purchased for us. "I didn't know where to start, so at one point I had three books open and one resting on my face—I was hoping to learn by osmosis."

He came over and plopped down onto the couch next to me, his face lined with exhaustion. "And how did that go?"

"It doesn't work." I snuggled up against him. "Was he impossible to work with tonight?"

Aidan sighed. "At one point, I told him to take a walk. He was in a piss-poor mood all night. I had to jump behind the bar and take over."

"No wonder you're late getting home," I muttered. "I came in earlier to see him."

"So he said."

"And yet he didn't tell you what we talked about?"

"Oh, I can guess," he remarked dryly, his hand rubbing up and down my arm. "Annie?"

I nodded. "I might've been too honest with him."

"In what way?"

"I told him he never really understood her, and he kept trying to change her."

"Ouch. That *was* honest of you."

"Do you agree with me?"

"I don't know, Sibby. Guys think differently than girls." He gently extracted himself from my side to lean over and kick off his shoes.

I rubbed my hand up and down his back, and instead of sitting up, he sprawled across my lap.

"How's Pierogi?" he asked, turning his head so he could kiss my belly.

"Firmly lodged in my uterine wall." He chuckled and

then it turned into a moan of pleasure as my fingers plowed through his dark hair. "I didn't mean to piss him off."

"He was already pissed off. He kept a pretty good lid on it, but tonight, you blew that lid off."

"Maybe I'll just steer clear of him, then," I said.

Aidan laughed, his breath teasing my shirt. "He just wants to be pissed, so I'm letting him be pissed."

"Sometimes that's all you can do."

"How's she doing?" Aidan asked.

"I don't want to talk about them anymore," I whispered.

"Oh?" He rolled over onto his back. "What do you want to talk about?"

"Ice cream sundaes."

"I love it when you talk dirty."

I nudged him off my lap. "Buy you a banana split?"

"You're really going to make me put shoes on after I just got home from work?"

"A happy wife is a happy life," I reminded him. "Come on, my treat."

I opened my eyes and stared at the ceiling. The November sun was out and peeking through the blinds of the bedroom. Aidan was asleep on his stomach, dark hair messy and adorable, his mouth slightly agape. I leaned over and sniffed him.

"Sibby," he whispered into his pillow.

"Gah!" I jumped back. "You're awake!"

"I heard you sniff me."

"I did no such thing."

"Liar." His mouth widened into a smile, but his eyes remained closed. "Were you watching me sleep, too?"

"Just for a minute."

"Right," he drawled, finally cracking an eye.

"I swear! I—" After covering my mouth with my hand, I flung off the covers and ran to the bathroom. As I bent over the toilet and vomited, I heard Aidan's footsteps treading on the wooden floor. I yelled, "Don't look! I'm disgusting." I would've said more, but my head went back over the toilet for round two.

Finally, when the morning sickness had completed its vile way with me, I managed to get up off the floor. I brushed my teeth, rinsed with mouthwash and splashed some cool water on my face.

I came out of the bathroom and saw Aidan sitting on the bed, wearing nothing but a pair of boxers. His hair was still askew, but the sleepy look had cleared from his eyes, and he was completely awake.

"How are you feeling?" he asked.

"Like I threw up all my organs." I collapsed onto the bed, belly first.

"You're beautiful."

I turned my head away. "I might need to hear that a lot in the next many months."

He flopped down and spooned me from behind. I felt him press a kiss to my hair. "Okay."

"I might need a lot of back rubs, foot rubs, and ice cream sundaes."

Aidan laughed and scooted closer. "Someone might be milking this for all it's worth."

"And sex, Aidan. I'm gonna need some sex. I'm going to need physical proof that I don't repulse you."

"What, you mean right now?"

I pinched his arm, making him squirm. "Not right now, you dingus. Maybe after a cup of coffee."

He swept my hair aside to brush a kiss against my neck. "I think that might be doable."

I glanced down at my unbuttoned jeans. Currently lying flat on the bed, I attempted to close them, but the button refused to stay put.

It popped open again.

"You will not defeat me," I stated. "Do you hear me?"

I tried one more time. Same thing happened.

It was official. I was too fat for my favorite pair of skinny jeans.

Slithering out of my pants was an endeavor. With a sigh of sadness, I folded up the jeans and stuck them on the top shelf of my closet. "So long, old friend. Hopefully we'll meet again."

An hour later, Aidan found me in the bedroom, standing in my underwear, all my pants scattered across the bed. "Hey. What's going on?"

"They turned on me, Aidan. Every last pair."

He sighed. "Riddles. My wife speaks in riddles."

"Pierogi is making me fat," I stated. "I can't button my jeans. And some of them I couldn't even get past my thighs. How? I'm like a minute pregnant. Have I already gained a bunch of weight?"

"God," he moaned. "Why would you ask me that? There's no way to win."

"Have I?" I demanded. "Be honest."

"Can't you"—he swallowed—"get on the scale?"

I glared at him.

"I'm failing at this comforting husband thing, aren't I?"

"No. I think you're in husband survival mode." My shoulders slumped. "Fine. I'll weigh myself." I marched into the bathroom. I pulled out the scale from underneath the sink. "We have a pretty good relationship," I said to the inanimate object. "But I have a feeling we're about to have a massive falling out."

"Sibby? Are you talking to the scale?" Aidan called.

"No!" I shouted back. With a deep breath, I stepped onto the scale…and watched the numbers blow past my normal weight. "Oh, my God!"

"What?" Aidan asked, shoving the door open.

I pointed to the scale in accusation. "It says I've gained six-and-a-half pounds. How Aidan? How did I do that in three weeks? Have I been eating too many ice cream sundaes?"

"You know, math is a tricky thing," Aidan said, slowly backing out of the bathroom.

I dismounted the offensive scale and stalked toward him. "Have I?"

"No. You haven't. But Sibby, you're pregnant."

"Yeah."

"You're *pregnant*," he said again, slowly.

"I know I'm pregnant," I snapped.

"You sure?"

"I'm eating right—except for the ice cream sundaes—I'm drinking coffee black, no added sugar, and I'm looking into prenatal yoga. I'm reading the books, I'm—"

"Completely disconnected."

I blinked. "Excuse me?"

He came forward and grasped my hand. Tugging me to the bed, he gestured for me to sit down. "Just listen for a second, okay?"

I nodded for him to continue. Aidan paused a moment, gathering his words. "I know this didn't happen the way you wanted it to happen. I know you weren't ready, and I know you wanted more time. And then—"

"And then the damn condom froze."

"Yeah. The condom froze and now we're having a baby."

"I know that."

"You're pissed at me."

"I'm not, Aidan. I swear."

"Well, something has you pissed. If it's not me, then—"

"I'm pissed at Pierogi, okay?" I snapped. "There, I said it. I'm pissed at my unborn child. And what kind of mother gets pissed at her unborn child? The timing of all this…ever since I found out I was pregnant, my whole life changed. Overnight. I'm sharing my body with another occupant. I think about Pierogi first—what can I eat? What can I drink? Am I getting enough sleep? And my career? Forget my career! I've barely been able to think about what I want to do with this book I wrote because I DON'T CARE. I don't care, Aidan, because there's something bigger going on than even my muse. Do you know how terrifying it is? To feel like you're losing yourself? It's like—it's like I'm on this rollercoaster, strapped in, unable to get off. And I just have to sit back and go along with it."

I ended my speech, trembling with emotion, my eyes filling with tears.

"Come here," was all he said.

I climbed into his lap and pressed my face to his neck. He held me and let me cry. And that might've been the thing I loved most about him. He didn't try to offer any words of comfort—he was just there—letting me have all my feelings, rocking me through the storm until it passed.

"Feeling any better?" Aidan whispered a while later.

I nodded against his neck. I did feel lighter.

Huh. Sharing feelings with my husband…a good idea. Always.

"Aren't you scared?" I asked, pulling back to look at him.

"Of what?"

"Of our lives changing?"

"Well, sure," he admitted. "But I guess—I don't know —I'm more excited than scared. Maybe…"

"What?"

"Maybe I should be more involved."

"You're involved. How can you be *more* involved?"

"Okay, involved is the wrong word. But you're on a limited diet and you can't drink. It's not fair that you have to abstain. So I'll abstain in solidarity."

I blinked. "You want to be miserable, too?"

He laughed and hugged me tighter. "I just meant, maybe I could be a little more understanding of what you're going through. I don't have the hormones to sympathize, so how about I go through caffeine withdrawal and cut out the drinking."

"You own a bar."

"Never said it was going to be easy."

"You'd do that? For me?" I asked, my heart becoming all mushy and gross.

"For you and Pierogi," he said with a soft smile.

I arched an eyebrow. "Then there's one more thing I want you to do…"

Chapter 19

#skinnygirlsmakemestabby #Iwillendyou

We were in a large open room on the second floor of a converted warehouse. Sunbeams shot through the floor-to-ceiling windows, painting rays of light onto the wood floors. The soft sounds of Native American flutes played in the background as women entered the yoga studio. They were all in different stages of pregnancy; some sported small baby bumps, while others looked to be far along in their third trimester.

Aidan and I had taken two spots in the middle of the room, and we were sitting cross-legged on our mats.

"They're judging me," Aidan whispered.

"No one's judging you," I stated.

"I'm the only guy here."

"You're sexy and wearing a pair of shorts that show off your lumberjack legs," I said. "The ladies are lookin'."

"I can't believe I let you talk me into this."

"How bad do you want a beer right now?" I teased him.

"On a scale of one to ten, about a fifteen," he muttered.

"You really don't have to give it up for me."

"I want to."

"Okay. Your choice."

"You're not allowed to make a bet with Annie on when I'll cave." He gave me a mockingly stern look.

"I would never do such a thing. That's like asking you to fail."

"On a scale of one to ten, how much faith do you have in my ability to be sober for the next eight months?"

"Oh, look the instructor is coming." I faced front and ignored Aidan's eye roll.

The young woman who came into the room looked neither pregnant nor homely. She was petite, with a dusting of freckles across the bridge of her nose and gorgeous red hair that trailed down her back in a long braid. Her yoga pants and sports tank showed off her killer, toned body.

She stopped in front of Aidan.

"Are you sure you're in the right class?" she asked, her blue eyes taking in all six feet hotness of my husband.

Aidan smiled, flashing his dimples. "I'm here to support my wife."

The instructor's eyes slid to me. I held up my hand and waved. "Oh, what happened to your wrist?"

"I tripped," I answered flatly.

"No backbends for you," she teased.

"What's a backbend?" Aidan asked.

I began to explain, but my words died as the instructor dropped to the floor and demonstrated. She grinned at him from upside down.

Limber bitch.

She unfolded herself and stood up. "That's a back-bend." With a wink, she stalked away, putting an extra sway in her step.

I looked at Aidan. "Next class better be taught by a gay guy."

After class, Aidan and I bought two green smoothies for the walk home. Aidan didn't even look like he'd exercised. Then again, he played basketball once a week with Caleb and stayed frisky with me.

He got his cardio.

Me on the other hand…my ponytail was limp, my skin was slick with sweat, and my heart rate still hadn't returned to a normal beat. And yoga hadn't even been that stressful. A lot of it had been breathing techniques followed by a few simple poses.

"That was fun," Aidan said when we got out onto the sidewalk.

I scoffed.

He looked at me. "Ah, come on, Sib, don't be mad. Trisha was just being nice."

"There's nice and then there's *nice*."

Aidan threw his arm across my shoulders. "I've only got eyes for you, love."

"I saw where your eyes were the whole class, Aidan. She was doing tricks for you. Like a little circus dog presenting her hind quarters."

"Sibby?"

"What?" I grumbled.

"Are you the love of my life?"

I sighed. "Yeah."

"Are you carrying my child?"

"Yeah."

"Are you the most beautiful woman in the world?"

"If I say yes, does that make me arrogant or delusional?"

He laughed and pulled me to him. "You've got nothing to worry about."

"You mean the only hind quarters you're interested in are mine?"

"Something like that."

"I want a meatball sub. It's a physical hunger—not an emotional one."

"Okay. I can make that happen."

He took my hand as we walked down the street. I finished the smoothie and chucked the plastic container into a trash bin. I heard the sound of barking, and when we turned the corner, there were people milling around, volunteers wearing black long-sleeved shirts and holding clipboards.

"Puppies!" I yelled in excitement, tugging on his arm. "Aidan, there are puppies!"

"Let's cross the street," he suggested.

"Why would we do that?" I hauled him toward the fray. "You like puppies!"

"I love puppies," he admitted. "I'm just afraid if we go into that mess, we're gonna come out with a dog."

"Scout's honor we won't leave with a dog."

"You were a rotten Girl Scout, remember? Your pledge means nothing."

"I'm ignoring you now."

"I thought you wanted a meatball sub."

"The meatball sub can wait. I want my puppy fix!"

There were dogs of all shapes and sizes, ages, and fur lengths. I bypassed the barkers and those that were surrounded by people. I kept walking, my eyes darting from dog to dog. I wanted to play with one that needed—

A medium-sized brown and white dog with wiry hair was lying on the sidewalk, taking a nap. He paid no attention to the hubbub surrounding him. The volunteer holding his leash smiled at my approach.

"Who's this little guy?" I asked, crouching down. I held out my hand. The dog raised his head, sniffed my hand, gave it a lick, and then went back to napping.

"This is Jasper. He's three years old, completely house-broken, and loves to take naps."

"My spirit animal," I teased. "Hi, Jasper."

Jasper lifted his head, bumped his snoot against my nose, and I swore my heart melted in my chest. I looked over my shoulder at Aidan who had a resigned look on his face.

I scratched Jasper's neck, and he rolled over, showing me his speckled belly. "Oh, my God. Are you the cutest?" I leaned over, and with no shame, buried my nose in his fur and sniffed.

Aidan sighed. "What's your adoption process?"

"Uh, they totally lied," Aidan stated as he dropped to his knees and cleaned up yet another puddle of Jasper's pee.

"They didn't lie," I said. "Jasper does like to nap."

"Yeah, and when he's not napping, he's peeing all over the house."

"It's been three days, Aidan," I reminded him. "This is a new environment for him and dogs are really sensitive. He's just settling in."

Jasper sat next to me on the couch, looking up at me with the sweetest brown eyes in the history of the world. "You're just settling in, aren't you?" I cooed. "Aren't you? Boop! Boop!" Tapping his nose, I grinned when his tongue lolled out of the side of his mouth.

Jasper flopped down onto his stomach and then rolled onto his back, putting his head in my lap. I rubbed his belly and sighed with contentment.

"It'll get easier," I told Aidan when he came back from washing his hands.

"It better."

"Pierogi will take way longer to house train," I reminded him.

"You mean potty train?"

"Yeah, that." I buried my nose in Jasper's neck, breathing in the scent of oatmeal and cinnamon. We'd given him a bath, and he smelled like Christmas cookies.

"He certainly got accustomed to the couch rather quickly," Aidan said.

"At least he doesn't shed."

"I draw the line at him ever being allowed in our bed."

"But—"

"Sibby…"

"Fine," I grumbled. "I'm sad we missed Halloween with him. He would've been a cute cowboy."

"Saints preserve us," Aidan muttered.

"Should we take him to meet Santa? That would make an adorable holiday card."

"Do you hear yourself right now?"

"What's bugging you?" I demanded.

"Aside from the pee I just cleaned up?"

"Uh, yeah. He's a dog. Dogs pee. I cleaned up two puddles yesterday."

He ran a hand over his face. "You've been ignoring me."

"I haven't."

"You have, Sibby. You've barely hugged me, or kissed me. All your attention has been on that dog!"

I covered Jasper's ears. "No fighting in front of him. Let's take this into the bedroom."

Aidan rolled his eyes but followed me into the bedroom. I closed the door and turned to face him. "Okay, let's hear it."

"I feel like you backed me into a corner," he said. "I wasn't ready for a dog."

I let out a mirthless laugh. "This conversation feels very familiar."

A muscle in his jaw ticked. "You can't compare an unexpected pregnancy to an unexpected dog adoption."

"You were the one who asked about it!"

"Because I saw you fall in love with that dog. I literally watched your face soften. What was I supposed to do? Tell you no?"

"Tell me no?" I crossed my arms over my chest.

He pinched the bridge of his nose. "Bad choice of words. But come on, Sibby. This has been a rough three days. We haven't left the dog alone because you've been worried about him acclimating. I miss you. I want to take you out to dinner tonight. It's the only night I don't have to be at the bar."

My anger eased. "Dinner, just the two of us, would be really nice."

"You'll date me tonight?"

I smiled. "Yeah, Aidan. I'll date you tonight."

We were at our favorite restaurant in our neighborhood. It had a long marble bar and a speakeasy feel to it. The lighting was low, the food was delicious, and they knew us by name. The bartender even sent over a round of mocktails because we had told him I was pregnant.

Yep, I used the word mocktail. My twenty-year-old self just cringed.

"Do you think Jasper's okay?" I asked.

Aidan looked up from his menu. "Yes." He smiled. "Did I tell you how gorgeous you are?"

"Yes, you did tell me how gorgeous I am. But tell me again," I said with a smile.

Aidan reached across the table to take my hand. He skimmed his fingers across my knuckles and said, "You're gorgeous." Letting go of my hand, he looked back at the menu. "What are you going to get?"

"The truffle risotto."

"If I get the chicken piccata will you share?"

"Yes."

"Done." He closed his menu and set it aside. "Thanks for taking me off the dating market."

I grinned. "You're welcome."

He reached for his water and took a sip. "I was just thinking about Caleb. I can't believe he has to start over and go through the whole dating process again."

"Yeah, I can't even imagine…but it's easier for men than it is for women."

"You think so?"

"Absolutely," I stated. "There's that whole ticking biological clock that most women have."

"Ah, yeah, that clock."

"I think my clock's broken," I admitted.

"Not broken," he assured me. "But maybe it's on Pacific Time when most clocks are on Eastern Time."

I blinked at him and then frowned. "Have you been drinking?"

"No!"

"Aidan?"

He sighed. "No, Sibby, I haven't been drinking, but"—he leaned across the table and whispered   "edibles."

"Cheater!" I accused.

The server chose that moment to arrive. "Um, would you like to hear the specials or should I come back?"

I looked up at her and smiled. "Specials, please."

She looked at me funny as she recounted the specials. After she left, I turned my attention back to Aidan.

"You mad?" he asked.

"Not even a little bit," I said. "I promise."

"I just needed a little stress reliever, ya know?"

"Aidan, we're good."

"We are?"

I nodded. "But there's no way in hell I'm sharing my truffle risotto with you."

He laughed. "If that's the price I pay…"

"I might demand a back rub."

"I'm game."

"And then I might let you take my clothes off."

He leaned forward, eyes darkening. "Best punishment ever."

Chapter 20

#donotmockthemocktail #battleoftheurine

After dinner, we walked down to the pier. It was chilly, so I used it as an excuse to huddle close to Aidan. Leaning my head against his chest, I watched the city skyline. A boat moved across the East River, clipping along at a steady pace.

We moved to a bench to share our dessert, a fluffy pastry from one of our favorite Polish bakeries. There were very few other people around, so it was almost like we had some privacy.

"This would've been a nice place to propose," Aidan said.

"I like how you proposed."

Aidan and I had gone on vacation. He'd proposed on a beach. It would've almost been a cliché except for the fact that a seagull pooped on me.

"Any regrets?" he asked.

"About marrying you? Tons," I teased.

"Not about that but in general. Anything you wish you could change?"

I thought about it for a moment. "I don't think so. Because if I changed anything, would I be in this place, in this moment? Even after getting fired from writing textbooks and walking in on Matt with another guy, all that crap led me to you, led me to writing books. Hard to have regrets, ya know?"

"I love that about you, Sibby. I love your optimism."

We fell silent. A few other couples and then a guy with a dog walked passed. Suddenly, I wanted to be home. "Can we go? I miss Jasper."

"Yeah, we can go."

Leaving the pier, I dodged around the people that wanted to meander and take it slow. "I really miss him," I said to Aidan.

"You know what? I kind of miss the little bugger too."

"I'm sure he misses us." I sped up the last few blocks, getting to the apartment before Aidan. I unlocked the door and went inside.

Jasper lay on a pile of stuffing and shredded gray cushions. He raised his head and cocked it to the side, his tail thumping in happiness to see me, yet he refused to get up from his spot in the middle of what used to be our couch.

"Oh, no," I whispered.

I heard Aidan come in behind me. "Son of a bitch!"

Jasper let out a low woof and then set his head down on his paws.

"My couch," Aidan moaned, stepping into the living room. "My beautiful, brand new couch."

"Let's hope that's all the destruction he did," I stated. We'd closed off the bedroom and the bathroom, so thankfully those rooms were untouched. I went into the kitchen, my jaw dropping open. There were at least four piles of poop.

"What did you eat? Indian food?" I yelled.

Jasper woofed again.

"What?" Aidan demanded.

"I think he punished us for leaving him," I stated, looking over my shoulder at Aidan, who was glaring down at the dog.

"You start cleaning, and I'll take him out for a walk," Aidan said. He reached for Jasper's leash and crouched down to Jasper's eye level.

"You sure?" I asked.

Aidan nodded. "Jasper and I need to have a talk, man to mongrel."

I grimaced at the mess in front of me. One thing at a time. The poop was the most important. Thank goodness it wasn't summer.

"I love you," I called to Aidan.

"Love you," he called back as he ushered Jasper to the front door. "Come on, beast. It's time we had a talk."

Four days later, I lamented to Annie over coffee. "I'm in the dog house."

"I thought Jasper was in the dog house for eating the couch."

"We're roommates." I took a sip of the decaf cappuccino, hating that it was decaf, but keeping my word to only have one caffeinated coffee a day. "Aidan is not a happy dude."

"So have sex with him."

"I did. It improved his temperament marginally. Now he's back to sulking—and working all the time."

"He needs to bond with Jasper."

"Yeah, they need a day together, doing guy stuff. Watching baseball, belly rubs, that sort of thing."

"It's football season."

"Whatever. Aidan resents the dog and the time I give to Jasper."

"Why did you get a dog?" she asked. "I mean, the timing was awful. You know that, right?"

"Oh, is that what we're doing now? Tough love?"

"You were there for me in my time of need, I'm just returning the favor." She reached for her Americano, which she drank black. "You had to know it was going to put an even bigger strain on things."

"Things aren't strained," I denied.

"Uh huh, right." Annie rolled her eyes and then played

with a raw sugar packet. "Your life would've been easier if you hadn't gotten a dog."

"But it's Jasper!" I held up my phone and showed her my wallpaper. It was the three of us, Aidan holding the camera for a selfie. He was smiling and my nose was buried in Jasper's belly fur.

"Adorable. Regular Norman Rockwell painting," she mocked.

"Aidan was the one who asked about the adoption process!" I said. "Why does everyone keep forgetting that?"

"I didn't forget it. But, Sibby, do you think just maybe he got you the dog so he'd feel like you guys were even?"

I sighed. "You mean like, he gets a baby before I was ready, and I got a dog before he was ready?"

"Something like that."

I drank the rest of my cappuccino in silence, thinking about how to bring my marriage back on track. It wasn't off the rails, per se, but it definitely felt like it had taken a detour.

"Can you puppy sit tonight?" I asked.

"Puppysit your little terror? No thanks."

"He's not a terror."

She cocked an eyebrow. "How many times a day does he pee in the house?"

"He's down to one."

"Are you lying?"

"Absolutely." I gripped her hand. "Please? I'll give you anything you want."

I walked into Veritas wearing a new, bright red, polka-dot dress and the highest high heels I owned. My eyebrows were newly waxed, my eyelashes were gooped with mascara, and I'd left my wedding ring on the nightstand at home.

Tonight, I would seduce my husband in a public place while pretending to be a 1950s vixen he'd never met before.

A dog with a bladder issue, an expanding waistline, and the propensity for having morning sickness in the evening would not stop me from proving to Aidan that he was the most important thing in the world to me.

Caleb wasn't working that night, thank goodness. Bailey, the bartender with tattoos snaking up his skinny arms, manned the bar. His gray vest and skinny red tie went well with the decor of the wine bar.

"Hey, Sibby," Bailey said. "Aidan's downstairs in the wine room."

"Thanks." I set my black clutch on the bar and shrugged out of my coat. The sweetheart neckline of the dress was fairly demure, but it showed off my shoulders and my upper back.

Bailey whistled. "Hot!"

I laughed. "Even with the blue cast?"

"Gives you some flare," he said. "Get you something to drink? Nonalcoholic, of course. Congrats, by the way."

I thanked him again and then asked, "Something cranberry-based, but can you put it in a martini glass? I wanna feel fancy."

"Your wish is my command." He bowed. "So should I tell Aidan you're here?"

I shook my head. "I want to surprise him."

"One lucky dude," he muttered and then started making my faux drink.

Fifteen minutes later, I was sipping on a spritzy cranberry mocktail when Aidan finally made his way up from the liquor room. He stopped, his eyes drifting down my body.

He strolled forward. "Hi, love. What are you doing here?" He leaned in to kiss me, but I turned my head and gasped in mock outrage.

"Excuse me, but do I know you?" I asked, fluttering my eyelashes.

Aidan frowned. "Huh?"

I let out a sigh and whispered, "We're strangers, get it?"

Aidan's face cleared of confusion, and then he grinned. "Oh, I get it." He casually leaned against the bar. "I'd offer to buy you a drink, but I see you already have one."

"If you play your cards right, I'll let you do more than buy me a drink."

"Is that right?"

I shrugged.

"So, Miss…" He raised his eyebrows as he waited for me to give my name.

I blurted out the first name that came to me. "Ah, Gertrude. My name's Gertrude."

Aidan choked on a laugh. "Gertrude. What an unusual name."

"It means strong spear in German."

I mentally smacked my forehead. How the hell was I going to seduce my own husband with a factoid like that?

A playful grin appeared on his lips. "I'd like to show you *my* strong spear."

"I'd like to be impaled on your strong spear," I admitted.

He looked at me.

I looked at him.

And then we both burst into laughter.

"I'm not very good at this," I admitted.

"Ah, Trudy," he teased, wrapping his arms around me. "I think you're better than you think you are."

"Aidan?"

"Yeah?"

"I'm not wearing any knickers."

He pressed his forehead to mine. "Why didn't you lead with that?"

"Are you sure no one heard us?" I asked, straightening a strap of my dress.

Aidan's button-down shirt was untucked, and his cheeks were flushed. "I don't think so. Bailey likes to play Classic Rock when he works, so hopefully any sounds of Steven Tyler wailing covered your wailing."

"I do *not* wail."

"Okay." He grinned and tucked his shirt back into his

trousers. "How come we never did this while we worked at Antonio's?"

"Because this would've been sexual harassment."

He laughed and came over to me. Trailing a finger down my shoulder, he kissed me and then said, "Harass me again."

"What, now?" I asked in amusement. "I've got news for you, bucko. This"—I gestured down my body—"took a lot of effort. I'm ready for sweat pants and fuzzy socks."

"Gonna curl up on the couch with Jasper, huh?"

"Yep."

"Did you leave the little rascal home by himself?" Aidan asked.

I chuckled. "Yeah, right. I've learned my lesson. Annie's at our place." I followed him out of the wine room and up the stairs. "By the way, you're never getting rid of the beard."

He scratched his jaw. "Yeah? You like it?"

Reaching up to stroke it, I smiled at him. "Oh yeah. You've got this manly, mountain man thing going on."

My clutch vibrated. Sighing, I dropped my hand and reached for my cell. "Aw, crap."

"What?"

I showed him the text.

"She's kidding right?"

I shook my head.

"The dog ate your underwear?"

"And is now throwing it up. I gotta get home."

So this was motherhood.

Chapter 21

#SibbyBalboa #whoops

"He's lying on your bed," Annie said the moment I walked in the door. She picked up the TV remote and muted the television, which was on some baking competition show.

Oooh, cupcakes.

"He's not allowed on the bed," I said. I set my clutch down and shrugged out of my coat.

"You want to tell him that after he puked up your underwear?"

"How did he get my underwear?" I demanded.

"The door to the laundry closet was cracked. Guess he

velociraptored his way in there. You owe me, by the way. Your dog is a terror."

"You cleaned up after him, didn't you?"

"Yep. Vile. Good thing I grew up with a dog."

Paws hit the wood floor, and then a moment later the menace popped his head out of the bedroom. His tail wagged, and then he bounded over, knocking into my legs.

"Why were you in my underwear, you little perv? Huh?" I scratched behind his ears, and his tongue lolled out of the side of his mouth.

"He was out about thirty minutes ago. I think I'll leave you to it," Annie said, rising from our newly purchased futon. We weren't getting a new couch until we could be sure Jasper wouldn't tear it apart.

Annie reached for her bag. "Going away party next Friday."

"Nope."

"Sibby—"

"I will not celebrate you leaving," I pouted. Jasper sank to the floor and rolled over. I squatted down to rub his belly, refusing to meet her eyes.

"I just cleaned up your dog's vomit."

I sighed. "Played that card, huh?"

"You know it."

"I can't believe you're actually leaving the city. " I stood up, and Jasper let out a little woof of annoyance.

"It's time, ya know?"

"I guess."

"Change is good, Sibby."

"I've had enough change. No more change!"

Jasper pawed at my foot.

I pointed at him. "He agrees."

Annie grinned. "I think he just wants you to keep petting him."

"So next Friday, huh?"

"Yeah. But I'll see you before then."

We hugged, and then Annie reached down to pet Jasper. "Bye, you little terror. It was fun before you ate a thing you weren't supposed to."

"You're a good dog aunt. I'll definitely trust you with Pierogi should the occasion arise for you to babysit."

"No babysitting for me. Dog sitting only."

Annie left, and then it was Jasper and me. I waved him toward the bedroom, and he padded after me. Without any urging, Jasper leapt up onto the bed and curled up on Aidan's side. I changed into pajamas and then crawled into bed.

"What do you think, Jasper? HGTV?"

Jasper's snore was the only reply.

"Best relationship ever," I said, scratching his back. "We never fight over the remote."

The next morning, I woke up to the best sight I'd ever seen: half of Jasper's body was sprawled on top of Aidan who was sleeping on his back.

Both my boys were breathing deeply, and I didn't want to wake either of them. I got out of bed and paused a moment just to make sure I didn't have to make a run to the bathroom. But the morning sickness god was on my side and everything stayed where it was.

After snapping a few photos, I quietly left the bedroom. I put on coffee and toasted bread. My phone vibrated with an incoming text. It was my agent, asking if I'd decided on what I wanted to do with the book.

I had to do something. Letting it sit wouldn't take my career to the next level. But I was tired of being out of control. So she couldn't sell the book? Fuck it. I'd publish it myself. No one would care more about my career than me, and it was time to own it. Stop whining, stop lamenting the fact that it hadn't gone my way, and do something about it.

Humming the *Rocky* theme song while pouring coffee, I felt myself get psyched up. I could do this. I could take charge. I set the coffee down and raised my hands into fists. Whirling, I let my hands fly with the excitement and adrenaline of power and control.

And I punched Aidan right in the eye.

"Shit!" he yelled, bending over and holding his face.

"Oh my God! I'm so sorry! I didn't hear you come up behind me!" I went toward him, but he held up his free hand to stop me.

"Not another step," he warned, voice tight.

Jasper trotted into the kitchen and sat down next to the refrigerator, patiently waiting for his morning relief break.

"I'm gonna take Jasper out, okay?"

"Great." His tone was flat.

"And I won't come back for at least twenty minutes."

"Fantastic."

"I love you."

"Love you, too," he muttered.

I went to the front door and called Jasper. He came flying at me. I threw on my UGGs and a coat. Grabbing my keys and phone in one hand and the leash with the other, I wondered if I'd be okay without a hat. The weather had finally started to turn.

Jasper dragged me to a nearly bare tree. We walked around the neighborhood, Jasper sniffing everything and trying to greet everyone. He was a friendly, sweet dog, and we'd really lucked out, and now that the peeing was under control, things were settling down into a routine.

"Sibby?"

I looked up from watching Jasper paw at a shriveled leaf. "Stacy," I greeted in surprise. "Hey."

The girl that had announced my pregnancy to the world stood in front of me, clutching a to-go cup of coffee. She was completely put together, wearing trendy skinny jeans and a flowing gray cape. The pink tips of her hair were bright, as if newly dyed.

I was wearing Bullwinkle pajamas, and I had no idea the state of my face.

"How are you?" she asked. "I mean, how are you feeling?" Her gaze darted to Jasper, who looked up at her and wagged his tail. He wandered over to her and brushed his nose against her jeans.

Traitor.

"I'm feeling pretty good," I said. "So, do you live in the neighborhood?" What were the chances that I'd run into her in Manhattan and now Greenpoint?

"I live in Bushwick." Stacy reached down to pet Jasper whom I swore moaned in delight. "My boyfriend lives in Greenpoint, so I'm here a lot."

"Ah," I said, not really sure what to say or how to extract myself from the conversation.

"Listen." She shuffled from one foot to the other. "I think I owe you an apology. That picture I posted of us… I didn't think. I just posted and didn't realize that maybe, you hadn't told people yet? I was just so excited to meet you, ya know? I kind of forgot you were a real person when I fangirled all over you. I thought about sending you a message, but I just didn't have the nerve. Anyway, I'm really sorry."

Stacy's attention was diverted to Jasper who was slutting it up and getting all the love.

As I watched them in silence, an idea popped into my head, and I rolled with it. "Stacy, are you free tomorrow?"

I was halfway through my chai latte when Stacy arrived. "Ugh! Sorry I'm late," she said, dropping her huge, black bag into the chair across from me. "My model for the makeup tutorial was twenty minutes late, so that threw everything out of whack from the start. And then I walked by the place twice because I wasn't sure I was in the right spot—who knew the coffee shop was fronted by a junk store."

I grinned. "It's a cool spot, right? And don't worry about being late." I closed the illustrated children's book I was perusing. "I haven't been here long."

She peered into my mug. "You're halfway done with your chai latte."

"It's all good. Seriously, don't worry about it."

"You're so nice," she gushed. "Okay, I'm gonna go get a coffee. Do you need anything?"

I shook my head. She reached into her purse and grabbed her wallet. "What's good here?"

"Everything."

She grinned. "Perfect. Back in a jiff!"

Back in a jiff? Who talks like that, I wondered in amusement. I watched Stacy interact with the barista behind the counter.

Scattered. That's the word I would use to describe her. And yet, she was a twenty-five-year-old Instagram and

YouTube sensation. She was running a successful business making real money, and it blew me away.

Stacy came back, carrying a mug topped off with a mountain of whipped cream and a plate loaded with pastries. "Ah, you got my favorite. The *pain au chocolate* is the best."

She grinned. "Dig in."

"Thanks," I said, reaching for the flaky pastry filled with chocolate. "I feel like I'm eating all the time. Like I'll finish breakfast and already be thinking about lunch. I've gained nearly seven pounds."

"Seven? Where are you carrying it? Because when my sister had a baby and gained weight, you could tell. Like, it was all ass and face. You don't look like you've gained any weight at all."

"You're just saying that." I snorted. "I haven't been able to get into any of my pants. And this is just the beginning. I think I need to go buy some jeans with the elastic-waist. And I'm *so* not ready to do that. It's why I've been living in yoga pants."

Truth be told, those were getting a little tight, too. If I didn't buy some new pants, I'd be forced to wear Aidan's sweats.

"Well, I can't tell, and I'm not lying," Stacy said with a grin. "Swear."

"My thighs touch," I muttered.

"All women's thighs touch. Unless you're a Sports Illustrated swimsuit model, and you're paid not to have your thighs touch."

"You're really awesome at this female empowerment thing."

She grinned. "You should watch my YouTube channel. I rant a lot."

"I have watched your YouTube channel. Well, I've

caught a few videos, anyway. I really like your style and delivery."

"Thanks, Sibby." She beamed. "I'm trying, you know? I never expected to have all this blow up in a big way. I grew up in a very conservative house. Wasn't permitted to wear makeup or dress how I wanted—like I wasn't allowed to express myself through my clothes."

"So New York is your dream place."

"Exactly!" Her eyes brightened. "Anyway, I'm super grateful that people relate to me because now I get to do what I love."

"I think that's really incredible," I told her. "I had no idea what I wanted when I was twenty-five. I really admire you, Stacy. And I'm not saying that to be condescending."

The more I talked to Stacy, the more I realized that she was scattered in a creative sort of way. I knew what that was like, where your mind was constantly going, but your mouth couldn't keep up with everything, so sometimes it all just came out in a jumble.

"I checked out your book blog, too," I told her. "You've reviewed a lot of books."

She nodded. "I started with the book blog, but I kind of parlayed that into the YouTube thing. I like talking on screen more than I like writing down my thoughts. Does that make sense?"

"It does." I bit my lip and pondered how I would approach her, but then I just went for it. "So, I wanted to talk to you about something, but I need your word that this won't get out."

Stacy had raised the cup of coffee to her lips and slowly set it down. Leaning forward, she put her hands in her lap. "You have my word. You can trust me, Sibby."

Chapter 22

#TMI #nojustno

I was locking up the apartment as Mrs. Nowacki was coming up the stairs. "Hi, Mrs. Nowacki."

"Hello, Sibby," greeted the old Polish woman who lived across the hall from me. She dressed like she still lived in the Old Country in the forties. Her rheumy blue eyes swept down my body. "It is cold out and sun is setting. You need to put on another layer. Or you need to eat more."

Oh, no. I had one mother already, and she had the smothering with love thing on lockdown.

"Thanks, Mrs. Nowacki, but I'm just going a few blocks."

"To visit your beautiful *mąż* at work?" she teased.

I smiled. "How did you know?"

She touched my arm with a mittened hand and leaned close. "Lust." She winked. "You have the love, but also the lust."

Just like I didn't discuss sex with my mother, I would not discuss it with my aging neighbor.

"I had the lust too," she said on a sigh.

"Your husband must have been a handsome man," I said.

"No." She leaned in closer. "But his brother—"

Aaaaaand uncomfortable.

"Okay, good to see you! Byyyyyyyeeeee!" I skittered past her and nearly ran down the stairs, escaping into the cool November air.

I headed to Veritas to tell Aidan about my morning coffee date with Stacy. The bar had a few people sitting in the comfortable booths in the back, so I had relative privacy when I delivered the news.

"You did what?" Aidan asked, his mouth agape.

I winced at his tone, as well as the black eye looming back at me. A black eye that was entirely my fault. Was it wrong that I found him really hot with the beard, black eye, and the flannel shirt? Yeah, I was so blaming the pregnancy hormones for that.

"Please tell me you're kidding," he said. "Please tell me you did not just give that girl—the girl who outed your pregnancy on Instagram—your unpublished book to read."

"You're sexy when you're mad."

He pointed a finger at me. "That won't work."

"Yes, it will," I replied cheekily.

Aidan pinched the bridge of his nose. "Why didn't you talk to me about this first?"

"Because you would've said no. I did a lot of thinking about this, and do you know what I realized? If Stacy likes this book—and she's loved everything I've written—then that means I'm not completely insane for thinking I can strike out on my own."

"Annie, Zeb, and I have all told you to strike out on your own. Why do you need Stacy to tell you that you can?"

I held up a finger. "Number one, you, Annie and Zeb are all people who love me and believe in me. That's all very nice and stuff, but it's not necessarily practical. Number two, Stacy is one of those people who has social proof."

"Oh my God. I think I finally understand what those pregnancy books mean when they talk about pregnancy brain."

It was my turn to glare at him. "When she uses a makeup product on her YouTube Channel, it sells. Companies *give* her products for free so she can try them out and use them. When she talks about how much she loves a new eyelash curler, people buy it. Her opinion matters."

"I get all that, Sibby. I really do. But don't you think you're giving her too much power?"

"Too much power? Aidan, I'm asking her to read my book. I didn't tell her why it didn't sell, I just asked her to read it and give me her honest opinion."

"And you trust her to do that?"

"Yeah, I do." I nodded. "Do you care that my thighs touch?"

His face screwed up in confusion. "Uh, what?"

"My thighs. They touch. When I stand."

"I don't get it. Don't all people's thighs touch?"

I leaned over the bar and plopped a kiss onto his mouth.

"What was that for?"

"For being you."

He sighed, frustration obviously diffusing. "You can't do that, you know."

"Yes, I can."

Caleb walked through the front door of Veritas, carrying a cardboard box. He hadn't seen me yet, and I briefly thought of darting around him to leave. Aidan's hand on mine stopped me.

"Hey," Aidan called out. "What's in the box?"

Caleb set it down on the end of the bar. He looked at me and then back at Aidan. I held my breath.

"Thanksgiving decorations from the kids at Mt. Sinai," Caleb answered. "Hi, Sibby."

"Hey, Caleb."

"Nice black eye you gave your husband there."

I rolled my eyes. "It was an accident."

"So she says," Aidan stated.

"It was! I was in the middle of my *Rocky* moment. I didn't hear you come up on me…"

Caleb shook his head. "You guys are so weird."

"My multiple personalities keep Aidan interested. Well, this has been fun. I'm off."

"To where?" Aidan asked.

"Home. Jasper needs a walk. And I've gotta do some online shopping."

"Baby stuff? I was kind of hoping you were gonna wait—"

"Pants. I need pants that fit. There, I said it."

"You know, your conversations have changed so much since you guys met," Caleb pointed out. "I remember when you guys were talking about whether or not we should do another round of shots, and now you're talking about babies."

I sighed. "I miss drinking."

"So do I," Aidan said. He leaned over the bar to kiss me. "I'll be home around eight."

I gave a salute and then headed outside. It had been a brisk morning, which turned into a chilly afternoon. Leggings and yoga pants were not viable options for actual warmth in the winter. As I was adjusting the red scarf around my neck, I heard the door of the bar open behind me.

"Hey, can I talk to you a second?" Caleb asked.

I turned and shoved my cold fingers into my coat pockets. "Sure."

Caleb raked a hand through his light brown hair. "Listen, I'm really sorry about how things went down with us."

I let out a breath and nodded. "I'm sorry too. Sometimes I just speak what's on my mind, and it gets me into trouble."

He shook his head. "Don't apologize for that. I got pissed because you were right, and I didn't want to hear it."

"Friends?" I asked.

"Of course." He wrapped me in a hug.

I silently cursed Annie for throwing away one of the good ones. "Can I just say one more thing, and then I won't say anything about it again?"

He stepped back and nodded.

"You're gonna find someone who deserves you. She didn't."

Caleb's mouth flattened. "I just want what you and Aidan have. I thought I had it, ya know?"

"I know," I said quietly. I didn't offer him any platitudes. It would've been a grave disservice. Even I knew that what Aidan and I had was special, and not everyone would find it. I wouldn't be a colossal bitch and lie to Caleb and tell him he'd find it one day. Because what if he didn't? Most people split up. It was just the truth. Annie's parents, for instance. They'd been unhappily married for over thirty years, and now they were divorcing.

"You want to come over for dinner some time this week? You can sniff Jasper's belly. That's what I do when I'm feeling down."

He smiled. "I heard you do that even when you're happy."

"I do it all the time. It's a real problem."

Caleb laughed and turned his head toward me as he said, "Dinner would be great."

I took my time walking home, thinking about the conversation I'd just had with Caleb. The idea of ever splitting up with Aidan gutted me—and now that Pierogi was on the way, it wasn't even a place my mind could go.

Did not compute.

Aidan and I had such a good time together. We were best friends as well as lovers. He just…*got* me. In a way no one else did. Aidan had become my family. You didn't just leave your family, but I guessed Annie had never felt that way about Caleb. The idea of ever hurting Aidan the way Annie hurt Caleb made my insides cramp.

Just as I was unlocking the door to the apartment, my phone vibrated in my pocket. I reached for it and saw Stacy's name flashing across the screen.

"Hey," I said. I set my keys down on the front table and dropped my purse.

"Oh, my God!" she screamed.

I held the phone away from my ear. "Aaaand I'm deaf. Thanks."

"Sorry! I just—Oh my God, Sibby!"

"Deep breath, Stacy."

"I finished your book!"

"But I just gave it to you this morning," I sputtered. I walked into the living room and collapsed onto the couch, not even bothering to kick off my boots.

"And I devoured it. I turned off my router so I wouldn't have internet. I turned off my cell. I locked myself in my room and I read, and I just couldn't stop."

"Wow."

"It's seriously the best thing you've ever written."

"It is?" I asked in sheer disbelief.

"Yeah! I mean, don't get me wrong I love your dirty chef trilogy. But OMG. This was something else. It totally sounded like you, but like, *better*. No, better isn't the right word. Hold on it'll come to me..."

"So did you...like the heroine?" I pressed.

"Loved her. She was so relatable."

"She wasn't a bitch?"

"Oh no, she totally was, but like, you *understand* why. And then when she grovels to her guy and he puts her out of her misery..." Stacy sighed. "She got her happy ending. She was real, ya know?"

"She was," I agreed slowly.

"When's this book coming out?" she demanded. "I'd love to interview you on my YouTube channel, so you can talk about it."

I let out a slight chuckle. "Funny story…"

Aretha Franklin was belting about respect as I pulled the baked salmon out of the oven. I heard the front door open and close, and then Aidan appeared in the kitchen.

"What's all this?" Aidan asked in amusement. Jasper got up from his spot on the kitchen floor to greet Aidan, tail whipping back and forth. Aidan crouched down to get some love from Jasper and after a few moments, stood.

"We're celebrating!" I said. After setting the glass dish on the stove to cool, I threw off the oven mitts and set them aside. "Hi."

"Hi." His grin was wide even as his brow furrowed in confusion. "What are we celebrating?"

I held up a finger and then went to the counter. "I made us a spritzy mocktail."

"What is it?" he asked, taking the glass from my outstretched hand.

"Pomegranate juice and Pellegrino."

"Ohh, getting exotic."

"Gotta keep it fresh," I said, sipping from my glass. "Tomorrow, I might try pineapple and Pellegrino."

He leaned over and kissed me. "I love it when you live on the edge. Why are we celebrating?"

"Let me turn down Aretha." I pressed the volume button on the wireless speaker and then faced Aidan. "Stacy loved the book."

"She finished it already?"

"Yep. Read it in one sitting. Said it was the best thing I've written."

Aidan grinned. "Cheers."

"Cheers!"

We clinked glasses, and then I set mine down. Picking up a plate, I looked at him over my shoulder. "Hungry?"

He nodded. "It smells great."

I served him a piece of salmon, some asparagus, and roasted potatoes. Aidan pulled out a kitchen chair and sat, placing the napkin in his lap.

"So you're going to publish it yourself?"

"Yes."

"Do you have a plan?"

I grinned. "Not even a little bit. I have no idea!"

"And yet you seem remarkably happy about it," he pointed out with a smile of his own. He picked up his fork and took a bite of salmon. "This is really good, Sibby."

"Thanks—and I guess that's not really true. I do have some idea of what to do. Stacy's gonna help me. Kind of like a PR agent."

"You must trust her despite what she did—outing your pregnancy on social," he said. "You sure you want to place something this important in her hands?"

"Yes. I trust her. Jasper. Come here." I cut off a small piece of salmon, made sure it was cool enough, and then put it in his doggie bowl. He wolfed it down like a beast that was starving. Which so wasn't the case. Jasper was the most spoiled dog in the world, I was sure of it.

"I really like her. She's oddly…put together," I said, picking up the thread of our conversation.

"If you say so."

"You don't like her."

"I don't even *know* her. My first experience with her wasn't ideal. She took a special moment from us, Sibby. Your Mom is never gonna forgive me."

"You? It wasn't even your fault."

He shrugged. "Like she'd really blame you."

"Is that why you sucked up to her when she came here? You were trying to make good?"

"Why are we talking about your mother? What just happened?"

"I don't know. This was supposed to be a celebration of my achievement. Why are we fighting?"

Aidan set his fork down and let out a sigh. "I don't know either. I just—I'm protective of you. And Stacy…" He shook his head.

"I made my peace with it," I said quietly. "Why haven't you?"

"Because I'm an introvert and you—you put it all on social media. You're even cataloguing your pregnancy journey."

I set my hands on the table and narrowed my gaze. "Where is all this coming from?"

<hr>

Chapter 23

<hr>

#girdyourloins #gentlemenlendmeyourshields

The buzzer sounded, interrupting whatever Aidan was going to say. Jasper ran to the door to greet whoever was downstairs. Aidan made a move to get up, but I waved him to stay seated.

I pressed the intercom. "Who is it?"

"Annie."

Releasing the intercom button, I sighed. She couldn't have come at a worse time. I was about to tell her that Aidan had a bad stomach bug (because you always use the husband as an excuse), but she fired off, "I'm about to flip my lid, and I need someone to talk to."

"Let her up," Aidan said.

I turned to look at him over my shoulder. I hadn't even heard him move. "But what about our fight?"

He rolled his eyes. "We weren't having a fight. We were having a discussion. I'm an introvert, you're not. It's weird for me that you put our lives on social media, but I'll get over it because it makes you happy to make other people laugh. Discussion over. Now buzz her in."

"I won the husband lotto." I leaned up to press a quick kiss to his lips and then buzzed Annie in. Two minutes later, she stood in the living room, out of breath and red in the face.

"My mother's getting remarried," she blurted out.

I frowned. "Isn't she still married to your father?"

Annie threw up her hands. "Technically. But apparently, as soon as the ink dries on the divorce papers, she's marrying Carl."

"That seems…fast. Who's Carl?"

"Her tennis instructor. And they've been having an affair for the past two years." Annie sank down onto the futon. Jasper hopped up and bumped his nose against Annie's hand. She absently reached out to pet him.

I looked at Aidan. He grimaced and shrugged. Neither of us knew what to say.

"Did she call and tell you this?" I asked.

Annie let out a laugh. "My father. My father called me after one too many Old Fashioneds and spilled the beans. God, and I thought I was bitter. He's wrecked." She looked up at Aidan. "Got anything to drink in this place?"

"May I offer you a pomegranate spritzer?" Aidan asked.

She blinked. "A what?"

"No alcohol, but high in antioxidants!" I said with a forced smile.

Annie put her head into her hands and moaned. "This is a nightmare. My mom is a total wanker, and now my best friends can't even drink to commiserate with me."

"I've been off the sauce for a few weeks, and I feel so much better," Aidan threw out. "Sleeping better, waking up easier——"

"Shut up, Aidan," Annie and I both said to him.

"I'm going to go watch sports in the bedroom," he muttered. He sent me a lovey-dovey look and then disappeared.

"You guys are nauseating—or that might've been the bourbon I had earlier."

"You drank bourbon?" I asked in shock. Holy hell, she never drank bourbon unless things were really bad. Bourbon made Annie want to fight.

"Sometimes the situation calls for bourbon."

"Let me get you some water. Okay?"

"It's just so fucking cliché, right?" Annie called as I filled up a glass. "Like really? Tennis instructor? Could she be more of a WASP?"

"You guys are Episcopalian," I reminded her.

She took the water and drank half of it in one go. "Thanks," she said. Setting the glass down on the coaster, she sighed. "When are you getting a new couch?"

"When we're sure Jasper will no longer punish us when we leave him alone."

"Futons are so college. We're done with that."

"Says the girl who wants to drink away her feelings," I pointed out.

She moaned and closed her eyes. "You're right. Damn

it. Just when I think I've broken all my old patterns of bad behavior, I fall back into them."

"Bad patterns don't break because you tell them to. Annnnnd, you have a habit of acting before you think."

"You sound just like my therapist."

"Therapist? Since when are you seeing a therapist?"

"Did I say therapist? I meant bartender."

I rolled my eyes. "Drink more water."

Just as Annie picked up the glass, the buzzer sounded again. I frowned. "Did you order Chinese to our place or something?"

She shook her head. "I wouldn't do that."

"You did it two weeks ago," I reminded her. "And you arrived *after* the delivery guy."

"My apartment is lonely."

"Way to lay on the Episcopalian guilt."

"It's got nothing on Jewish guilt," she fired back.

"Truth."

The buzzer sounded again.

"Who's at the door?" Aidan called from the bedroom.

"No idea," I called back, heading for the buzzer. I pressed the intercom. "Who is it?"

"Caleb."

I glanced at Annie as I replied, "Thought you were at the bar."

"Swapped last minute with another bartender. I'm taking you up on your offer for dinner. Oh! Door's open. See you in a sec!"

The intercom went silent. My finger slowly fell from the button. I looked at Annie again.

"I'm fine," she said.

"You just found out your mom is having an affair." I paused. "And more importantly, you've had bourbon."

She inhaled a deep breath. "I'll keep it together. Promise."

"Aidan!" I shouted, sending Annie a worried look. "Caleb's here!"

"Uh, is Annie still here?" he called from the other room.

"Yes."

"This is gonna be really bad…"

"She says she's fine."

"I love how you guys talk about me like I'm not here," she pointed out.

I raised an eyebrow but didn't reply. There was a knock on the door. I sent up a silent prayer to Moses.

"Hey," Caleb said when I opened the door. "Sorry to just drop by."

Jasper hopped down from next to Annie to greet Caleb. Caleb crouched down to give Jasper a scratch.

"It's okay," I said, looking over my shoulder, glad to see Aidan coming out of the bedroom. "It seems to be the theme of the night."

"What do you mean?" Caleb asked, completely enthralled with Jasper.

"She means I did the same thing," Annie replied.

Caleb froze when he heard Annie's voice.

"Hey, Caleb," she said softly, rising from her spot on the futon.

He lifted his head to meet her gaze. "Hey."

I felt Aidan come up behind me. He rested a hand on my shoulder, and I backed into the warmth of his body. I looked up at him, but Aidan's gaze was on his best friend.

"I brought dessert," Caleb said. He gave Jasper one last pat on the head and then stood. "Here." He thrust a bakery bag into my hands.

We all stood in silence, the tension mounting. Jasper sniffed the bakery bag, and I hauled it closer to my chest.

"I really wish you guys had alcohol," Annie stated.

"Right?" Caleb agreed with an awkward laugh. "So, listen, I'll go—"

"No, you stay," Annie shot out. "I'll go."

"No, you were here first, I'll—"

"It's okay. I've got laundry—"

"Maybe we should go?" I whispered to Aidan.

"It's our apartment," he whispered back. "And if we leave, they might get into a fist fight."

"Or have sex on our futon."

"I'm not giving them the opportunity to defile it."

"So we stand our ground," I stated. I let out a sigh. "I wish I'd prayed to Mary instead of Moses. I think Mary might've had more clout in this situation."

"Let's pray to all of them and cover our butts."

"Who wants ice cream!" I bellowed like a camp counselor.

Annie shook her head. Caleb didn't reply.

"Uh. Okay. Aidan, find a game we can all play. How about Taboo or something?"

"Are you sure that's a good idea?" he asked through the side of his mouth.

Annie and Caleb were acting like two dogs at a dog park. Sort of sniffing around each other, checking out if the other one was rabid. Jasper had gone to his doggie bed in the corner of the room, head resting on his paws, eyes bouncing back and forth as if he somehow understood more in that moment about human nature than we did.

"Oh God." I pressed a hand to my mouth.

"Hold it together, soldier," Aidan whispered. "Don't leave me alone with these two. They clearly can't decide if they want to eye-fuck each other or rip each other's throats out."

"Can't!" I ran to the bathroom and got my dose of evening sickness. A few minutes later, red-faced but otherwise unharmed, I came back.

The Pictionary easel had been set up—guess Taboo wasn't happening—and Annie was standing with a marker in her hand. "You okay?" she asked.

I nodded. "I'm never eating salmon again."

She crinkled her nose. "And now I'm never eating it again either, thanks."

Caleb let out a laugh but stopped when Annie looked at him with a knowing grin. Their faces closed off when they both appeared to realize they still remembered the intimacy of being a couple, but were no longer one.

Why were we doing this? Subjecting ourselves to awkwardness when it would've been easier if Annie and Caleb both left.

"Boys against girls?" Aidan voiced.

"Okay," Caleb said.

I shrugged and took a seat on the futon next to Aidan. Caleb was in the chair, arms resting on his knees. The only one not uncomfortable was Jasper, who had since fallen asleep and was now on his back, legs spread, showing his goods to the world.

"I'll go first?" Annie asked.

Aidan nodded. "Yeah."

Taking a deep breath, Annie drew a card. She blanched and then tried to stick the card underneath the pile.

"Hey, that's cheating," Caleb stated. "You have to draw that card."

"Okay," she said, voice low and quiet. She uncapped

the marker and Aidan flipped the timer. Annie turned to the easel. She pressed the marker to the paper and drew.

"Moon?" I called out just to fill the silence.

She shook her head and kept drawing. A moment later, she finished, her eyes aimed down to the floor. Annie had drawn two halves of a heart with jagged lines. She'd drawn a broken heart.

"You've got to be kidding me," Caleb muttered.

"I tried to pick another card," she stated. "But you called me a cheater."

"You *are* a cheater!"

"I'm not a cheater!" she yelled back. "I never cheated on you!"

Caleb jumped up from the chair. "Yeah? And what if we hadn't shown up? You would have if you'd had the chance and another shot of vodka!"

"That was a low blow!"

"You know what's a low blow? Letting me propose *four* times!"

She put her hands on her hips. "Yeah, because I held a fucking gun to your head!"

I looked at Aidan, and we slowly backed out of the living room. "What should we do?" I said in my normal tone of voice. Caleb and Annie were still yelling at each other, so they didn't pay us any attention.

"Leave," Aidan said with a grimace.

"You never even apologized for how you treated me!" Caleb shouted.

"I absolutely did!"

"No, you didn't. Looking beaten and defeated and making our breakup all about you isn't an apology! It was about both of us."

"Annnnnd, this is about to get nasty," I said. "Let's take Jasper and get the hell out of here!"

I grabbed Jasper's plaid sweater, which rested on the table by the front door, and softly whistled for him. He got up, stretched, and then cocked his head to the side when he looked at Caleb and Annie screaming at each other.

Aidan patted his thigh and Jasper lunged toward us. I got him into his sweater and then snapped his leash onto his collar, and then we were out the door. I doubted Annie and Caleb even heard us leave.

Chapter 24

#mouthwash #itwasthedog

We went to our favorite neighborhood German beer hall. It was chilly out, so most people were inside by the wood burning fireplace. But because we had Jasper, who was decked out in his plaid sweater, we had the outside to ourselves.

I'd given Aidan a pass to get a beer, but he'd remained steadfast. We were both drinking hot tea and enjoying each other's company.

Aidan grinned. "Another bratwurst?"

I shook my head and leaned back. "Nope. Three is my limit."

"When do you think we can go home?" he asked, reaching down to pet Jasper's head, which was resting in his lap.

I pushed away the empty plate and reached for my tea. "When either one texts that the smoke from the cannons has cleared."

"They're totally having sex right now."

"Yeah, I bet they are," I agreed. "All I want is to go home and rest in our bed."

"Speaking of bed… Is now a good time to talk about the nursery."

"The nursery," I repeated.

"For Pierogi."

"Well, of course for Pierogi." I rolled my eyes. "Who else would need the nursery?"

"We need a crib and a changing table. And a diaper genie, and—"

"A diaper *what*?"

"Genie." He plucked a lone French fry from my plate and stuck it in his mouth. He chewed quickly and swallowed before explaining. "It's a thing where you can dispose of all the dirty diapers so you don't have to keep taking the trash out. Traps the smell or whatever. My sister swears by it."

"Okay. But babies are small for like the first year of their lives. We can get away with the crib in our room."

"But eventually we're going to need a real nursery. We could convert your office into the baby's room."

I swore I heard the sound of a bomb detonating in my brain.

"You're kidding, right?"

"No, I'm not kidding."

"Where does my office go?" I demanded.

"We could put your desk in the living room," he suggested. "Get you one of those desks that has tons of storage and built-in bookcases.

I sighed. "The curse of living in an apartment."

"We could move."

"We *just* moved—and where would we move?"

"We could buy a place in the city," he suggested.

"Not feasible. Especially since you want a place Upstate."

Aidan said nothing but stared at me with blue eyes. He waited. And waited.

I sighed again. "Guess my office is being moved to the living room."

"Ah, fuck," he muttered.

"What?"

"You're unhappy again."

"No," I assured. "Unhappy isn't the right word. But, I'm just—the changes. They keep coming."

He reached across the table to grasp my hand. "The changes are never gonna stop. Not now. Not with Pierogi on the way."

My jaw dropped. "Oh, God."

"What is it?" Aidan got up and immediately came to my side. "Are you feeling okay?"

I grasped the lapels of his coat. "Pierogi's gonna turn into a—a *teenager*!

Aidan smiled. "Yeah."

"He or she is gonna have hormones, and what if it wants a motorcycle and dyes its hair blue?"

"We can't do much about the hormones," Aidan said. "But I do think we have some say in the motorcycle thing. And even though I'm not a fan of blue hair, at least it's not permanent."

"I want to find out the sex," I demanded. "As soon as Pierogi has the parts, I want to know the sex. I gotta know what I'm dealing with."

Aidan kissed my nose. "We'll find out the sex."

My phone vibrated in my pocket. "The angry exes have left the building."

"We can go home? Great, let me go close out our tab."

Aidan handed me Jasper's leash and then headed inside the bar. My phone buzzed again with another text from Annie.

Annie: Never drinking bourbon again. It makes me do stupid things.

Me: Like doing Caleb?

Annie: Yep. Exactly.

Me: Not on our new futon, I hope.

When she didn't reply right away, I thought it might be time to start looking for steam cleaner rentals in Greenpoint. Luckily, she texted while we were on the walk home.

Annie: No sex on your brand new futon. Or on your floor. Swear.

Me: Then where did you do it?

Details were important.

Annie: We went back to my apartment. He left already.

Me: You okay?

The conversation went silent. I had my answer. We got back to the quiet apartment and everything appeared intact. I released Jasper, who bounded to the bedroom.

"You coming to bed?" Aidan asked when he saw me heading to the kitchen.

"In a minute. Just gonna clean up dinner remains."

"I'll help."

I shook my head. "No, go ahead to bed. I just need a minute."

He nodded in understanding and then disappeared

into the bedroom. I cleaned up the kitchen, put the dishes in the dishwasher, and then made myself a cup of tea. I took it into my office and flipped on the light. Sitting at the desk, I swiveled around in my chair, taking in the walls covered in collaged corkboards. This was my space. All mine.

And I had to give it up.

Would I ever be ready? Each day Pierogi grew a little bigger, and my world grew a little smaller. My dreams would have to wait, or fit in around a baby—a baby that couldn't fend for itself.

A baby that needed me.

But what did I need? I wasn't sure anymore. Our two-bedroom apartment was the perfect size for two adults and one medium-sized dog. I had my office, a place to work and write. Add in a baby…

My thoughts continued to swirl out of control as I sipped on lemon ginger tea. My career was in a state of transformation. I hadn't planned for it. Just like I hadn't planned for a baby. That was life, though. You could plan and plan, and then the universe laughed and said, "Just kidding."

"Sibby?" Aidan asked from the doorway of the office. "You okay?"

I tapped my finger against the mug and nodded slowly. "Yeah. I'm okay." Surprisingly, I meant it.

I woke up with a burst of energy, and I bounded out of bed before Aidan. When the coffee finished brewing, I went to wake him up. Aidan was sleeping on his back, and Jasper was resting his head on Aidan's chest. Jasper yawned right into Aidan's face and Aidan grimaced.

"God, Sibby, your breath stinks."

I marched over to the bed, picked up my pillow, and hit him directly in the face with it.

"What the—"

"That was the dog, breathing his doggie breath in your face," I informed him.

His hands pushed the pillow to the side. Staring up at me with sleepy blue eyes, he smiled. "You're a goddess, did you know that?"

"Uh huh."

"A beautiful, pregnant goddess—and your breath smells like cream soda and cotton candy."

Climbing onto the bed, I let out a laugh. I leaned over and kissed him. "Cinnamon toothpaste."

Aidan wrapped his arms around me and pulled me to him. Jasper slithered out of the way and jumped onto the floor. His collar jangled as he scratched behind his ear.

"Good morning, Trudy," he teased. He kissed me and then nuzzled my ear.

"Good morning." I ran my hand along his jaw, loving the feel of his beard. Jasper jumped back up onto the bed, and we spent the next few minutes having a morning love session that involved belly scratches and kisses.

For both Aidan and the dog.

"Has he been out?" Aidan asked, finally swinging his legs over the side of the bed. His dark hair was mussed, but his eyes were bright and clear.

"Not yet."

"I'll take him."

"Coffee's ready for when you get back."

Aidan suited up the dog and himself and then was out the door. I poured myself a cup of coffee and took it to the couch. I was getting ready to turn on the TV when my cell phone vibrated.

"Hey," I said, answering Annie's call.

"Hey."

"How are you doing?"

She sighed.

"Got it." I blew on the coffee, hoping to cool it down a bit.

"So, listen. I canceled my going away party."

"But that's tonight!" I stated. "And I was looking forward to going out! To a bar."

"Why?" Amusement colored her tone. "You can't drink."

"No, but I like the jukebox. Why did you cancel? Is it because of last night?"

Annie paused, and then I heard her inhale a deep breath. "I'm in Montauk."

"Um, how?"

"I left early this morning. My cousin picked me up at the train station here a little while ago and we're already home."

"But—why?"

"Really? You're asking me *why*?"

I pinched the bridge of my nose. "What about all your stuff?"

"My uncle's gonna take care of it."

"You're not coming back to the city, are you?"

"Sibby, it's not like we're never going to see each other again. You'll come to Montauk."

"Yeah." I felt lost. My best friend had left the city, and we hadn't even had a proper goodbye. "I wasn't ready for you to just be…gone.”

"Story of your life lately, right?" she asked. "You're never ready, but things happen anyway."

"You're mean to point that out."

"You love me."

"I do. You've been with me longer than Aidan."

"I'm still with you, Sibby. I just had to get out of there."

"I know. I'm just bummed." I took a sip of the now cooler coffee. "How's the view?

"Currently? I have a perfect view of my aunt doing jazzercise. I'm staying in the apartment over the garage," she explained. "My kitchen window looks right into the living room of the main house."

"Main house? Apartment over the garage? What is this, the servant's quarters?"

"Nah, it was the original mother-in-law suite. But Grandma Betty decided cruise living was a better way of life."

"And now you get to reap the rewards. Just do me one favor…"

"What?"

"Don't hide from your life. Lick your wounds, feel through your feelings, because I know you have them—"

Annie laughed.

"And then move on."

"Thanks, Sibby."

"Love you."

"Love you too. Tell Aidan bye for me."

"I will."

We hung up, and I set my phone aside. I was a jumble of emotions. On one hand, I totally understood Annie's need to quietly get out of town. On the other, I was miserable thinking about the fact that my two closest girlfriends now didn't live close by.

I suddenly wanted to get back into bed and stay there.

The front door opened, and Jasper bounded inside. He ran to the futon and sat at my feet. I freed him from his leash, and then he took off for his water bowl. Aidan shrugged out of his coat and hung it on the hook by the door.

"It's freakin' cold out. I think we might get snow." He pulled off his black beanie and ran his hand through his flat hair.

"Hmm," I replied, pulling my legs up to my chest.

"Sibby? What's wrong?"

"Adulting. I don't want to do it anymore."

He came over to sit down beside me. Reaching for my coffee with one hand, he put his other on my leg. "Don't think you have a choice there, Gertrude."

"Give me my coffee back or prepare to meet a most sudden death." He handed it over with a smile, but not before he took a sip. "Annie left this morning for Montauk."

"But her party—"

I shook my head.

"Ah. I see."

"Nat moved to Houston, Annie moved to Montauk, and Zeb works all the time."

Aidan plucked the coffee from my hand again and set it on the table. "Come here." He pulled me into his arms and pressed my head to his chest. "It will be okay."

"How do you know?"

"Because I do."

"That's it?" I looked up at him. "I'm supposed to just take your word for it that everything will be okay?"

He smiled and kissed the end of my nose. "You got any other ideas?"

Chapter 25

#hormonehostage #rightinthefeels

I set my glasses aside and rubbed my tired eyes. My back ached from sitting at my desk for hours, pouring over the plan I was creating for the release of my new book. I had lists going with names of editors, graphic designers, proof-readers, and bloggers.

So began the process of DIY.

"This is exhausting," I said to Stacy, looking at her through our video Skype window.

Her blond hair was pulled into two pigtails, her bright pink ends curled. "I can only imagine. Find an editor yet?"

I shook my head. "I combed through the list of the editors you recommended and sent most of them emails. No one's emailed me back yet."

"Don't worry. You'll find a good one."

"If that were the only issue it wouldn't be that bad, but there's so much to worry about."

She smiled in sympathy. "I know."

"I gotta get out of the apartment, get some fresh air."

"Don't forget to rest," she reminded me. "Drink orange juice. That always helped my sister when she was getting… ya know."

"Uppity?" I supplied.

"Yeah, uppity."

I glanced down at Jasper who was stretched out on the wood floor. How I envied his life. Naps, food, belly rubs, and walks outside. Repeat.

"Call me later if you need anything," she said. "I'm just gonna be hanging out at home, playing with makeup."

"And getting paid to do it," I pointed out.

She grinned. "Yep. I used to dream of this when I was a little girl."

I closed our connection and pushed back from my desk. Reaching my arms over my head, I stretched out the muscles of my back that were tight, and in desperate need of Aidan's hands. Unfortunately, Veritas was closed for a private event, so he wouldn't be home until late.

"Hey, Jasper. You wanna go outside?" I asked.

The lazy mongrel stretched and then flopped back down. I shook my head. Not that I blamed him. The temperature had dropped, and the weather app was predicting snow. It was always wrong, so I didn't put much faith in it, but when I looked out the window, the late afternoon sky was grey and white.

Jasper wasn't at all prepared in case it snowed. The city streets would be heavily salted, and it would burn his paws. "Okay, buddy," I said, going over to him and crouching down. He wormed his head toward me and closed his eyes in doggie bliss when I scratched his belly. "We gotta get you outfitted for winter so you have to come with me."

I stood and headed for the front door. I threw on all my layers including a hat, gloves, and a scarf. I wasn't taking any chances with the cold. I leashed Jasper up and prepared for the misery.

The wind was whipping through the streets, stirring up the fallen dried leaves. I burrowed my face so only my eyes were visible. Thankfully, the pet store was only three blocks from the apartment. The owner behind the counter already knew Jasper, and Jasper loved him due to all the treats he got whenever we came in.

"Sit," Julio said.

Jasper dutifully planted his behind on the floor as he eagerly waited for his reward.

"Good boy," the owner said. With a smile, he held out his hand, and Jasper lapped up the treat. It was gone in one bite.

"How are you today, Julio?" I asked him.

"Tired," he said. "The grandchildren came over yesterday."

I laughed. "Full house, huh?"

"They ran us in circles. My wife and I collapsed before they did." He clapped his hands together. "What brings you in here today?"

"Dog boots. For winter."

"Ah." He waved for me to follow him. Jasper was on the man's heels, hoping for another treat. We went to the back of the store in the corner and stopped. "Here." He picked up a pair of plain black dog boots, sized small. He ripped them out of the package. "Let's try these on him."

I scooped Jasper up into my arms. The owner got the front two booties onto Jasper before he squirmed to get away. He slipped out of my grasp, landed on the floor, and darted to the other side of the pet store, out of sight. A moment later, Jasper ran back to us, boots off his paws and in his mouth. He dropped the boots and then immediately started chewing on them.

I looked at the pet storeowner and sighed. "How much do I owe you?"

After throwing away the ruined boots, I leashed up Jasper and left. He dragged me down the street when he saw a fluffy white ball of fur in a pink coat. "He's friendly!" I called out.

The owner of the white puff turned up her nose and scooped up her dog. Jasper whined when his new friend disappeared around the corner. I stuck out my tongue at her behind her back. "This ain't Park Avenue, lady. We're in Brooklyn. No need for the 'tude," I muttered.

Jasper looked up at me with sweet brown eyes, his tail thumping against the sidewalk.

"You should've played it cool, dude. You were too eager. Come on, let's get home. Mama needs some hot chocolate."

I kept my eyes on Jasper as we walked, not paying attention to where I was headed—or whom I might run into—until a familiar voice called out my name.

"Matt?" I gaped in astonishment.

My ex smiled as he strolled closer. His hair was gelled and styled, his slate gray wool pea coat was accented with a bright red scarf, and he was tan.

Very tan.

He leaned over and brushed his lips against my cheek. "It's good to see you." His gaze dropped to Jasper. "And you got a dog!"

"Yeah about three weeks ago," I said, still marveling at the changes in Matt. When we'd been together, he'd dressed conservatively—and had been decidedly in the closet. Now he was out, proud, and the last I'd seen via Instagram, he and his boyfriend had just spent a weekend in Vermont making cheese together. "You look great!"

He peered at me. "So do you."

I shook my head. "No, I really don't."

"You do," he insisted, letting his gloved hand drop near Jasper's nose. "Your skin looks amazing. What skin regimen are you doing?"

Rolling my eyes, I snorted. "The pregnancy regimen."

"You're pregnant!" He grinned. "That's awesome! Congratulations!" He moved in for a hug, but Jasper let out a low woof.

I looked down at him. "Hush, you. Matt's a friend."

Matt laughed. "Protective, isn't he?"

"Not usually," I admitted. "How are you and Taylor doing? I saw the photos on Instagram. Very nice."

"We had fun. And now we're back to the grind. And the gray city. How's Aidan? And the bar?"

"Both are good."

"And the writing?"

"Good."

Once upon a time, I'd been planning a life with Matt. When I'd walked in on him and another guy having sex in our bed, I'd been furious—and embarrassed. Embarrassed that I hadn't realized why we would never work long-term. His betrayal had come as a shock. But, it had all worked out. Matt was happy with someone. I was happy with Aidan. And life went on.

"Taylor and I just looked at an apartment on Clay Street."

"To rent?" I asked.

He shook his head. "We want to buy."

"Oh, wow."

"We looked in Boerum Hill and Park Slope, but they're too far away. And they're so family-friendly." He winced. "Sorry."

I held up my hands. "No worries. Greenpoint is rapidly becoming the new Park Slope."

"I know. But Greenpoint is closer to the city than Park Slope. And I refuse to buy in Bushwick. It's still an overpriced shit hole over there."

We laughed. "Some cool stuff is popping up," I said. "That taco place we went to a few years ago…"

He shook his head. "Life's weird, isn't it?"

"It really is."

"It was good seeing you, Sibby. Congrats again on the baby."

"Congrats on being able to buy a place."

We hugged briefly, and then went our separate ways. Eight point five million people in New York, and my world was still tiny.

I got home, and once I peeled all the winter layers off me, I settled down onto the futon. Jasper snuggled up next to me, and any motivation to work on my release plan went up in smoke.

"I should work," I told him.

He rested his head on my lap. Sighing, I reached for the remote. "Let's see if there's some great bad TV to watch. I can work later."

Three hours later, I was sobbing when I answered Aidan's phone call. "Hello?" I hiccoughed.

"Sibby? God, Sibby, what's wrong?"

I hiccoughed again and inhaled a shaky breath.

"Sibby, talk to me. Are you okay? Is it Pierogi? Is it Jasper? What is it?" he asked, voice desperate. "I'm leaving the bar, I'll be home in—"

"I watched a Hallmark Christmas movie," I blubbered.

"Christmas?" he repeated. "But it's not even Thanksgiving yet. Why are they playing Christmas movies in November?"

"Because it's Hallmark."

"Okay," he said slowly. "Aside from the Hallmark tears, is everything okay?"

"Uh huh."

"Any emails from potential editors?"

"I haven't looked in a few hours."

"Why?"

"Because."

"That's not a valid answer."

"Tunnel," I said. "Going through a tunnel. I can't hear you! Losing service—"

"You're sitting on the futon," he drawled in amusement. "Just check your email. If an editor doesn't want to work with you, then that's on them. Not you."

I buried my nose into Jasper's neck fur, the phone still pressed to my ear.

"You there?" Aidan asked.

"Yeah." The word came out muffled. "Fine. I'll check my email. How's your night?"

"Corporate dudes can really drink," he said.

"That's because they're miserable and the company is paying for the drinks. Dulls the pain of having to go into work in a suit and tie every day."

He laughed. "They've already polished off three bottles of Grey Goose. It's amazing."

"It's not even seven o'clock."

"It's gonna be a long night," Aidan said with a sigh. "I better get back to it. Caleb needs help slinging drinks."

"Do not!" Caleb called from somewhere in the background.

I let out a laugh.

"Order some food, don't cook, relax. Check your email," Aidan said.

"Aidan Kincaid, good at marriage," I quipped.

"Check your email," he said again.

"Okay, I'll check my email!" I groused. "See you later. Love you."

"Love you."

"Love you!" Caleb called mockingly in the background.

Shaking my head, I hung up. I looked at Jasper. "Am I being a wimp?"

His ears twitched, but otherwise, he acted as though he hadn't heard me.

"Should I just suck it up and see if I've been rejected?"

His ears twitched again, and still he didn't move. With a sigh, I gently urged him off my lap. I went into my office and sat down at my desk. I shook my mouse to wake up the computer screen. A moment later, my inbox pinged with replies.

"Hot diggity!" I yelled in excitement. As I scrolled through the emails, I realized most of them were polite brush-offs. They were booked or not taking on new clients. Out of thirty emails only three had openings. I discarded one because I didn't like the tone of the email. The other two, I replied back, asking if they'd mind looking over the sample. I wanted to make sure we were a good match.

Finding the right editor was harder than dating in New York. Then again, I had dated a closeted gay guy for two years.

I looked at Jasper who stood in the doorway to the office. "Tell me I'm great."

He let out a woof.

"Tell me you love me."

Woof.

"You want a treat, don't you?"

Woof.

Nodding, I got up. Jasper dogged my heels as I went to the cookie jar in the kitchen that held his organic, gluten-free duck nuggets.

"Sit," I commanded.

He sat.

"Paw."

He gave me his paw.

"Edit my book."

He let out a whimper. With a sigh, I gave him his treat. "You really don't pull your own weight around here, dog."

Instead of listening to me tell him what a lousy house-guest he was, Jasper bounded over to the futon and jumped up on it.

"All right, you ruffian. What do you say to another Hallmark movie?"

Chapter 26

#Aidandoesthemorphine #nofilter

I woke up to a vibrating cell phone. Searching for it on my bedside table, my hand encountered air. It took me a minute to realize I'd fallen asleep on the couch.

"Crap," I muttered. I somehow reached the lamp and turned on the switch. Bright light illuminated the living room. Jasper was asleep, his head resting on my legs. The DVR read 3:11 a.m.

Frowning, I grabbed my phone. I didn't recognize the number, but I answered it anyway. "Hello?" I croaked.

"Mrs. Kincaid?"

I licked my dry lips. "Yes, this is she."

"I'm Dr. Campbell at Beth Israel. Your husband was brought in, and we rushed him to emergency surgery—"

"Emergency surgery!" I screamed. "What happened? Oh, God. He was hit by a car, walking home—"

"Mrs.—"

"He got robbed and they stabbed him!"

"Mrs.—"

"He fell and hit his—"

"MRS. KINCAID," the doctor boomed. "Your husband's appendix burst!"

"His appendix?" I repeated. Blood slowly returned to my head. "You sure?"

"Yes, ma'am. He's sleeping soundly. He'll make a full recovery in no time."

"Thank you," I whispered.

"My pleasure. You can visit him tomorrow in room three fifteen."

"Tomorrow?"

"Yes, Ma'am. Tomorrow. Visiting hours are between—"

"Doctor, you just called me at 3:11 in the morning to tell me my husband is in the hospital. Do you really think I'm just gonna be able to go back to sleep and wait until tomorrow?"

"I know its difficult, but—"

"I'm pregnant!" I shouted, causing Jasper to perk up. "I'm pregnant, and undue stress is bad for a woman in my condition."

He sighed in defeat. "All right, Mrs. Kincaid. I'll have a nurse bring a cot to your husband's room. Do me a favor. Take a deep breath. Good. Another one."

"Thank you," I said as I felt my blood pressure begin to stabilize.

"You have nothing to worry about. He should recover quickly."

"Are you married?" I blurted out.

"Yes."

"Happily?" I needled.

"All right, Mrs. Kincaid. I concede your point. You're going to worry no matter what. But you were right about stress. Try to minimize it. As you said, a woman in your condition shouldn't have undue stress."

"Thanks, Doc."

I hung up and then burst into tears. A knock on the door startled me out of my meltdown. Jasper jumped up and barked at the door. I shushed him and then went to peer through the peephole.

It was my Polish neighbor from across the hall, Mrs. Nowacki. She was in a blue terrycloth bathrobe and red slippers.

I opened the door. "I'm so sorry, Mrs. Nowacki. Did I wake you?'

She waved a hand at me and stepped inside. "I am always awake at this hour," she said, Polish accent thick. "My colon…"

"Er—sorry." I wiped the tears from my eyes.

"I hear you yell and I come to make sure you are all right."

I was instantly grateful not to be alone. My lip wobbled. "Aidan's in the hospital. His appendix burst."

She frowned. "Appendix?"

Since I had no idea the Polish word for appendix, I gestured to the lower part of my stomach and then made a burst motion with my hands.

Her face cleared of confusion.

"He's okay," I assured her. "But I want to go to the

hospital immediately. Only…" I looked at Jasper who was sitting at Mrs. Nowacki's feet.

"I watch the *szczeniak*," she offered, patting Jasper's head.

"Are you sure?"

She nodded. "We have nice conversation about life."

"You and Jasper?"

She nodded again. "They speak, but no one listens."

"Um. Okay." I handed her Jasper's leash. "He usually goes out around 7:30. Is that okay?"

"It's okay."

"Thanks, Mrs. Nowacki," I said, relief in my voice. "I'll try and be back by nine."

She waved me away. "I use spare key to feed him breakfast."

When we'd moved in, Mrs. Nowacki had informed me that she had a key to our apartment. She'd gotten it from the tenants who'd lived there before us. Eccentric as she was, she'd never abused the privilege of having a key to our place and she was a good person. Our relationship was growing stronger by the day.

"Thank you," I whispered, feeling emotion getting the better of me.

"Go to your *mąż*. Give him kiss for me." She winked and then opened the door to the apartment. Jasper looked at me. I shooed him away. He trotted after her, and the door to her apartment closed.

Inhaling a deep breath, I threw on my coat and boots and then arranged for an Uber. There was almost no traffic since it was so early, and thirty minutes later I arrived at the hospital. I checked in with the nurse who directed me to Aidan's room. He was sound asleep when I crept in. I closed the door slowly, so as not to wake him.

I gently ran my hand across his hair and tried to choke

back the tears. It was just his appendix. He'd be fine. I desperately wanted to climb into bed next to him, but he needed his rest. Besides, a bunch of tubes and wires were attached to him, and I didn't want to accidentally pull one out.

Making sure a blanket covered him, I had to force myself not to keep petting him. I settled into the cot and curled up into a ball. Pressing my face to the pillow, I let the tears rip.

"You're beautiful," Aidan rasped.

My eyes peeled open, swollen and gritty. I had no doubt my hair was in a dark, frizzy cloud around my face, and judging by the dry mouth, I had been sleeping with it gaping open.

Beautiful, my ass.

I sat up slowly, my head throbbing with one of those headaches I knew I'd have all day. There wasn't enough sleep or aspirin on the planet to get rid of it. Stress did that to me.

"How are you feeling?" I asked as I came to his side.

"Groggy. And thirsty."

There was a pitcher of water on the bedside table. I filled the plastic glass and held up the straw to his mouth. He drained three quarters of the glass and then rested his head against the pillow.

"So your appendix ruptured?" I asked. "Where were you when it happened?"

"On my way home. I collapsed on the sidewalk. Someone called an ambulance."

"It's my understanding," I drawled, running my fingers through his messy hair. "That there are symptoms of an inflamed appendix. Is that right?"

"You should know. You watch *Grey's Anatomy*," he teased.

"Aidan." I said his name in a warning tone.

"You sounded exactly like a mom just now." His glassy blue eyes brightened, and he smiled. "Did you know that?"

"I'm gonna count to three and then—"

"Please make it dirty. Please make it dirty—"

"*Aidan*," I growled.

He sighed. "Yeah, my side kind of hurt. But nothing bad. And the Advil I popped during the event seemed to help."

"You mean you were so busy pouring shots for the suits that you didn't notice."

"Something like that."

I shook my head.

"How did you get a cot in here?" he asked. "Visiting hours—"

"I played the pregnant card." As soon as I said the word, it was like my bladder filled instantly. "Be right back."

After using the bathroom, I came out to a nurse taking Aidan's vitals. She was a cute little thing, blond, perky. Better suited to being a dental hygienist or a realtor than a nurse.

"Breakfast will be right up," she cooed. "Unfortunately, it's going to be pretty bland, but that's the post-surgery diet everyone gets."

He flashed her a white grin. "I'll survive. Thanks, Susie."

I rolled my eyes.

"Feel better, Aidan." With a quick glance in my direction, she paused. "Oh. I didn't know Aidan had a visitor."

"I'm not a visitor," I cooed in the same stupid flirty tone she'd used. "I'm his *wife*."

"Nice to meet you." She quickly darted out the door.

I glared after her. Aidan's chuckle had me whirling. "You shut up."

He tried to laugh and then gripped his side. "Ow."

"Serves you right," I muttered, going to his bed and fluffing the pillow behind his head.

"What did that pillow ever do to you?" he asked. "You're punching it, not fluffing it."

Leaning over, I brushed a kiss to his forehead. "I'm pretending it's your face." I shook my head. "Un-fucking-believable. You're lying in a hospital bed, missing part of your anatomy—"

"Not a vital part, thank God."

I ignored him. "You're gorked out on pain meds, and yet you still manage to be charming and have women fawning over you."

"It's the Kincaid gift."

"The Kincaid curse is not knowing when to keep your mouth shut."

"Ooooh, I like it when you're rough."

I laughed.

"But seriously, Sibby. Aren't you glad you reeled me in when you did?" He waggled his eyebrows. "Locked me down." He held up his hand and gestured to his ring finger. "Tiniest prison ever."

"I'd hit you with a pillow right now if I thought it wouldn't hurt you."

"Best prison ever." He smiled. "Give me a good morning kiss."

"We both have morning breath," I pointed out.

"Just a quick peck."

The breakfast tray arrived a few minutes later, and Aidan grumbled when all he saw was oatmeal and cold toast without butter. "What is this?" he demanded. "How am I supposed to get my strength back?"

A tall, thin orderly set the tray down in front of Aidan. "You get bland food for a few days, and if it sits well, you get an upgrade."

"Didn't you hear me? I need my strength back," Aidan repeated. "See my wife?" Aidan pointed and the orderly's gaze went to me. I waved. "Well, she's pregnant. I've done a lot of reading—pregnant women want it all the time. How am I supposed to service her when—"

"Okay, that's enough out of you," I said, covering Aidan's mouth with my hand, my face heating with embarrassment. "Must be the morphine…"

The orderly's shoulders shook with laughter. "I've heard worse. Believe me."

"Yeah?" I asked.

"Oh yeah. Let's see. I've been propositioned more times than I care to count. I've been asked if I was into swinging, BDSM—"

"So morphine removes all filters then?"

"Who says they were on morphine?" The orderly winked and then slipped through the door.

I looked at Aidan who was staring up at me with mischievous blue eyes. I lowered my hand. "You're pure trouble."

"And that's why you love me."

"Actually I love you for your huge—"

"Good morning, Mrs. Kincaid," Dr. Campbell greeted with a knowing smile.

"Just shoot me. Please," I muttered.

Aidan made a gun gesture with his fingers and pretended to fire it at me, making toy gun pellet sounds. I shook my head. "Do you think we can lower his morphine?"

"We want to keep him comfortable. We're going to keep him here for a few days. Normally, we'd send him home today, but because he had open surgery we want to monitor him for signs of sepsis. When he goes home, he needs to be on bed rest for a week. No heavy lifting. Minimal movement, and definitely no work."

"I feel like a part of me is missing," Aidan lamented. "Is that normal?"

"Dear Lord," I muttered. "A husband on bed rest? Isn't it supposed to be the other way around? *I'm* the pregnant one."

Chapter 27

After breakfast, I left Aidan as he enjoyed a steady flow of morphine. Before I went home to relieve Mrs. Nowacki of doggie-sitting, I stopped off at the Polish bakery on the corner. The girl behind the counter grabbed a box, a pair of tongs, and waited for me to decide what I wanted to order. When I was just getting ready to ask for a toasted everything bagel, I felt my any-time-of-day sickness rear its head. I darted away from the counter, hand pressed to my mouth, and ran to the back.

I turned the handle of the single bathroom, but it

wouldn't budge. Pounding on the door, I yelled, "Hey! I need to get in there immediately!"

"Back off!" someone yelled from the other side.

There was no way I'd make it through the entire bakery without losing it. The bathroom was across the hall from the back kitchen, and I spied an empty dish tub. Grabbing it, I hocked my guts until there was nothing left. As I was bent over the dish tub, clutching it like a lifeline, the bathroom door opened.

"Ew. If you're sick, you should've stayed home."

I glanced up at the willowy blonde who had come out of the bathroom and glared at her. "I'm pregnant."

She blinked. "Oh."

"Yeah." Another surge of nausea came about, and I hunched over the dish tub again.

A plump grandmotherly woman came out from around the counter to stand in front of me. "Nothing to see!" she snapped at the busybody customers. "Come have a seat in the back." Taking the dish tub with one hand and tugging me along with the other, she urged me away from the main room and into the kitchen. She threw the dish tub in the economy-sized sink, sprayed it out, and then turned back to me.

"I'm so sorry."

She waved a hand at me. "Sit, sit."

I plopped down in a folding chair, inhaling the scent of sugary goodness baking in the ovens. Rows and rows of cookie sheets lined the big island, the pastries cooling in the fresh morning air.

"You eat this," she said, handing me a croissant in a napkin. "When I was pregnant with my third, it was the only thing that would calm my stomach and stay down."

"Thank you." I tore a piece off of the buttery crois-sant and pushed it into my mouth. And then I made a noise better reserved for the bedroom. The woman laughed.

I polished off the croissant and immediately my stomach rumbled. "May I have another? I'll be glad to pay for—"

She hushed me and then handed me another.

"Thank you." I held out my hand to her. "I'm Sibby. I live around the corner."

"Marta." She took my hand and gave it a vigorous shake. "So, your morning sickness. It's pretty bad?"

I nodded. "I don't just get it in the mornings either. It comes at different times every day."

Sibby's Law, meet pregnancy.

"Hmmm," Marta said. With a smile, she gestured to my crumbled napkin. "Another? I won't judge."

Shaking my head, I stood. "No. Thank you so much. I left my box of pastries at the counter." I followed Marta out of the back kitchen. The bakery had cleared out a bit, the late morning rush was over.

Marta spoke in Polish to the counter girl. The girl reached underneath the counter and lifted my box of pastries. When I tried to give them money, Marta covered my hand.

"Come back and see me," Marta said.

I took the box and dropped the money into the tip jar, smiling as I left. The cool air on my cheeks refreshed my mood and my stomach. The walk home was quick. Mrs. Nowacki answered her door almost immediately. Jasper leapt toward me; he was so happy to see me his entire behind wagged.

"How was he?" I asked Mrs. Nowacki, reaching down to pet Jasper.

"We watched late night *Jeopardy!* reruns. He got all answers wrong."

I grinned and handed her the box of pastries. "For you. As a thank you."

With a smile of pure delight, she took the box from my hands. "Thank you. And how is handsome *mąż*?"

"Recovering. He'll have to be in the hospital for a few days."

She shook her head. "He needs his own bed. He'll recover much faster."

"Oh, he won't be leaving his bed for a week. Doctor's orders."

And I was going to have to take care of him. Aidan very rarely got sick, but when he did, he turned into the biggest baby. For Aidan, a little cold became as serious as the Plague in his mind. He hated the loss of control over his body. Recovery from an appendectomy would be interesting.

"Enjoy the pastries." I gestured for Jasper to come, but he let out a low whine and then ran to Mrs. Nowacki's side.

"We had fun, didn't we?" Mrs. Nowacki said, petting Jasper's head. "You come back and visit. Next time, don't try to eat Aiko."

"Who's Aiko?"

"Cat."

"You have a cat? Since when?"

"Since always. Is good for woman my age to have something to look after." She tapped her head. "Keeps me here."

I touched her arm. "You are always welcome to come over."

She waved her hand. "I don't want to be a bother."

"You're not a bother," I said with a sincere smile. "Come over soon. Jasper would love it."

Mrs. Nowacki thought for a moment and then nodded.

"I make Hunter's Stew. Secret family recipe. It will help your *mąż* to get well."

"He'd like that."

"Sibby," Aidan whined. "Sibby, I'm thirsty."

I briefly closed my eyes, remembered that I loved my husband, and then went to tend to him. There should've been a rule that hospitals weren't allowed to release sickly husbands into their wives' care. It had only been a few hours since I'd gotten him home with Caleb's help, and already I wanted to drop him back off at the hospital. Every time I sat down, Aidan called for something else.

Was it bad form to spike your husband's tea with NyQuil to knock him unconscious?

"Help! I'm parched!"

"Coming!" I called back. I went into the kitchen and grabbed him a glass of water. Aidan was propped up in our bed, Jasper sleeping on my side of the bed, keeping Aidan company. The dog hadn't left Aidan's side since he'd gotten home.

I handed him the glass of water. He stared into it. "It doesn't have ice in it."

"No, it doesn't. Do you want ice?"

"Yes, please."

I took the glass back to the kitchen and added a few large ice cubes before bringing it back.

"It's too cold to drink now."

"So you want less ice?" I asked in an overly sweet tone.

"Yes." He gave it back to me.

I reached into the glass and pulled out a couple of ice cubes. "There. All good, right?"

Aidan wisely didn't say anything; he took the glass and drank the water.

"Anything else I can do for you?"

He shook his head.

"You sure?"

He nodded.

With one last long look, I left the bedroom, dumped the extra cubes in the kitchen sink, and went back into my office to get back to work. I'd finally found a great editor to work with, and she currently had my manuscript. Now, I was fielding graphic designers for my cover. It was an interesting evolution—it was up to me to tell them what I wanted. They hadn't read my book, so I had to find a designer who had a good eye, but also one who would bring the vision I had for my cover to life.

"Sibby!" Aidan called.

I put my forehead to my desk.

"Sibby, I'm hungry!"

Of course he was hungry.

"Okay!" I called back to let him know I'd heard him. I was never getting any work done ever again. Maybe I should've taken Aidan's mother up on her offer—she'd volunteered to come to the city to look after Aidan. I'd brushed it off, but for the sake of maintaining a healthy marriage, it might be necessary.

"Sibby! Can I have marmalade on my toast?"

"Sure!" To myself I stated, "He's the father of my unborn child. He makes cute puppies. A body part ruptured. He's allowed to be insufferable."

"Sibby!" Aidan called again. "I need you."

"The father of my unborn child is a dead man," I told my computer screen. I got up and went to Aidan. He was scratching his beard and staring out the window. There would be snow any day now.

"You bellowed, my love," I stated, trying to keep the sarcasm from my voice.

"Thank you."

"For what?"

"For all that you do. I love you. I know this isn't easy. I know I'm a big baby. But I love you, and you're gorgeous, and I can't wait until I'm well again so I can take care of you and Pierogi."

My eyes misted. "Damn it."

"What?"

"You weren't supposed to be sweet or apologize. You were supposed to be annoying, and I was supposed to yell at you."

"You can still yell at me."

"You can't yell at an invalid."

"I'm not an invalid."

"Could you get up and fight me?" I demanded. I held up my fists and started swinging them in small circles. "Put up your dukes."

"You're in fine form today."

"I had an acai smoothie." My tone changed. "I'm really sorry."

"For?"

"For not being patient."

"I haven't made it easy, have I?"

I shook my head.

He sighed. "I'm going crazy. Caleb is running the bar. He'll have to handle the ordering, tend to customers, everything—while I'm in this bed."

"Anything you can do to change your situation?"

"No."

"Do you trust Caleb?"

"Yes."

"Then relax."

"You shouldn't be waiting on me hand and foot," he stated. "Call my mom."

"Nope."

"But—"

"I got this."

"You're trying to release a book."

"I'm aware." I smiled. "Maybe you just…don't call me every five seconds when you need something."

"I miss you."

"You do?"

He nodded. "Can't you take the day off and rest with me?"

I looked at Jasper snuggled up against Aidan. And then I looked at my husband. His beard was long, and his neck was due for a shave. His hair was mussed, but his blue eyes were clear.

"Yeah," I said, climbing into bed next to him. "I can take the day off. Let's watch TV together."

"What do you want to watch?" he asked.

"Nope. You choose. You're the sick one."

"I don't want to tell you."

"We're married. We have no secrets."

"Oh, I have secrets. And I have guilty pleasure TV shows."

"Let me guess." I smirked. "*Cops*?"

"Nope."

"*Antiques Roadshow*."

"Try again.

I thought for a moment and then grinned. "*Keeping up with the Kardashians.*"

"Damn it! How'd you guess?" he demanded.

"We *are* married," I reminded him.

"Right. So can we watch it?"

"I guess. But you have to promise not to tell anyone we did this. I've got street cred to think about."

"You? What about *my* street cred? I've got a beard. And I wear flannel. Caleb would never let me live this down."

I held up my pinky. "I swear to take this secret to my grave, or let a subway rat feast upon my fleshy remains."

Aidan wrapped his pinky around mine. "I swear."

Chapter 28

#thebestpartofwakingup #prayforme

"Before I leave, do you need anything else?" I asked.

Aidan glanced at the bed. A water bottle, an L.L. Bean catalogue, his laptop, his phone, and the TV remote were all within reach. Jasper was on his back, legs spread eagle, enjoying doggie dreams.

"I think I'm good," Aidan said with a boyish smile.

I ran my hand through his hair and then leaned down to kiss him. "Doctor cleared you for real food. I was gonna pick something up on the way home. What would you like?"

His eyes dilated. "You."

I kissed him again. "Doctor didn't clear you for strenuous activity yet. A few more weeks, champ."

"My own wife, cock-blocking me," he teased.

"I promise to make it up to you."

"Yeah? How?"

"I asked the doctor if we could do other things…"

He looked hopeful. "Please give me good news, Gertrude."

I whispered something filthy in his ear. "After I get this cast off, I plan to make you really happy that you married me."

"Go to the doctor. Go to the doctor now."

I laughed. "I should be home in a few hours, okay? Text me what you want for dinner."

The first snow flurries of the season were falling when I stepped out of the apartment. I was bundled from head to toe, but I still grumbled about being cold on my walk to the subway.

Aidan had been bedbound for three days, and already I was completely exhausted. Even though he'd gotten less needy, it was difficult being the only one to walk Jasper, tend to Aidan, and figure out my book stuff. And I didn't even have a kid yet.

How the hell did single parents do it? They should get a freakin' medal.

The subway ride into Manhattan to my doctor's office would take about forty-five minutes. I thought about reading, but lately, reading while on a train gave me motion sickness—and I'd been sick in enough public places.

Leaning my head against the subway car wall, I closed my eyes. The train went around a curve, and immediately it slowed down until it came to a halt. Trains frequently stalled, and it was no cause for concern, but when we didn't move after a few minutes, some of the commuters started to grumble.

The intercom switched on, and the conductor's voice boomed, "Ladies and gentlemen, please be patient. We should be moving shortly."

"Fucking train," the middle-aged guy next to me complained.

I silently commiserated with him. Thankfully, the subway car wasn't completely packed, so I didn't feel like a clown in a clown car.

It started to heat up, so I removed my hat and scarf. When that only gave me marginal relief, I unzipped my coat and tugged at my turtleneck in an attempt to cool off.

"It's hot in here, right?" I said out loud.

A few people looked at me. One shrugged and another said, "It's not that hot."

As my body temperature continued to rise, I began to panic. I dug around in my purse for a bottle of water—these days, I never left home without one. I drank half the thing in one go. Screwing on the cap, I realized I had to pee.

"Crap," I stated. My hands were turning clammy, and I was squirming in my seat.

The guy next to me glared.

"Sorry," I said. "But I'm pregnant—and I have to go to the bathroom."

Apparently saying I was pregnant was my get-out-of-jail-free card. His scowl dissolved. "How long do you think you can hold it?"

"Um, about five minutes? If I think about something else—maybe seven."

He stood up and moved his way toward the intercom at the end of the subway car. "Hello? Hello, can you hear me?"

There was a crackling on the other end of the inter-com, and then the voice of the conductor came through.

"We've got a situation," the guy said. "There's a pregnant woman in this subway car, and she's gotta go to the bathroom." He looked at me. "You doing okay?"

I hunched down in my seat as other people began looking in my direction. "Yeah, doing okay—nope, wait, I lied."

I was definitely on the verge of peeing my pants.

Oh God.

Puking humiliation I could get over. Not so much with urine...

"What do you mean you don't know the hold up?" the guy yelled at the intercom.

Sweat broke out along my brow. I crossed my legs and straightened my back as much as I could, trying to relieve the pressure in my balloon-like bladder.

"Someone talk to me!" I yelled. "Distract me!"

"You don't look pregnant," a young college guy said. "I think you're making it up."

"You're an idiot," an older woman said. "Anyone can tell she's pregnant."

I looked up. "What do you mean you can tell I'm pregnant?"

The older woman shot a glance at my stomach.

Great. So on top of embarrassing myself in public, I'd also been eating one too many ice cream sundaes and it all went to my belly.

The man came back to my side and put a hand to my shoulder. "You don't look well."

I moaned. The train showed no signs of moving again. Even if it did, I knew I wasn't going to make it to the next station, up and out of the subway system and to a bath-room. That ship had sailed.

My eye caught the Folger's label on a red container nestled in a woman's plastic grocery bag near me, and an idea sparked.

"I'll give you twenty bucks for that Folger's container," I said to the woman carrying the grocery bags.

"Sold!" The woman dug out the Folger's container and handed it to me.

"What are you thinking?" the man beside me asked.

I opened the Folger's container and ripped off the seal. "I'm gonna pee in this thing."

"You're kidding."

I shook my head. "I need a few volunteers to stand in front of me." I headed for the corner of the train where there was no seat, only a handrail. Five people made a human wall of privacy in front of me.

"Let's just hope the train doesn't suddenly lurch," the guy muttered.

"Gotta keep the faith," I called, tugging at my tights.

Just as I had relieved myself and was standing again after managing the awkwardest of all squats, two cops pushed open the doors between the train cars and stepped inside.

In a not-so-amused tone one of them asked, "What's going on in here?"

"You will not believe the afternoon I just had," I said,

coming into the bedroom. I reached down to pull off one of my boots and then thought better of it. Jasper was looking at me like he needed to go outside.

"I have a pretty good idea the afternoon you had."

When I frowned in confusion, Aidan turned his laptop toward me, showing me a YouTube screen. He pressed the space bar and immediately the five people that had shielded me from prying eyes while I peed in a Folger's canister came into view.

"No," I whispered. "No, no, no…"

I watched video Sibby stand up just as the cops came into view.

"Close it," I demanded. "I don't need to see anymore. I know how it ends."

It had ended with me receiving a public urination citation and a summons to attend an administrative hearing to pay a fine.

"At least it's just a ticket and not a criminal offence anymore," Aidan stated, trying to hide his smile.

"Can you not be Mr. Glass is Half Full? This is not funny."

"It's sort of funny. Okay, it's *very* funny."

"Why are you so calm about this?" I demanded.

"Sibby," he said. "People sometimes pee in public. When you gotta go, you gotta go, and it's a lot better to pee on a tree or in a corner than it is to pee your pants. It's not that big of a deal."

"It's a *huge* deal. Embarrassment and law breaking aside, this video is on the internet!"

"You like your life on the internet."

"This is bad publicity. People don't like to support criminals."

"I could make so many political jokes it's not even funny."

I rolled my eyes. "Focus. Please. This could ruin me."

"Or—you can use it to your advantage."

"What do you mean?"

"I mean, make a public statement. Go on Stacy's YouTube channel. Or your own Instagram account. You have enough followers. Just explain yourself."

"Hmm… Yeah. I guess I could say, with the help of some nice people I was able not to pee my pants. I mean, the choice was to pee in a coffee container or just let it rip and get it *everywhere*—yeah I did the right thing."

"Or maybe something more eloquent? You're a writer, right?"

"Right." I thought for a moment. "I got nothin'."

"Just say that you don't normally condone this kind of behavior, but there were extenuating circumstances."

"Right. The train had stopped and even the conductor didn't know when the issue would've been resolved."

"See? There you go. Also mention the nice people who helped you. Mention that you're pregnant, and mention that the cops were nice even though they wrote you the ticket anyway."

"Good. This is all good stuff." I paused. "Can you repeat all that?"

He raised his eyebrows. Jasper woofed, letting me know he needed to go out. After I took him for a relief break, I ran into Mrs. Nowacki in the hallway.

"Hi," I greeted. "How are you?"

Jasper ran up to her and wagged his tail. She gave him a good scratch under his chin and said, "I make a cake for your *mąż*. I bring it over once it is cool."

"Thank you."

She touched my bare wrist. "You are free."

I nodded. "Got it off this afternoon." It felt weird to be

without the cast. I wouldn't have to cover it to shower. "Have a good night, Mrs. Nowacki."

After letting Jasper off his leash, I fed him dinner and then put the groceries away. I went into the bedroom and flopped down on the bed. Aidan held out his arm, and I scooted into the nook of his body.

"What can I do to cheer you up?" he asked.

"Nothing."

"Nothing?"

"Don't make me cook," I said.

"No cooking. What else?"

"I'd love a foot rub."

"Grab the coconut oil. What else?"

I sat up and reached for the jar of coconut oil on my nightstand. "I think you know."

"Really?"

"Yep."

He sighed. "Thai food and *Legally Blonde* it is."

I nodded vigorously. "My soul hurts."

"Okay, okay, I know when I'm beat. Just don't tell Caleb I lost my dude card today."

"Uh, you lost it last week when we watched *While You Were Sleeping* and you got misty-eyed."

He rolled his eyes. "Sandra Bullock is so hot she made me cry."

I handed him the lotion. "You just volunteered to also give me a back rub."

Aidan took the bottle and sighed. "Yes, dear."

"Before we watch the movie, let's play a game."

"Ohhh—"

"Not that kind of game. Sorry."

He grinned. "What kind of game?"

"Guess how many items were in my cast."

"I don't understand," he said, gesturing for me to take

off my tights, so he could rub my feet. "What do you mean items *in* your cast?"

"The arm itched, right? So I stuck a pencil down there to scratch it, but it was too short to get back out so I just left it…"

Aidan held back a smile. "What else was in there?"

I flashed him a smile. "Aside from the pencil? Three bobby pins, a chopstick, and a peanut."

Chapter 29

#Ifoughtthelaw #thelawwon

"You wanna tell me why there's a video of you peeing on the subway?" my mother asked.

"How did you know about that?"

"Your cousin Aaron emailed his mother, and his mother forwarded it to me."

Damn my cousin. And damn my aunt. And damn email forwarding.

"Explain yourself, Sibyl Ruth."

"Lift the phone," I told her. "So I can direct my answer to your face and not your boobs. And for the love of God, stop middle-naming me." FaceTime with my mother was always an interesting experience. She'd had an iPhone for years, and yet she still couldn't figure out how to use it properly.

"I can never get this angle right." The screen shook, and then my mother's face appeared. "Hello, there you are."

I waved.

"So this video—" she began.

"The train stopped in between two stations underground. I was trapped in a subway car full of strangers, and there was no sign of when we were going to move again. I was hot, thirsty, and panicky. My bladder filled, and I had to pee so bad I couldn't hold it anymore. I had two choices. Pee in the Folger's container, or soil myself."

"Well, when you put it that way—"

"Exactly. I plan on releasing my own video to the masses to explain the situation."

"Remember to smile," she told me. "And tone down the hostility. And tell people you are pregnant. People are forgiving of women who are pregnant. And you told the cops all this?"

"Yes."

"And they still gave you a fine?"

I shrugged. "City has to make money, right?"

"Let me call Mel."

"Don't call Mel," I pleaded.

Mel Silverman had been the family attorney for as long as I could remember. He was on his third wife and fourth toupee. Still, he could get shit done.

"I'll just go to the administrative hearing, pay the fine, and be done with it."

"At the courthouse? You have to *go to court*? My baby's in the system!" my mother wailed.

"Ma, put some hemp oil under your tongue."

"I do not *use* hemp oil, Sibyl Ruth."

There she went again, middle-naming me. She only middle-named when she was vexed with me.

"Where's your lavender body mist?" I demanded. "Spray that around and take a deep breath. Calm yourself, please."

"I don't need to spray the lavender." She scrunched up her nose at me. "Let me say hi to my grandbaby."

Thank goodness for Pierogi's distraction. I pressed a button to turn the lens, and then I directed it at my belly. My mother instantly lost the ability to speak in a normal tone and began cooing nonsense at my stomach.

"And that's enough," I said.

"Five more seconds…"

"Ma," I warned.

"Fine, I'm stopping, I'm stopping. Where's Jasper? I want to say hi to my grandpup, too."

"Jasper is napping with Aidan." I was jealous of naptime. Lately, it seemed harder and harder to get out of bed. I'd close my eyes at night, and it felt like only moments later I was waking up to a new day.

"How's he doing?" she asked.

"Crabby. Which I guess is good because that means he's healing, and he wants to get up and get moving."

"No heavy lifting for a while," came my father's voice, followed by his head popping into the frame. He still had a full head of salt and pepper hair, and it was combed off his forehead neatly. Total silver fox material, or so my mother liked to inform me.

Yuck.

"You're not going to lecture me, too, are you?" I inquired.

He held up his hand. "Nope. But I really do think we should call Mel. What happened to you is atrocious."

"Um, they didn't cuff me or take me to the station."

Dad shook his head. "A Goldstein mixed up with the law. We need to clear the family name."

I raised my eyes heavenward. "It's no longer a criminal offense in New York City to pee in public. It's just an administrat—"

"This is so embarrassing," my mother stated. "What am I gonna tell *Bubbe* and *Zayde*?"

"You tell them nothing," I said. "Do they even know how to use a computer?"

"*Bubbe* uses the internet to search for flash mob scenes," my father said.

Dear. Lord.

"Just say nothing, okay?" I pleaded. The last thing I needed was my German-accented grandmother calling me. Because apparently being unable to hold one's bladder had brought shame upon the entire family.

Mom shook her head. "First you can't come for Thanksgiving and now this."

My dad looked at his watch. "Gotta get to the hospital." He kissed my mom's head and then saluted me. Great, he was leaving me to deal with my mother alone.

"Blame Aidan's appendectomy," I said, returning to the holiday conversation. "He's stuck in a bed."

"So you would've come to Atlanta for Thanksgiving if his appendix hadn't ruptured?"

Probably not, I didn't say. I was exhausted. Before the appendix thing, Aidan was working all the time. Leaving town for the holidays was a luxury we weren't able to afford—not as business owners. We didn't punch a clock or get paid sick leave. This was something my mother had never understood.

"I'm getting an ultrasound," I voiced, changing the subject. "The day before Thanksgiving."

Thankfully, my mother took the bait. "I want a copy. I want to get it framed and put it on the mantle."

Somehow I held in an eye roll. "I'll get the doctor to send it, okay? Mom, I gotta go, I love you so much. Bye!"

I hung up with my mother before she could start talking about something else and then went to the bedroom. Aidan was sitting on the side of the bed, his legs touching the floor. "I need a shower," he said.

"You just had a shower."

"No, I had a sponge bath. And that was two days ago." He threw me a heated look. "I enjoyed it immensely."

Smiling, I approached him. "Yeah, I'm aware. A certain part of you definitely rose to the occasion."

"I can't wait for the doctor to clear me. I'm ready for some more invigorating exercise."

"Horn dog."

He grinned and pushed off the bed to stand. "Come on, I'm ready to try my hand at standing in the shower."

"Mind if I ogle your wet, naked body?"

"Ogle away." He took a small step toward the bath-room. "But please don't let your ogling get in the way of making sure I stay upright."

I left Aidan in Mrs. Nowacki's care while I met up

with Stacy. She lived in a two-story, two-thousand-square-foot loft in an old warehouse in Bushwick. Her other roommates were the typical nine to fivers, so we had privacy.

The second floor was her studio space. Though there was a ton of natural light, she had light stands and interchangeable backdrops. As Stacy did my makeup to ensure I was camera ready, she asked, "Are you sure this is a good idea?"

I frowned. "Why wouldn't it be a good idea?"

She gently tapped the end of the makeup brush to the furrow of my brow. "Don't frown. You'll get wrinkles—and then you'll get Botox, and that's a slippery slope."

Laughing, I let my forehead smooth out. "You speak like you know that's how it's gonna go."

"I've met enough people in my circle and trust me, plastic surgery is like regular maintenance for them."

"Duly noted."

She held up a hand mirror, and I had to admit I was impressed. I hardly looked like I was wearing any makeup, but my skin tone was more even, and she'd hidden the bags under my eyes.

"Um, can you do this for me every day?" I asked. "I feel pretty again."

With the thickening of my waistline, it was difficult to feel feminine. And with a husband on bed rest who couldn't get frisky, my feminine parts were feeling ignored.

"I love dressing other people up," she admitted. "So yeah, I would totally do this for you."

I gave her a thumbs up. "Let's do this."

"Okay, but you didn't answer my question. Are you sure this is a good idea? Wouldn't it be better just to leave it alone? Let the video die?"

In the three days since the video of me on the subway

went viral, it had only gained more traction. "I feel like I need to set the record straight."

She nodded. "I get it, but sometimes its better just to keep your head down. And if you apologize, it means you did something wrong, and I don't think you did."

"And I'm hoping other people feel that way, too. This is the second time I've been in the spotlight—and not through any fault of my own. I call it Sibby's Law. If there's something to spill or mess up, it's got my name all over it. And my readers… I'm launching this book on my own. It's more important than ever that I make good with them, ya know?"

"Have you thought about being completely unapologetic?" she asked. "You're a pregnant woman, and you were trapped on the subway. If you're going to do anything, then you should be calling out the injustice of getting a fine."

"I don't have an agenda, Stacy. All I want is to release my book, have it do well, and write my next one."

"But it's complete bullshit!" she argued. "And you shouldn't be penalized."

"I broke a law," I said simply.

"It's not as black and white as saying you broke a law. You broke a law—but what about the guy that posted the video of it all going down? I'd sue. Defamation of character or something."

"I don't think it works that way. My mother wanted to call the family lawyer."

She raised blond eyebrows. "You have a family lawyer?"

"Yeah." I nodded. "Doesn't everyone?"

"No, not everyone—oh, you're kidding." She let out a laugh when she saw my smile. "Why didn't you take your mom up on the offer?"

"Because I'm an adult? I don't know. When my mom gets involved, things have a habit of spiraling out of control." I told Stacy about my mother stalking me and the showdown in Starbucks.

Stacy laughed so hard I thought her mascara would run down her face, but then I remembered she was a makeup queen, and her mascara was probably indestructible.

"Can we do this video? I want to post it tonight." Exhaustion was tugging at my eyelids. I'd already had my one cup of caffeinated coffee, and yet it seemed to do absolutely nothing.

Stacy tucked a stray hair behind my ear and then said, "Yep. Sit in that chair. Let me light you."

Five minutes later, I was talking into the camera. Short and sweet. I wrapped up my heartfelt apology, the entire time Stacy's words playing in the back of my mind.

Did I really owe anyone an apology? Maybe not, but I definitely wanted to give my own version of the story.

"How was I?" I asked when Stacy touched the screen to end the video.

"Honestly? A little fake."

I blinked. "Seriously?"

"Yeah. You didn't really sound like you. You sounded kind of insincere."

I stood up in a fit of frustration. "I was sincere! I am sorry for what I did!"

She cocked her head to the side. "Are you? Because the way I see it? You have nothing to be sorry about, and I wish you hadn't apologized. You're a pregnant woman who couldn't hold her bladder, and some asshole got your humiliation on video and posted it."

"Yeah. He's a dick."

She laughed. "And what's his handle?"

"I dunno." I shrugged. "Big tool?"

"Monster wanker? Asshat? That guy's account blew up, but *you* were the casualty. Your reputation was the casualty."

"You really think my reputation is a casualty?" I asked, biting my lip.

"People think they know you because they've seen your clips on Instagram. It's the same with me on YouTube. But they have no idea that we're not always the face we show them."

"You sound like you're sick of being in front of the camera."

"I am," she admitted. "I'd much rather be behind it. What about you? Do you like having your life on display?"

"I like it—making the videos, showing people that I'm clumsy and ridiculous—because that *is* who I am. I don't feel like I'm giving up anything by including them in my life."

"That's good." She smiled. "You've made a career out of being clumsy."

"The cork video. Yeah, you're right." I shook my head, remembering how this had all begun. Me pinging Matt in the eye with the cork from an exploding champagne bottle. Someone else had captured that video of me, too.

"I feel like you're the viral video version of Lucille Ball," Stacy said.

"Best compliment ever."

"It's bullshit, you know," she said. "Thinking you owe anyone an explanation or an apology."

I sighed. "Yeah, kinda wish they would stick it where the sun don't shine."

Chapter 30

#surprise #ofcoursethiswouldhappen

"Make no mistake," Aidan said that night at dinner. "Mrs. Nowacki may come across as this sweet old woman, but she takes no prisoners. I lost twenty bucks to her in a few rounds of Pinochle."

"I should've warned you. She's a total card shark." I held up the serving spoon. "More green beans?"

"Yes, please. They're really good," he said. "Food also tastes better because I'm finally eating at a table and not in bed."

Jasper was resting at our feet. I slipped him a piece of beef, loving that we spoiled him.

"What do you think about inviting Mrs. Nowacki to spend Thanksgiving with us?" I asked.

"We're doing Thanksgiving?" He scratched his stubbly jaw—he'd shaved the beard, but had left the stubble—no doubt to drive my hormones insane. "Who's cooking?"

"I was thinking I could make Thanksgiving sides, some pies, and maybe we could just have turkey sandwiches."

He frowned. "Who are you and what have you done with Sibby?" He put a hand to my forehead. "Aliens have taken over your body, right? They sucked your brain out and now you're one of them, is that it?"

I waved his hand away. "What? Thanksgiving would be a nice idea, right? We're not traveling anywhere. I'm not ready to make a real turkey. Maybe next year, but this is a nice lead up to that."

"I think so. Yeah."

"Caleb can come after he closes the bar. Mrs. Nowacki will make it four. I can see if Stacy and her boyfriend are going anywhere. We could have a Friendsgiving."

"But I don't want you doing all the cooking alone," he said. "I can help."

"You'll help?"

"Sure. Just no heavy lifting—and since we're not getting a turkey, no lifting is involved. I can peel, chop, dice, and talk you off a ledge when you realize you bit off way more than you can chew."

I laughed. "Thanks for the vote of confidence. Text Caleb. I'll text Stacy."

"This'll be nice," he said after he texted Caleb. "We've never done Thanksgiving on our own."

"Like a Bat Mitzvah, this is a right of passage. Every

woman must make her own Thanksgiving dinner. It means she's arrived."

"What are you even saying right now?"

"No idea. I'm faint from hunger." I reached for the spoon resting in the casserole dish of scalloped potatoes.

"That's your third helping."

I looked at him, eyes narrowing. "What's that now?"

"Just making an observation." He held up his hands in defense. "You're really sexy, by the way."

"Yeah, right," I muttered.

"No, you are," he insisted.

"My girl parts miss your boy parts."

"My boy parts miss your girl parts," he said.

"I think I'm revirginizing."

"You know that's not really a thing, right?"

"Tell it to my neglected hoo-hah."

Aidan's gaze lowered, and he opened his mouth to speak, but I cut him off. "Yeah, please don't actually talk to my crotch."

We laughed. As I cleared the dinner table, I said, "So this is a slice of what marriage in our eighties is gonna be like."

"Great conversation and laughter, but no sex?" Aidan rested his hands on the table and slowly stood up.

"Yeah."

"I'd rather laugh with you than have sex with anyone else."

My eyes misted. Loading the dishwasher, I tried not to let him see I was on the verge of crying. Everything set me off lately. Just the day before, I'd watched a Walgreens commercial about gum where a couple kissed and I'd burst into tears.

I didn't hear Aidan come up behind me, but suddenly he was there. His arms wrapped around me. "You really are the best. You know that, right?" he asked against my ear.

Sinking back into him, I closed my eyes and just let him hold me. "It's all going to be okay, isn't it?"

"Of course it is."

"You don't know what I'm talking about."

"Nope. But it doesn't matter. We got this, Sibby."

I raised his hands to my lips and kissed them. "Go sit down. I'll clean up the rest of this."

"Movie?" he asked, releasing me.

"Whatever you want."

I ran a sponge across the counter and then started the dishwasher. Filling Jasper's water bowl, I looked over my shoulder. Husband and dog were on the futon, snuggled up together. It was a perfect picture, and it made me think about a year from now when it would be four of us.

Shaking my head, I dispelled the image. But it was a nice picture all the same.

I made it through half the movie before I fell asleep. Sometime during the night, Aidan got me up from the futon. "How did you fall asleep during *Jaws*?" he marveled.

"Hormones." I pushed my head into the pillow, already curling up to get comfortable and wanting to sleep for days.

"I'm gonna take Jasper out."

I started to get up. "No, I'll do it."

Aidan gently rested his hand on my shoulder, and I plopped back down into the plush foam top. "I need some air. I miss the outside, and it's time for me to try stairs. You rest."

I wasn't going to fight. "Okay," I murmured. I didn't hear him leave.

I pulled on my giant black parka, the one with the faux fur trimmed hood, and turned to Aidan. He zipped his coat slowly, shaking his head when he saw my getup.

"It's not that cold," he said. "Oh, that's right. It's below seventy, which means you're practically an icicle."

"You know the movie *Aliens*?"

"Yeah."

"You know when the alien opens its mouth and a tiny tongue alien pops out, salivating and screaming with those nasty teeth?"

He smiled, dimples flashing. "Yeah."

"They modeled that after me when I get cold, but they toned it down a bit."

Aidan laughed, a deep belly laugh that had me instantly worried. He was up and moving, more and more each day, but I was still concerned about his recovery. We'd gone to see the doctor a few days prior. He had checked the surgery site and removed Aidan's stitches.

Aidan still wasn't cleared for the horizontal hora, and we were both feeling…antsy. To the point where we'd started snipping at each other. We needed a good romp to set us right—and with all the extra hormones running through my body, I was in danger of devouring him. He might not be able to walk once I was through with him.

I sighed.

"What's that sigh mean?" Aidan asked, handing me my scarf.

I took the soft plaid scarf and wrapped it around my neck. No way was any cold air getting to my skin. "I think you know."

"I don't—ohhhh."

"I need the doctor to clear you like, now."

He grabbed the zipper of my coat and tugged me to him. "I think we need to go somewhere this December. How do you feel about Christmas in Puerto Rico?"

"Really?"

"Yeah. Escape the holiday fray. Lie on a beach. Do lots and lots of dirty stuff."

"What do we do with Jasper?" I reached for my bag and slung it across my chest. "Mrs. Nowacki can't handle him for a long time."

"We'll take him Upstate. My parents would love to have him."

"Turn him into a country dog." I smiled. "Okay. I'm in. Puerto Rico. Tan skin here I come."

"Let's not get ahead of ourselves," he quipped.

I swatted his behind in good humor. To Jasper I said, "Be a good boy while we're gone."

Aidan locked up the apartment, and then we took the stairs slowly. When we got to the foyer, I arranged for an Uber. Aidan leaned against the wall to catch his breath.

"You okay?" I asked as I put a hand to his chest.

He covered my hand with his. Nodding, he pushed away from the wall. "Caleb will definitely kick my ass at basketball now."

"You'll get your stamina back."

"I can only hope."

"I was talking about basketball."

"I was talking about sex," he pointed out.

"Gee, ya think?"

The Uber arrived, and Aidan held the back door open for me. I scooted in and he followed, though he was slow. This was the most movement he'd done in weeks, but there was no way he'd have missed this appointment. I'd rescheduled my ultrasound twice already. If I tried to reschedule it again it would've been after Thanksgiving, and I didn't want to wait. So an appointment the day before Thanksgiving was the only option.

Aidan reached for my hand and gave it a squeeze. We were quiet on the ride into Manhattan. Traffic was a nightmare due to the looming holiday travel and people taking time off early in the week, but I wasn't about to let Aidan traverse the subway system. It would've been too much.

We finally arrived, and even though we were five minutes late, Dr. Hayden was behind on seeing patients so it didn't matter. I checked in with the smiley nurse in pink scrubs with neon pink hearts all over them.

"There's a lot of pink in here," Aidan whispered when I took a seat next to him.

Guess he'd seen the nurse. And the walls.

I looked around. "Yeah. Why do I feel like I'm in one big square vagina?"

Aidan burst out laughing, causing a few heads to turn in our direction. He clutched his side and pressed a hand to his mouth, but laughter still escaped.

I shot an apologetic look to a woman who appeared ready to pop. Her belly was huge, and her belly button was visible through her shirt. Was that how I would look? Could my body even handle that?

The nurse called my name and held open the door that led to the exam rooms. Aidan followed. She drew my blood, making small talk to distract me.

"Are you going into the stirrups today?" Aidan asked

once we were alone. "Because that might impact our sex life."

"You don't think watching your child's head come out of my birth canal will impact our sex life?"

"Well played." Aidan looked around the room, his gaze resting on the plastic models of the different stages of fetal growth. He reached for one, but I stopped him.

"You look with your eyes, not your hands," I said and then immediately balked. "Oh God. I just became my mother. Sorry. Pick that up, and we'll play catch with it."

The door opened and Dr. Hayden walked in. She was in her early forties, her brown hair twirled up into an elegant chignon. She smiled warmly at both of us and set my chart on the exam counter.

"Well, let's hear a heartbeat," she said with enthusiasm. She had me lie back on the table as she asked me a bunch of questions, nodding at my answers.

I lifted my shirt and pulled my yoga pants down to expose my lower belly. Dr. Hayden squirted cool gel across my skin and turned on the ultrasound machine. She put the wand to my stomach, and after a few seconds, we heard the rapid beat of a heart. I looked up at Aidan who looked glassy through my teary eyes.

With a gloved finger, Dr. Hayden pointed to the screen. "There's your baby. I'll give you two…" She frowned as she trailed off.

"What is it?" Aidan asked. "Is something wrong?"

"No, not wrong," she said slowly. She moved the wand to another part of my stomach. I heard the heartbeat again, but it also sounded like there was an echo. Dr. Hayden looked at the monitor and then back at me. She smiled. "Congratulations. You're having twins."

#doubledoubletoilandtrouble #myuterusisnotaclowncar

"Twins?" I repeated. "As in *two*?"

Dr. Hayden smiled gently. "Yes."

"I'm having two babies. There are *two* babies growing in my uterus. There are two babies that are gonna come out of my—*two*?"

"Two," Dr. Hayden said. "Any history of twins in your family?"

"No," I said.

"Nope," Aidan said. "Not in my family either."

"Are you sure?" I asked the doctor. "I mean, it's really too early to tell, right? I mean, you could be wrong."

"I have to wait to look at your blood work—but I'd guess your HCG levels are high, which is usually a multiple birth indicator. Plus, combined with the extreme fatigue, severe morning sickness which happens at random times throughout the day, not to mention the amount of weight you've gained so early on..." She put a hand to my arm. "I'll give you both a minute."

Dr. Hayden left the room, leaving us alone again. I pulled down my shirt, hauled up my pants, and then got off the exam table.

"Sibby," Aidan began.

"You are *so* fired," I snapped, grabbing my parka and purse. I heard him sigh as I stormed out of the exam room.

Twins? I was having twins?

Sibby's fucking Law at its finest.

My phone vibrated with a text as we headed to the reception desk.

Annie: How'd the ultrasound go?

I shoved my phone back in my pocket.

"Mrs. Kincaid, would you like to schedule your next doctor's appointment now?" the nurse wearing the pink heart scrubs asked.

"I'll call." I shoved my arms into my coat. Not bothering to wait for Aidan, I left the doctor's office, took the elevator to the lobby, and stood there, staring out the large glass windows at the street traffic. Car horns, people yelling—none of it registered as my mind tried to process.

The elevator doors dinged, and a moment later, I felt Aidan stand behind me.

"Am I allowed to touch you?" he asked.

I thought for a moment and then nodded. He wrapped

his arms around me from behind and rested his chin on my head. We stood like that for a moment, before I stepped out of his embrace.

"I need to walk," I told him. "Alone."

"Okay." He didn't sound happy.

"Can you get home by yourself?"

"Yeah," Aidan said.

I took a step toward the revolving door.

"Sibby…" His hands were in his coat pockets, his eyes bright. "I love you."

Inhaling a shaky breath, I turned and walked out.

"Hit me, barkeep," I said.

"You only say 'hit me' at the black jack tables," Zeb stated. "And I'm not a barkeep because this isn't the Wild West in the 1800s."

My eyes rested on the empty shot glass. Zeb sighed, took the shot glass, and filled it with cranberry juice.

"This is your sixth one," he said, putting it back in front of me. "I might need to ask for your keys."

I downed the shot of sweet, tart cranberry juice and slid the empty glass along the bar. After I'd left Aidan at the doctor's office, I'd walked west. About fifteen blocks later, I'd given up walking and caught a cab to Zeb's quaint restaurant. I'd plopped my jiggly butt on the stool in the corner and refused to talk. He was filling in behind the bar

because a bartender had called in sick, so he was relent-
lessly pursuing a line of conversation—a line of conversation I didn't want to talk about.

"I'm cutting you off until you tell me what's going on."

"Went to the doctor today. First trimester ultrasound."

"Oh God, Sibby. Is everything okay?" He placed his
hand on mine, and I instantly laced my fingers through his.

"I'm okay. Everything's fine."

"Then why—"

"Twins. I'm having twins."

Zeb didn't say anything, and then he let out a laugh.
"Of course you are."

I glared at him. "It's not funny." My response only
made him laugh harder until he pulled his hand away so
he could bend over the bar.

"Twins," he repeated. "Damn. That's hilarious."

"It is *not!*"

"It is! Oh man, this is gonna be so good." He shook his
head. "Why aren't you happy?"

"Happy? I was just getting used to the idea of one. But
two? Two babies? Two of everything?"

He scratched his jaw and looked thoughtful. "Twice
the fun? Twice the laughs?"

"Twice the poop, twice the puke."

"You're overwhelmed," he pointed out. "Did you talk
to Aidan?"

I lowered my forehead to the bar. "No. I ditched him at
the doctor's office."

"You ditched your recovering-from-an-appy-husband
immediately after you guys found out you're having
twins?"

"I'M FREAKING OUT!"

He shook his head. "Give me your phone. Right this
minute."

"What are you going to do?" I asked.

"I'm going to call your husband."

"No!"

"Unlock your phone, Sibby."

"No!"

"You're being a butthead."

"You're the butthead."

An older couple sitting at a table near the bar area looked at us. Zeb called out, "She's having twins, and she's nervous about it."

"*Mazel tov*!" the older gentleman called.

"Two is such a blessing!" the woman added.

"Whatever you two are drinking"—Zeb said—"next round is on me."

The couple grinned and then went back to eating.

"Don't call Aidan," I said to Zeb. "I'll call him."

"You know what, don't call him. We need to get you an Uber. You need to talk to him face to face."

"Oh. Yeah. Probably for the best."

An hour later, I walked into the apartment, but Jasper and Aidan weren't there.

I sent Aidan a text letting him know I was home. He didn't reply right away, and so I set my phone on the coffee table. He was walking Jasper, no doubt. I wandered into my office and plopped down onto my office chair. Swiveling, I took in the space. I'd made my peace with making it a nursery—and I'd even started looking at Pinterest for nursery room inspiration. One baby in here would've been doable in the short-term.

But two?

I heard the apartment door open, and I got up. Aidan was setting Jasper's leash on the table as I came into the living room.

"Hey," I said.

"Hey." He shrugged out of his coat and hung it on the hook by the door. Bending over, he lifted one foot to unlace his boot.

"I'm sorry."

He continued to take off one boot and then the other. "Okay, you're sorry."

"And you're pissed. You have every right to be."

"Do I?" he asked. "Thank you. I'm so glad I'm entitled to my feelings."

I flinched.

"Is this how it's always going to be? You get news you don't want to deal with and you run?"

"I needed space and time—"

"And what did *I* need, Sibby? Did you stop to think about what I needed? I'm about to be a father, Sibby. This isn't all about you."

My shame intensified, but I held his gaze. "What would you like me to say, Aidan?" My tone was soft, curious. "Because I apologized and—"

"An apology is not enough," he growled. "We found out we're having twins and instead of celebrating, instead of holding each other, you left. Why do you keep leaving me?"

What could I say to him? How could I tell him that even though *we* were expecting twins, I felt like we were experiencing different emotions, different journeys. I wasn't trying to negate Aidan's feelings; his excitement, his enthusiasm. But his emotions weren't mine.

Was I happy?

Yes.

Was my fear sometimes greater than my joy?

Definitely.

Would I change anything?

No. Not at all.

"Have you ever been pregnant?" I asked him.

He blinked. "No."

"Neither have I. This is all new territory for me. It's new for you, too. I'm not disputing that. But Aidan, I've got two babies growing inside me. I'm responsible for their well-being. And there aren't enough books or advice out there that will make me feel any less terrified that I'm gonna fuck this all up." Aidan reached for me and pulled me into his arms. I spoke against his chest. "I don't mean to run. I never want you to think I'm leaving you, but sometimes, I need more than the space in my head."

"You need physical space."

"Yes." I hugged him closer. "Not right now, I don't."

"I wish," he sighed. "I just wish I could take some of your worry from you, but I know I can't."

"No, you can't. But I'm glad you're my partner."

I woke up the next morning with Aidan spooning me from behind and Jasper curled up next to my belly. I would've gladly stayed there, but I had to pee. I scooted out from underneath Aidan's arm and gave Jasper a pat on my way to the bathroom.

While I was brushing my teeth, the intercom buzzed. Frowning, I glanced at my cell phone resting on the sink. It was seven thirty in the morning. I headed for the living room.

Aidan came out of the bedroom, scratching his arm and yawning. "Did you order anything?"

I shook my head, toothbrush resting against my cheek. "Do they deliver stuff on Thanksgiving?"

Aidan went to the intercom. "Hello?"

"Hi, sweetie!" Aidan's mom called.

Aidan glanced at me as he answered, "Hey."

"Will you buzz us in? Your father is struggling with the turkey."

"I am not," Aidan's father grumbled in the background.

Aidan released the intercom and pressed the unlock button.

I removed the toothbrush from my mouth. "Why are they here? And why do they have a turkey?"

He shook his head. "I don't know."

A few moments later, the door to the apartment burst open, and Aidan's parents crowded into the living room.

"I got the turkey," Aidan's father boomed, holding up a covered roasting pan. "Shot it myself."

Nancy shrugged out of her coat and hung it by the door, and then she bent down to give Jasper some love. He was itching to go outside, yet he was excited by the arrival of new people. After she greeted her grandpup, she embraced me.

My arms went around her automatically. "Hi, Mom."

"Where can I set this bird down?" Bud's gaze darted around the room in question.

"Kitchen counter," Aidan said. "Um, so. What are you guys doing here?"

"Not that we're not happy to see you," I added quickly.

Nancy released me and then went to hug her son. "It's Thanksgiving."

"Yeah," Aidan said. "We know."

"Well, I was talking to Sibby's mom—"

"You talked to my mom?" I asked with raised brows.

"Yeah. She called me, actually. She was pretty upset that you both weren't able to make it to Atlanta for Thanksgiving. And I told her I was upset because you weren't going to be Upstate for Thanksgiving, and she had the genius idea of Thanksgiving in the city!"

Now wasn't the time to tell Nancy that Aidan and I never had plans to go to *either* place for Thanksgiving. Aidan's appendectomy had given us an out. But I hadn't counted on my in-laws randomly showing up. That kind of behavior was strictly relegated to my parents.

The buzzer sounded again.

"That must be them!" Nancy exclaimed. "Sit down, Sibby, you look a little flushed. I'll buzz them up."

Chapter 32

#nottonight #Ihaveaheadache

My mom smothered me in her arms, squashing me against
her chest. And then she wrapped her arms around my
waist. "I'm just dying to see the sonogram!" she cooed.

"Oh, me too!" Nancy added, handing my mother a
cup of freshly brewed coffee.

"Thanks, Nancy," my mother said.

"Honey, sit down," Nancy said to Aidan. "You're still
recovering."

"And you sit down too," my mother commanded me.

I sank down onto the futon next to Aidan, still in dumb

shock. My father and Bud were in the kitchen, talking about the turkey and its size. Nancy and my mother *kibbitzed*. Jasper jumped up onto the futon and put his head in my lap.

"You really should've gotten another couch," Mom said. "I think Jasper is past his rip-stuff-to-shreds stage."

"Yeah, we'll look into that," I said absently.

"Do you want to cook the turkey?" Nancy asked, shifting my mother's attention.

Mom shook her head. "Bud shot it. I think you two have earned the right to cook it." They laughed and headed into the kitchen to join their husbands.

"My parents are making it a habit to drop in unannounced," I said.

"And now my parents are doing it too."

"Gah, there's four of them!" I buried my head in my hands.

"I think our Thanksgiving just got hijacked."

"Ya think?"

"Don't panic."

"Panic? Why would I panic?"

"Because you're not ready to tell them we're having—"

"Sibby? Are you hungry?" Mom called from the kitchen.

"Nope. I'm good," I called back. Lowering my voice, I said to Aidan, "I'm nauseated."

Aidan's hand went to my back. "Morning sickness?"

"Sure, let's go with that."

"Well, I think we should get to cooking," Nancy said.

I heard the sound of the fridge opening. "This won't be enough," Mom said. "We'll need more groceries."

I'd gotten a delivery from Whole Foods the previous morning. It had been more than enough to feed six. But now we were feeding ten.

"Let's send the men to the store," Nancy suggested.

Mom snorted. "With a list. Otherwise they might come back with ice cream and nothing else."

"Is it too soon to go back to bed?" I asked him.

"They'd only follow us," Aidan said.

"We're on borrowed time. When do you think they'll ask to see the sonogram again?"

"Let's get Sibby to show us the sonogram," Mom said, excitement in her voice.

"Oh, good idea," Nancy said.

I pinched the bridge of my nose. "I'm getting a migraine."

"No, you're not."

"Let's pretend. I'm gonna go"—I lifted my fingers and did air quotes—"sleep it off." I stood up, and Jasper made a move to follow me. "He needs to go out."

"You're just gonna leave me out here alone?" Aidan asked, mouth agape.

I pointed to my belly.

He sighed. "You can only play that card for six more months. You know that, right?"

Smiling, I went to the bedroom. With my hand on the door, I said, "And then I'm gonna play the 'I gave birth to your legacy' card."

"Damn it. I'm never winning again."

Just as I was closing the door, I heard my mother ask, "Aidan, where's the sonogram?"

I woke up from my nap to the delightful smell of a roasting turkey. I took a few moments to enjoy it, and then I was running for the bathroom. Guess it was time to cross turkey off the list, too. After cleaning up, I threw on some jeans with a lot of give in the waistline and Aidan's forest green wool sweater. I lifted the collar to my nose, inhaling the comforting scent of his Gucci cologne.

The door to the bedroom quietly opened. Aidan stood in the doorframe and smiled. "Whatcha doin'?"

I dropped the collar of his sweater. "Nothing."

"Liar." He strolled forward. "I was just coming to wake you up. They're gone."

"Gone, gone?" I asked hopefully.

He brushed a strand of wavy hair behind my ear. "No. I sent them to Veritas. Caleb is getting our parents hammered as we speak. They took Jasper so we could have some space."

"But the turkey—"

"Mom gave me instructions on how to baste it and when. Smells good, doesn't it?"

I nodded. "Don't think I'll be having any, though."

"Made you throw up, huh?"

"Yep. Another food ruined."

He took my hand and led me out of the bedroom and into the quiet living room.

"It's really quiet in here," I stated. "Kind of weird."

"You hungry?"

I nodded.

"Your mother made some fruit salad before they left for the bar."

"Fruit sounds good."

"Sit. I'll get it for you."

"Thanks." I sank down in a chair at our six-person kitchen table. "How long did I sleep?"

"Few hours. The moms prepped everything and then wrote down when things needed to go into the oven at what time."

"You mean I don't have to make Thanksgiving dinner? Score." I looked around the living room. "We don't have enough space for everyone."

"Dad has a long folding table in the back of his truck. Seats twelve. I fended off the mothers for a while about the sonogram. Told them it was your thing to share."

"My thing? You mean you left it up to me to tell everyone we're having twins?"

"You're having twins?" Mrs. Nowacki asked, holding the key to our apartment in one hand and a baked good in the other.

I stood up to relieve her of the pie.

"Meat." She gestured. "Not sweet."

"Looks good," I told her. "And yes, we're having twins." She patted my cheek and smiled. I took her hand and squeezed it. "We haven't told the parents yet. Our secret?"

Mrs. Nowacki nodded. "I am good at secrets. I have many secrets."

I raised my eyebrow. "What stories do you have tucked away, Mrs. Nowacki?"

"I tell you." She grinned. "Maybe."

"Can I get you something to drink, Mrs. Nowacki?"

Aidan asked as he came into the living room, holding a bowl of fruit salad. He handed it to me, and I took a bite immediately.

"You have *Krupnik?*" Mrs. Nowacki asked.

Aidan grinned. "Of course we have *Krupnik*. We've been experimenting with a cocktail recipe using *Krupnik* as the base. Can I make it for you?"

She nodded and took a seat on the couch. I missed Polish honey vodka. Actually, I missed all booze. And soft cheeses. But then I thought about what I was gaining.

Definitely worth it.

Before the parents were due back, I uploaded my apology video to Instagram. I debated on whether or not I should do it—I was still firmly in the camp of "I have a career to think about." Sometimes we had to do things we didn't want to do, or we'd suffer the consequences. It was kind of like going to the dentist. You went to the dentist, promised to floss more, and then conveniently forgot about it until the six-month mark rolled around right before your next check up.

I had a point. Didn't I?

Right—adulthood. Sometimes you had to do things you didn't want to do. This was one of them.

"How long have they been at the bar?" I asked Aidan, setting my phone down. The screen immediately lit up with Instagram notifications. I turned the phone face down.

"Few hours."

"They're gonna come back sloppy!"

"Probably. Your dad loves Caleb's Brooklyn."

"I know."

At our wedding, Caleb had jumped behind the bar for a bit and made his signature cocktail: The Brooklyn. Unlike a Manhattan, which called for whiskey, a Brooklyn called for reposado tequila. By the end of our reception our parents couldn't walk straight.

"What's Thanksgiving without a little sloppiness?" Aidan added. He handed Mrs. Nowacki her cocktail and then sat down next to me. "You guys okay if I watch football?"

Mrs. Nowacki took a sip of her drink and grinned. "I like. And yes, watch the football. I like the football."

"Oh yeah?" Aidan reached for the remote. "You have a favorite team?"

"Detroit," she said. "They have the best—" She patted the side of her rump and winked.

"Oh my," I muttered.

"You're in luck Mrs. Nowacki. The Lions are playing the Cowboys." Just as the two of them were settling down to watch football, the buzzer to the apartment went off.

"Who is that?" Aidan asked.

"Stacy and her boyfriend, if I had to guess." It was already two o'clock, and I'd told her to come by any time, since I thought all I'd be doing was cooking.

I pressed the intercom button. "Hello?"

"It's me!" Zeb called out. "And Terry!"

I buzzed them in. "It's Zeb and Terry."

"I thought they were going to some island for the holiday?"

"Thought so too." I opened the door as their footsteps sounded just outside. "I thought you guys were going away and couldn't make it."

"There's a hurricane in Costa Rica right now," Terry said. He held up both hands full of grocery bags. "We've got wine."

"Is this okay?" Zeb asked. "Sorry to just show up—"

"Theme of the day," I said, wrapping an arm around him. I looked at Aidan. "I'm glad your dad brought a big table."

"Your parents are here?" Zeb asked Aidan.

"Yep," I said. "And so are mine. They all showed up as a surprise."

"And where are they?" Terry wondered. "Because it's a little quiet in here."

"At Veritas," Aidan said. "Having some pre-dinner cocktails."

"What did you bring?" I asked, peering into Zeb's grocery bags.

"Cheese. So much cheese—oh shit," he said, face falling. "You can't have cheese, can you?"

"Or wine," Terry added. "God, we're the worst party crashers ever."

I laughed. "You're not. You're never crashing. And I can have hard cheeses."

"I got a few of those," Zeb said.

"Hang up your coats, get comfortable," I said, taking the grocery bags from them. Aidan got up, eyes still glued to the TV as he went to get two chairs from around the kitchen table.

"Zeb, Terry, this is our next door neighbor, Mrs. Nowacki."

"Both so good looking," Mrs. Nowacki said, her cheeks rosy from the *Krupnik* cocktail.

Zeb plopped down next to Mrs. Nowacki. "Hi, new best friend."

"You're so shallow," Terry said with an amused smile.

"Uh, you were the one who took the longest getting ready this morning."

Terry gestured to his perfectly styled hair. "It takes effort to look this good."

"Some of us come by it more naturally," Zeb stated, tone dry.

Terry blew him a kiss.

"Quit it. I'm not allowed to have a lot of sugar," I teased. Terry and Zeb were too cute. They'd met eight months ago in the ethnic food section at Dean & DeLuca. It was the perfect meet gay cute. Though they didn't technically live together, they spent every night together.

"Oh my God, I totally forgot—congratulations! Twins?! That's so exciting!" Terry gushed.

I put my hands to my belly. "Yup, frying up two Pierogis in here."

"Pierogis? Who has pierogis?" Mrs. Nowacki interjected.

I tried to explain to her the American cultural tradition of nicknames for fetuses while in utero. I wasn't sure she understood. It might've been the mild language barrier. It might've been the alcohol.

"Where's your cheese plate?" Terry asked, standing up.

"Try the cabinet over the fridge," I said.

"Ah, the place where you put all the crap you hardly use but never want to get rid of," Terry said with a nod. "Zeb's got one of those."

"I need all those cheesecake pans," Zeb defended.

"One in each size?" Terry said. "You're gonna have to downsize when we move in together."

"You're moving in together?" Aidan asked, finally pulling his eyes away from the TV.

I raised my eyebrows. "Did you just follow that entire conversation while watching football? I'm impressed."

Aidan put his hand on my thigh and squeezed.

"Now who's just too adorable?" Zeb wondered. "And yeah. We're shooting for April. My lease is over then."

"Anyone mind if I open a bottle of wine?" Terry asked.

Stacy and her boyfriend Joe showed up not thirty minutes later, bags in hand and adding to the growing pile of liquor. Joe was a musician who wore all black. His ears were pierced, and Mrs. Nowacki took it upon herself to examine the ink on his arms in an incredibly un-subtle fashion. While Joe was occupied and Aidan was playing bartender, Stacy pulled me aside.

"Saw your video…"

"Yeah, I posted it about an hour ago."

She nodded and bit her lip.

"What? What is it?"

"I sent you the entire video, Sibby."

"I know."

She shook her head. "You didn't watch the whole thing, did you?"

"What do you mean?"

"I mean, I never stopped recording like I thought I did. And it recorded the part where you said you didn't really want to apologize. And you didn't trim off the part where you thought you weren't being recorded…"

I felt my face drain of color. "You mean—"

"Yeah, Sibby. You just told everyone where to stick it."

#breakingtheinternet #zenthefuckout

"I shouldn't be allowed around technology," I said. "Or people. I shouldn't be allowed to talk to people."

"Have you"—she swallowed—"checked your phone?"

I shook my head. "I posted the video and then my phone blew up, so I set it aside."

"You're getting some nasty comments."

"Sometimes I wish you weren't such a straight shooter."

"You didn't let me finish. You're getting a lot of support, too."

"Oh. Well, that's good." I pressed a hand to my forehead. "How do I diffuse this?"

"For the love of God, just do *nothing*," she said. "Let it run its course, and don't add more fuel to the fire."

"I think we've passed that point," I muttered. "Me posting an unedited video of myself is a prime example of Sibby's Law. It's what I *do*. But you know what? This is all gonna be okay."

"Yeah? How do you figure?"

"I could take it down, but that would do more harm. People would feed on the censoring and denial of reality. So there's nothing to do but enjoy Thanksgiving and let it go."

"Wow, your chi must be in major alignment because I'd be freaking the fuck out right now."

I shrugged. Let the *zen* begin.

"Thanksgiving selfie time?" she asked. She lifted her phone, and we made stupid kissy faces at the screen. "I'll tag you."

"Awesome." We headed back into the living room. Joe and Aidan were absorbed in the football game and Zeb and Terry were playing cards with Mrs. Nowacki.

Hope they had cash.

The timer on the oven dinged, and I went to check the turkey. I gave it a nice baste and closed the oven door, not wanting too much heat to escape.

"I thought we were having turkey sandwiches and a bunch of sides," Stacy said, sipping on a *Krupnik* cocktail.

I reset the oven timer. "Change of plans. My parents showed up. So did Aidan's."

"Unannounced?"

"Yup."

"Wow."

"They're grandbaby hungry," I explained. "So I'm sorry if the conversation turns into baby stuff."

She waved a hand. "All okay."

I was ready for the parents to come back. Sitting on news of twins was driving me batty. I was fairly certain once I told them my mother would faint. And then when she woke up, she would probably attach herself to my body, barnacle style.

"Hello? Sibby?" Stacy waved her hand in my face.

I shook my head. "Sorry. I was fast-forwarding my life in my head by a decade and got lost in thought."

"Come back to the present, come back to the present," she teased, her voice sounding like a cheesy hypnotist.

"The present. Right. Aidan!" I called.

"Yeah, love?"

"Any ETA on the parents?" I asked.

"I don't know. Call your mom."

"Can I use your phone?" I didn't want to look at my cell. The notifications were no doubt out of control and I wouldn't be able to ignore them.

Stacy hopped down from the counter and didn't even spill her drink. She headed to the coffee table and made a cheese cracker tower and then plopped down onto the floor.

"I'll get you a chair," I said.

"Nah, I'm good." She crossed her legs and reached out to touch Joe's ankle.

He looked down at her. "Hey, baby."

I stage whispered to Aidan, "Everyone's in love."

"Yep." He didn't take his eyes off the TV.

"I've become obsolete and you don't love me anymore," I muttered.

Aidan handed me his phone without reacting.

"The game can't be that interesting," I said as I looked

at the other occupants for support. All eyes were glued to the TV, even Mrs. Nowacki, but we knew why she liked football.

I took Aidan's phone and called my mom. She didn't answer. I called my dad. He didn't answer. Then I called Aidan's parents and they didn't pick up their phones either.

Super weird.

I called Caleb, and he answered on the third ring. "Hey, bud."

"Hey Caleb, it's me."

"Hey! How's that turkey looking?"

"Juicy. Are my parents around?"

"No. All the parents left the bar fifteen minutes ago."

"Then they should be here…"

"Call them."

"I did," I said. "I called all of them. None of them answered." I walked away from the living room—Aidan and Joe were yelling at the TV, and I could barely hear Caleb.

"Oh, hold on, I'm getting another call," I said to Caleb, looking at my phone. "It's my mom." I pressed a button. "Mom? Where are you guys?"

"Sibby, it wasn't my fault—"

There was a siren in the background, and it made it impossible to hear what she was saying.

"Ma, hold on! I can't hear you!" When the siren passed, I asked, "Okay, what did you say?"

"I said, it wasn't my fault. I had a firm hold on the leash, I swear I did, but Jasper saw a squirrel and he lunged so hard that his collar snapped and he—"

My hand gripped the phone. "*He what?*"

"He took off, Sibby. And we've all split up to look for him, but we can't find him."

There was no time for fear. I snapped into drill-sergeant mode. I commanded my mother to call the others and get them in the same place and wait.

"Are they on their way?" Aidan asked as I walked back into the living room.

"Uh, no. Jasper got loose. They've been scouring the neighborhood but can't find him."

"Jasper got loose?" Aidan jumped up from the futon. "We have to go look for him. Now."

"We'll help," Terry added.

Everyone rushed to get their coats. Everyone except Mrs. Nowacki, who had fallen asleep.

"Let's make a video," Stacy said, sticking her hipster beanie on her head.

"Now's not the time for a freakin' Instagram video," Aidan snapped.

She flinched. "Okay, I know you hate me, but between both Sibby's and my account, if we show a picture of Jasper and make a video, other people can help find him."

Aidan's face softened. "I'm sorry, I—"

"Later," I said. "You guys can become besties later."

"Where should we look?" Zeb asked.

"Where have your parents already been?" Joe added.

"Who knows. They're all drunk," I said. "So I'm getting them together in one place. You guys"—I pointed to Zeb and Terry—"head north."

"Got it," Zeb said.

"You guys," I said to Joe and Stacy, "head south."

Joe nodded.

"I'll visit all his favorite places—"

"We," Aidan cut me off. "We will visit all his favorite places."

"He has favorite places?" Terry asked, following Zeb out the door.

"Pretty much every fire hydrant in Greenpoint," Aidan stated.

"You sure you're up for this?" I asked Aidan, worry in my tone for him—and for Jasper. He was out on the streets of Brooklyn. Alone. It was cold. Traffic. No, I couldn't think about that.

Aidan cupped my cheek. "Yeah. I'm healed enough to go. We'll find him."

Stacy held up her phone. "Video?"

I nodded. It was quick and to the point, and within a few minutes it was uploaded to Instagram. I took a deep breath, grabbed Aidan's hand and we were out the door.

We split off from the others, but had to take it slow so Aidan didn't re-injure himself. Aidan's phone pinged with a message. "My mom," he said. "They're wandering the streets of Greenpoint calling for Jasper."

"The four of them together?" I asked.

"Yeah. My parents met up with your parents—"

"I told my Mom to stay put."

"Don't be mad at her," he said, shoving his phone back in his pocket.

"I'm not mad at her."

"Yes, you are."

"She got drunk and lost our fur baby."

"It wasn't her fault. You know how Jasper gets around squirrels."

"I'm freaking out! Why aren't you freaking out?"

"Because if you freak out, and I freak out at the same time, then the world will spontaneously explode. Come on," he said, grabbing my hand. "I bet I know where he went."

Jasper was running around in the dog park, tongue lolling as he stalked after a black miniature poodle. The poodle's owner was sitting on a bench, bundled up to the extreme in a white parka and pink earmuffs. I opened the gate of the dog park and called to Jasper.

He came over immediately and jumped up onto my legs. I scooped him up and buried my face in his fur. Aidan stroked Jasper, and we had a not so private, highly emotional reunion.

"He didn't have tags on him," the owner of the poodle said, getting up. "But he seemed friendly enough, and my Claudette took a fancy to him."

"Thank you so much," Aidan said. "He saw a squirrel and—"

"It happens. Claudette has slipped away before."

"I'm gonna call my dad. Let them know we found him." Aidan got his phone out of his pocket. He stepped away to make the call.

"The dog I had before Claudette was a hound mix. He

pulled a lot. A harness was the only way to keep him under control. A collar alone wouldn't hold him."

"Harness. Got it. Thank you. My name is Sibby. This is Jasper." I gestured with my chin. "That's Aidan."

"Mae," she said with a smile. "Claudette and I are here most days between three and four."

"Excellent. We'll be back." I waved Jasper's paw at her. "Happy Thanksgiving."

"Happy Thanksgiving."

I was finally able to take a deep breath as I carried Jasper out of the dog park. Aidan followed, shoving his phone into his pocket. "The parents have been corralled to Veritas."

"Great, just what they need. More booze."

"Caleb is making them hydrate."

"Good."

"We should call the others, let them know the search has been called off."

"Send a mass text from my phone," I said, turning my body so he could get my cell out of my pocket.

"I'll get us an Uber first." While we waited for the car, Aidan sent off a mass text to everyone, telling them to head back to our apartment. "Well, this has been an exciting Thanksgiving so far," Aidan said as we climbed into the cab.

"We haven't even told our parents about the twins yet."

"Yeah, it all kind of got away from us, hasn't it?"

"Next year's gonna be even crazier," I told him. "Two extra humans. With my DNA."

"They have my DNA too," he pointed out.

"Won't matter. Sibby's Law is strong. Even diluted Sibby's Law."

"Stop with the Sibby's Law. There's no such thing as Sibby's Law."

"Instead of the cut version of the apology video, I posted the entire thing where I basically told the law to fuck off. Stacy was caught on camera saying behind-the-scenes-stuff, so who knows what I've managed to do to her career. I might've tanked my career too and—"

Aidan blinked. "So, Sibby's Law, huh?"

I sighed. "Sibby's Law."

The car stopped. "Can't go any further," the driver said.

"Why not?" I asked.

"Road is blocked off. There's a fire truck down there."

Aidan and I looked at each other. He opened the door and got out. I scooted across the seat with Jasper in my arms and stepped out onto the street. We darted around the closed road sign and briskly trotted toward our apartment building. Jasper was getting heavy in my arms, but he rested his face against my shoulder, so at least he wasn't squirming to get down.

We got to the middle of our block, and my mouth dropped open.

The second floor of our apartment building was on fire.

Aidan's face went slack. "Okay. I'm an official believer in Sibby's Law."

#paininchampagne #notagain

The mood in Veritas was somber. We'd pulled a few tables together; the parents sat at one end, sobering up—while the rest of us stared at our hands. Even Jasper seemed to know something was wrong because he was lying down on a towel near my feet, face on his paws.

"I set. Our house. On fire," I said.

"No," Mrs. Nowacki said. "It was my fault. I fall asleep."

I grabbed her hand and gave it a squeeze.

"No, it's my fault," my mom chimed in. "I wasn't paying attention and Jasper—"

"Stop," I said. "Everyone please, stop. This is just one of those things that happens. The important thing is that we're all safe—and no one in the building got hurt."

All of our neighbors were gone for the holiday, and the fire had been contained to our apartment. Windows were open to air out the smoke, but we had to wait a few days to go inside and assess the damage.

"This is going to be an insurance nightmare," I muttered. Luckily, we were covered out the wazoo.

Because, well—me.

Caleb was behind the bar, mixing cocktails and bringing them over to us. For our parents, he brought water.

"Where are you guys gonna stay?" Stacy asked.

"A hotel, probably," Aidan said.

"Absolutely not." Nancy said as she stood. "You'll stay with us."

"We have to be close to the city, Mom," Aidan said gently.

"Why? You're not going back to work for another week or so," Bud said.

"Still," Aidan said. "Sibby needs to be close to the city."

"I do?" I asked.

He nodded with a look. Oh, so *he* didn't want to be in his parents' home for any length of time. Got it.

"You should just move to Long Island and be done with it," Terry said.

"Yeah. I mean, you need the space, now that you found out you're having twins," Zeb said, slugging back his second cocktail.

The entire bar went silent.

Mom looked at Zeb. "What did you just say?"

Zeb's eyes widened. "Nothing. I said nothing."

"No." My mom stood. "You said twins."

"Did not," Zeb denied.

"*Did too*," she shot back. To me she said, "Sibyl Ruth, are you having twins?"

Oh boy.

"Yeah," I said slowly. "We're having twins."

Nancy stood up and looked around the bar. "And how many of you knew before we did?"

Zeb slowly raised his hand, followed by Terry and Caleb. Even Mrs. Nowacki raised her hand. My mom stared down Stacy and Joe. "You two didn't know?"

Stacy shook her head. "Though to be honest, I kinda guessed."

I looked at her. "Seriously?"

"Yeah." She nodded. "I'm like seriously awesome at guessing if a woman's gonna have multiples. I usually guess the gender right, too."

"It's true," Joe said. He looked at her fondly. "It's like her carnic trick."

"And yet again, I'm the last to know what's going on in my own daughter's life!" my mother bellowed.

I winced.

"Honey," my father said, standing slowly.

She waved him back down. "You, hush."

My father sat and then threw me a sympathetic look and mouthed, *I'm sorry* followed by a *congratulations*.

"This isn't how this is supposed to go, Sibby. I'm your mother. I'm supposed to know before everyone else. Before your friends. Before social media. EVERYONE."

I stood up and pressed my hands to the table. "You lost my dog."

My mother stared at me.

I stared at her.

"Call it even?" she suggested.

I grinned. "Sounds good."

She clapped her hands together, all traces of anger gone. "Twins!"

"Twins!" everyone echoed.

The parents stood up and came to us. Mom grasped me to her, and for a moment, I closed my eyes. We were all happy, healthy, and safe. Sometimes that was all that mattered. Everything else would be okay.

My phone rang. It was Annie calling to wish us a happy Thanksgiving. I missed her so much, but she was already starting to sound like her old self. Her time away from the city was clearly doing her some much-needed good. As I hung up with her, Caleb came out from behind the bar, holding a bottle of champagne.

"Do you want to do the honors?" he asked me.

"Sure." I took the bottle from him and removed the cage. "Who wants champagne?" As if on cue, everyone ducked.

"Ha-ha," I said. "Like that would happen again—"

The cork shot from the bottle, whizzed through the air, and hit one of the champagne flutes that Caleb had lined up on the bar. The flute smashed on impact and caused the flutes on each side to wobble, and in domino style, all the flutes toppled, one by one in a chain reaction.

"Huh," I said. "What do you know? I still have magical powers."

Everyone rose slowly. Aidan took the champagne bottle from my hands and said, "I've been good this entire time. I gave up drinking in solidarity, but now—" He brought the bottle to his lips and took a sip. He passed the bottle to Stacy who also took a sip. As the bottle made the rounds, Aidan took me into his arms.

I sighed. "Sibby's Law. Still going strong."

He grinned. "I wouldn't want it any other way."

Mother Shucker (Sibby Series Book 3)

This is Sibby's Law...on hormones.

Sibzilla is on the loose. She's coming for your pastries, chicken wings, and pie.

She's coming for bigger pants.

No one is safe. Especially not her husband.

Watch out, Mother Shuckers. It's about to get real.

Chapter 1

Lox: [laks]

1. Smoked or cured salmon, usually thinly sliced.

2. First comes the toasted bagel and a nice schmear. Add a hefty amount of lox, top it off with sliced onion, tomato, and capers. Squeeze a lemon over the top to bring out the salmon flavor. Take a *big* bite.

3. Congrats, you just became an old Long Island Jew.

"Okay, now let's talk about the perineal massage," Shana said, holding a plastic baby under her arm like a football.

"Let's not," I voiced. "Some things should stay in the bedroom…"

A couple of people in our birthing class sniggered.

Shana glared in my direction, expecting it to silence me.

I clamped my lips shut and Aidan put his hand on my thigh. I chanced a look at him. His eyes were trained on our class instructor, but I saw his ears turning red as he attempted to hold in his laughter.

"Sibby," Shana said with a lamenting sigh, "what did I say?"

"That I was supposed to keep my thoughts to myself," I repeated, like a kindergartener being chastised.

"And have you done that?"

"No."

She held up her index finger. "First, we watched a birthing video, and when the baby was coming out of its mother, *you* likened it to a scene in *Aliens.* Then, when you saw a baby in the video still in its amniotic sac, you made the cry of an orc from *Lord of the Rings.*"

"Oh come on, it tore through the membrane like a Tolkien character!" I looked around, expecting someone to agree with me. But no one would meet my eyes.

"Sibby," Aidan whispered, "don't argue."

Clearly Shana wasn't done publicly listing my transgressions because she put her hand on her hip and went on. "When we broke up into groups, you were supposed to write down your biggest fears. And what did you do?"

"I might've drawn a pornographic sketch…" I looked at my lap. "Yeah, probably not one of my finer moments."

"And now I want to discuss perineal massage—something that will legitimately help you all as you go through labor—and *you* won't take it seriously. I'm sorry, Sibby, but I'm going to have to ask you to leave."

My head whipped up and my jaw dropped. "I'm being kicked out?"

"You're clearly not taking this seriously and the rest of the class is. You're disruptive and frankly, you're acting like a frat guy."

"Awesome!"

"It wasn't a compliment!" she snapped. She pointed to the door. "Go."

"But—"

"GO! You too, Aidan."

"Wha—what did I do?" he demanded, looking offended.

"You didn't keep your wife quiet."

"Keep his wife quiet?" I repeated.

"Oh boy," Aidan muttered.

I rose slowly. Not for any dramatic reason, but because I was physically struggling to get out of the chair.

"Fine. I'll leave," I said, tossing my hair over my shoulder. "I'll find another class with a sense of humor."

I stomped through the open doorway, belatedly realizing that I'd forgotten to grab my winter coat and bag. There was no way I was going back in there. I'd rather freeze.

The door opened and Aidan met me in the hallway. Thankfully, he'd gathered my belongings.

"You were ready to rumble," Aidan said, holding my coat out to me.

I slid my arms into it and zipped the coat closed. "She started it, but I ended it."

"She didn't start it. *You* started it. And you didn't end it. She did because she kicked us out."

"We don't need a birthing class."

"Do you know what's going to happen during labor?"

"Sure, I'm reading the baby books."

"Putting them on your face and joking that you'll learn by osmosis isn't reading," he said in dry amusement.

"Fine, I'll actually read them," I rolled my eyes and we headed for the elevator.

"We need a tribe, Sibby," he said. "These people were supposed to be our tribe."

"Those people are weird. They don't know how to laugh and I need laughter to get through this."

He wrapped his arm around me. "I know you miss Annie, but even if she were here, she wouldn't know what the hell to do with babies or birthing class or strange fluids that come out of—"

"Ack! Aidan! What did I say about mentioning fluids?"

"My bad."

I felt a pang in my chest at the mention of my best friend. My life hadn't been the same since she'd left the city for Montauk. We still talked all the time. Our text-message thread was a long list of memes and emojis. Still, it wasn't the same as having her living in the same neighborhood. We couldn't just grab dinner and chat about whatever.

The elevator arrived and we rode it to the first floor. "That was all Sibzilla back there. Let's blame her for my inability to keep my mouth shut."

"I don't think you can blame your alter ego for this one."

"Are you mad at me?" I asked when we got out onto the street. Brooklyn was bathed in darkness, the sun having set some time around five. December in New York was no joke. At least all the holiday lights were up in the neighborhood, so we had some cheerful light early in the evenings.

"I'm not mad," he said with a sigh. "But you've just made it harder. And it's already hard, you know?"

"I'm sorry. I know I can be—and I don't think—and my filter—" I sighed. "Can I buy you a drink?"

"Absolutely. I need beer and you need chicken nuggets."

"Another piece of pie?" Aidan asked in amusement.

I shook my head and blotted my mouth with a napkin. "Nope, three's my limit."

Aidan discreetly signaled for the check. A moment later, a cute waitress brought it over. She batted her eyelashes at my husband.

It ruffled my craw and stuck in my feathers, or something like that.

"Hi," I said to her. "I don't think we've met. I'm Sibby. This is my *husband*, Aidan. We're expecting twins. We have a dog, and we're happily married."

Aidan snorted into his beer.

The waitress looked at me in disbelief. "Okay…"

I tried to smile, but I was pretty sure it came across as a grimace because she backed up a few inches out of fear.

Aidan put his credit card in the check presenter. The waitress swiped it up and dashed away.

"I know I'm not supposed to encourage this kind of behavior, but I kind of like it."

I rolled my eyes. "You do not. You're just saying that

for self-preservation. You're afraid I'm going to sit on you and crush your ribs."

He took my hand and smiled. "You're beautiful. You're even more beautiful now that you're going to be the mother of my children."

I sighed. "I'd really like to have sex with you. Tonight."

"That can be arranged."

"We have to do it under the cover of darkness."

"Sibby…"

"No, Aidan. I don't want you to see my thighs rubbing together—it's awful."

"Your thighs have always rubbed together."

I gasped. "Um, how are we supposed to have a happy marriage if you don't learn to lie to me?"

"I don't care if your thighs rub together." He grinned and then leaned over the table and whispered something into my ear that made me want to get home, fast.

The waitress returned with his credit card. He quickly signed the slip and tipped her and then got up. He held his hand out to me and helped me slide out of the booth.

We walked north up Manhattan Avenue, the main drag in Greenpoint, and every now and again Aidan urged me ahead of him so we could walk single file and let others pass. People were boisterous and happy as they ducked into bars and restaurants, filling the city with life.

I shook my head. "Strange."

"What?"

"They're just getting their night started and we're already going home to our dog and footie pajamas."

"I don't have footie pajamas. *You* have footie pajamas."

"I can't zip up my adult onesie anymore. It's been retired."

"It'll come out of retirement."

"Yeah, in eighteen months."

"Why such a specific time frame?"

"I still have months before my due date. And then I need at least a year not to feel like an utter failure while I try to squidge my body back into my regular clothes. I'm allowing a few extra months for wiggle room. No pun intended."

"If you want to get your figure back you might have to—"

"Don't say it."

"—join a gym."

"I hate your face."

"You love my face," he countered.

I nodded and sighed. "Yeah. Which is how I got knocked up with twins."

"My face had nothing to do with it. Do you need me to show you the pop-up book again?"

"Now I *really* hate your face."

After a slow climb to the second floor, we finally got to our apartment. "Whose idea was it to live in a walk-up? We should've moved to an elevator building," I huffed.

Prenatal yoga didn't do much for endurance training.

"I don't remember." He reached into his pocket for his keys. "It's going to be a bitch getting a double stroller down those stairs."

"Oh man, you had to remind me of that. Not that I'll be leaving the apartment for the first three months after the twins are born, anyway."

He pushed the front door open and let me step inside first. Jasper was in the middle of the couch. He lifted his head and started to wag his tail.

A six-foot Christmas tree that Aidan had chopped down himself when he'd gone Upstate, rested in the corner of the living room. It was garnished with colored lights, candy canes, a little tinsel, and handmade ornaments from Aidan's childhood. A menorah rested on the fireplace mantle nearby.

"I think the tree covers the smell of charred turkey a little bit," Aidan said, his nose sniffing the air.

"Mostly, yeah a bit. I've got a super nose now though so I can still smell it." I shook my head. "We're never cooking Thanksgiving dinner again. From now on, it's turkey sandwiches all the way."

Aidan grinned.

The insurance claim had been a nightmare, but we got lucky and there was very little actual damage. Most of it had been cosmetic. With the insurance money that came through, we were able to repaint the kitchen slate gray to match all of our brushed-chrome appliances.

I sat down on the edge of the couch and patted my leg. Jasper came to me and jumped into my lap. I smushed his face between my hands and made a bunch of nonsense noises.

"Don't fall asleep," Aidan warned.

I rolled my eyes. "I'm not going to fall asleep."

"It's winter, it's dark out, and you're pregnant. The odds of me getting laid tonight shrink every minute you're on the couch."

"Wow. You must burn a lot of calories being so snarky."

He grinned. "I learned from the best."

"Flattery will get you nowhere."

"Flattery will get me into your pants."

Jasper let out a whine, which was dog speak for, "Take my ass outside or I'm going to poop on your floor."

"Once around the block," Aidan said. "And then I'll be back. Please be awake."

I saluted him and when he grabbed the leash, Jasper supermanned off the couch toward Aidan.

The door shut and I heard the patter of Jasper's paws as he scrambled down the stairs and then Aidan's hearty chuckle, laughing at something Jasper had done. I shucked out of my down coat and then moseyed to the bedroom. I turned on the lamps and then sat on the bed.

Leaning over, I attempted to reach my feet. It was a regular struggle between the frumpback whale and her boots. Unfortunately, the boots won.

I fell back against the pillows. My belly loomed before me. It was all I saw. Somehow in the last few weeks, I'd gone from sorta pregnant to when-are-you-due pregnant.

I closed my eyes.

I'd realized I first had the bump when I was getting dressed for my administrative hearing. I had to deal with the ticket I'd been given for peeing in a Folgers container on the subway. In public. I'd put on a black sweater dress that all of sudden had been a little too tight around my middle. I hadn't had anything else to wear, so I showed up to the courthouse feeling like I looked less than stellar. But breaking down in front of the woman who was handling my fine—who happened to be a mother of three—had turned out to be a saving grace.

Ticket and offense dismissed.

Something buzzed underneath my butt. I awkwardly rolled to the side and managed to get my cell phone out of my back pocket.

Grinning, I pressed answer. "Well, if I do declare…"

"Why does your Southern accent sound Polish?" Annie asked with a laugh.

"Yeah, about that…I think I've lived in Greenpoint too long. Mrs. Nowacki even left handmade pierogis in my refrigerator the other day. Tell me you want my life. Don't lie."

"I want your life," she said automatically.

"How's Montauk?"

"Boring. And exactly what I need. I can't get into any trouble up here. Because the only people below the age of fifty-five who live here are my cousins."

"So what do you *do*? I mean, when you're not working in your uncle's restaurant?"

"You mean when I'm not mediating my aunt and uncle's fights?"

"Yeah. That."

"I walk on the beach and contemplate life."

"See, I don't know if you're kidding, so I don't know whether or not to laugh."

"I'm serious, Sibby. I don't drink anymore and I run on the beach in the mornings. Still off all social media. It's been really good for me."

"When did you start doing that stuff?"

"Not too long ago. The healthy habits seem to be sticking, so I felt like I could finally tell you."

I heard the front door open. "Gotta go. Husband's home. I have to have sex with him before I fall asleep."

"Wow. You are really selling this marriage thing."

I hung up with her, tossed my phone aside, and struggled to sit up.

"Sibby?"

"Bedroom!"

I heard Jasper run to his food bowl and a moment later he was chowing down. Aidan appeared in the doorway, his dark hair disheveled. "Whatcha doin'?"

"Trying to sit up."

I held out my hands. With a chuckle, he came forward and gave me a boost. "Anything else I can help you with?"

"Nope, I'm good."

"Really? Like maybe you want some help with your boots?" Before waiting for me to reply, he dropped to his knees. He unlaced my boots and pulled them off. He tweaked my big toe.

"Cute socks."

They were red-and-black plaid, and fuzzy.

I wiggled my toes. "My favorite pair."

"Who bought them for you?"

"Someone who loves me."

"You mean someone who doesn't want you sticking your ice-cold feet on his legs in the middle of the night."

"Yeah, he's the best," I said with a smile.

"A real *mensch.*"

"Way to go on the Yiddish."

"I've been listening to a podcast on Yiddish since your mom told me I needed to know some of the lingo."

"Who would have thought that listening to three old Jewish men complaining in Yiddish would be so popular? They have thousands of subscribers. Like, how, just how?"

He grasped my right sock around the ankle and worked it off, flinging it into the corner of the room. Its mate followed suit.

Jasper's furry body appeared in the doorway, his tail wagging. He had that look like he was about to make himself at home on the bed.

"Go," I commanded, pointing in the direction of the living room.

Jasper whined, but dutifully turned and trotted away.

"There's nothing weirder than our dog watching us do it," I said.

Aidan laughed. "Are you going to continue cracking jokes or do you want to get down to business?"

I waggled my eyebrows. "Can't I do both?"

"No. And if you're cracking jokes it means I'm not doing a good enough job. Now be quiet and let me work my magic."

The next morning Aidan and I were both awakened by the buzzer. Aidan launched himself up, his hair askew, eyelids at half-mast. "Wha—what happened? Are you in labor?"

I sat up more slowly than he had, but I was more alert. "You're a few months too early, love. It's the buzzer."

"It's seven-thirty in the morning," he muttered. "Who the hell is here?"

I gently pushed him back down onto the bed. "UPS guy, most likely. Go back to bed; I'll get it."

Sure enough, it was the UPS guy.

"Package for you," he said abruptly.

Ha. Package.

I fake-signed his electronic thingy and took the box. "Thanks."

"Happy holidays," he said, and then left.

I closed the door and immediately took the box to the kitchen table. I grabbed a knife from the knife block and was just about to slit the box's tape when Aidan trekked into the kitchen. He was walking around without a shirt and his flannel pants rode low enough on his hips that I could see his appendix scar.

That had been one terrifying experience. A call in the middle of the night… I'd thought the worst. Memories rushed to me.

"You're not allowed to die," I blurted out.

He raised dark eyebrows as best he could, still half-asleep. "You're the one holding the knife. You might want to stop gesturing with it in my direction. Then I have a chance at living."

I lowered the knife.

"Thank you." He took a deep breath and ran a hand through his hair. His cowlick stood straight up, making him look like a cartoon character. "I hadn't planned on dying."

"Good. In fact, we should do everything in our power to become vampires and then we can live forever."

"Sounds like a plan," he said, not at all taking me seriously.

And to think, he was putting up with my crazy all before a cup of coffee.

I nodded. "Glad that's settled."

He gestured with his chin to the box. "What did you order?"

"A bread maker."

"Why?"

"Because I want to learn how to make bread. Obviously."

"Obviously. Give me that," he said, reaching for the knife. "I don't trust you with that thing."

Couldn't say I blamed him.

While he cut open the box, I got the coffee going. While it brewed, we oohed and aahed over the bread maker.

"This looks really high-tech," he said. "We have to read the manual."

"Whoa. Call the press. A *man* just admitted to needing to read directions."

"Har-har."

"Annie suggested this specific bread maker. She thinks even *I'll* be able to use it properly."

Aidan poured himself a cup of coffee while I flipped through the recipe book.

"Hey, look! We can make Jewish Rye!"

"Coffee?" he asked.

"Yes, please."

He fixed it the way I liked it and then set it down in front of me. While I was engrossed in my new bread maker, the buzzer sounded again. A few moments later there was a knock at the front door and Aidan let Caleb in. He was dressed in running clothes and the hair at his temples was dark with sweat.

"Did you jog here?" I asked.

"Yep."

My face torqued into a picture of confusion. "Why?"

"Why what?"

"Why do you jog, is what she wants to know," Aidan said.

"Because it's good for you. It's how I stay in shape."

I stared at him blankly. "I don't get it."

"Dude," Caleb said, conveniently ignoring me and

looking at Aidan, "put on a shirt. You're making me feel inadequate."

"Why would you want to cover up a work of art?" I asked.

Aidan laughed as he started for the bedroom, and Caleb helped himself to a cup of coffee.

This was our morning routine. Caleb had grown needy since his split with Annie, but I didn't mind.

"Will you let me take Jasper for a jog one morning? I'd like a running buddy."

Aidan came back into the kitchen with his chest covered. "You can try, but you will fail."

"Huh?" Caleb asked, taking a sip of his coffee.

"I've tried running with Jasper. He's not a running dog. Every time I get going, he comes to a crashing halt. Then I come to a crashing halt. I might have fallen over into some trash cans once…"

"It's true. He came home with a banana peel stuck to his shirt. I think Jasper likes to make asses of us on purpose," I said. "The other day, I left the dog park with dog crap on my yoga pants."

Caleb chuckled. "Your dog is a menace."

"But we love him."

"So what did you get?" Caleb asked, touching the bread maker. "Looks like a time machine."

"Bread maker."

"Oh, yes! Can you make me a cinnamon loaf? Oh and banana bread?"

"Sure."

"Sweet."

Aidan smiled. "You might want to wait until Sibby works out all the kinks."

I glared at Aidan for alluding to my supervillain powers of appliance destruction.

"I'll be a guinea pig, no problem," Caleb said.

"Poached eggs okay for everyone?" I asked. They nodded in approval.

We spent the next hour devouring a dozen eggs and two packages of bacon. I could eat like a six-foot man. No shame. I'd started wearing Aidan's sweats for big meals and I owned it.

"Thanks for breakfast," Caleb said as he loaded the last plate into the dishwasher. "Aidan, I'll see you at the bar later."

Caleb gave me a hug, rubbed Jasper's ears, and then left.

When the front door shut, Aidan said, "You don't have to feed him, you know."

I pressed the dishwasher start button. "I'm afraid if I don't feed him, he'll starve. Have you seen how much weight he's lost?"

"He'll gain it back. Caleb was fine before Annie came along. He'll be fine after. He just needs more time."

Hmm. I wasn't sure I believed that. Annie was a one-woman emotional wrecking ball.

"What do you have going on today?" Aidan asked, switching the direction of our conversation.

"Book-release stuff and coffee with Stacy."

"Say hi to the millennial for me," he said.

"Uh, Aidan? *You're* a millennial."

"Yeah, but she *acts* like a millennial. Who has pink hair nowadays unless you live in San Francisco?"

"Congratulations, you just became a seventy-five-year-old man. Let me grab you some ointment—"

He shuddered and cut me off. "You know how I feel about that word."

I hugged him. "I have to pick up all the bread-making

stuff at the store. While I'm there, I can grab you some Metamucil and Grape Nuts…"

"You're thoughtful, Sibby. Really. By the way, let's ban the words Metamucil and ointment from our vocabularies."

"Hey, just thinking about the health of your plumbing."

"Let's also vow not to mention my plumbing. That's a conversation between me and my proctologist."

I blinked. "We're too young for this sort of talk."

A Quick Guide To Yiddish

Bubbe: Grandmother.

Gatkes: Long johns.

Gefilte Fish: A dish of stewed or baked stuffed fish, or of fish cakes boiled in a fish or vegetable broth and usually served chilled.

Kibbitz: Chit chat.

Mazel tov: Congratulations.

Plotz: Collapse or be beside oneself with frustration, annoyance, or other strong emotion. Literally 'to burst'.

Tuchus: Slang for butt or rear-end.

Zayde: Grandfather.

About the Author

Wall Street Journal & *USA Today* bestselling author Emma Slate writes romance with heart and heat.

Called "the dialogue queen" by her college playwriting professor, Emma writes love stories that range from romance-for-your-pants to action-flicks-for-chicks.

When she isn't writing, she's usually curled up under a heating blanket with a steamy romance novel and her two beagles—unless her outdoorsy husband can convince her to go on a hike.

Emma also writes rom-com and contemporary romance as E. Slate.

Additional Works

<u>Writing as E. Slate</u>

The Sibby Series

Queen of Klutz (Book 1)
Sibby Slicker (Book 2)
Mother Shucker (Book 3)
Sibby's Spawn (Book 4)
Hot Mess Express (Book 5)

Others:

From Stardust to Stardust

<u>Writing as Emma Slate</u>

The Tarnished Angels Motorcycle Club Series:

Wreck & Ruin (Tarnished Angels Book 1)
Crash & Carnage (Tarnished Angels Book 2)

Madness & Mayhem (Tarnished Angels Book 3)
Thrust & Throttle (Tarnished Angels Book 4)
Venom & Vengeance (Tarnished Angels Book 5)
Fire & Frenzy (Tarnished Angels Book 6)
Leather & Lies (Tarnished Angels Book 7)
Heartbeats & Highways (Tarnished Angels Book 8)

SINS Series:

Sins of a King (Book 1)
Birth of a Queen (Book 2)
Rise of a Dynasty (Book 3)
Dawn of an Empire (Book 4)
Ember (Book 5)
Burn (Book 6)
Ashes (Book 7)
Fall of a Kingdom (Book 8)

Others:

Peasants and Kings